First published 2023
ISBN 978-1-3999-4417-5

This book is a work of fiction and, except in the case of historical fact, any resemblance to actual persons, living or dead, is purely coincidental.

This one goes out to all the pigeons, you feathery guardians of the sky.

And also to Logan and Sydney, without whom such nonsense would have no meaning.

And finally to Griff, my Editor-in-Chief, my muse and my biggest supporter.

The Department of Conspiracy

One Flew Over the Cuckoo's Nest

Sam checked himself in the mirror. His outfit looked great. The shiny two-piece tracksuit was a bit tight around his chest, but he'd loosened the zip which only added to the 1970s vibe he was going for. He adjusted his peroxide white wig and carefully placed the big square sunglasses on his face. Veronica's party invite instructed *Childhood Heroes* – Sam was sure his outfit would go down a storm. Everyone loved Jimmy Savile when they were a kid, right?

Sam usually felt a little bit awkward at parties and could reliably be found hanging around the kitchen making small talk. But he was feeling pumped about this one. He was actually surprised Veronica had invited him at all as she rarely spoke to him – he wasn't altogether convinced she knew he existed up until that point. But there it was, a powder blue party invitation tucked into the top of his locker on their last day of college. Perhaps she *had* noticed him all those times he'd been sat two tables away in the cafeteria. Maybe she *hadn't* been blanking him in their sociology class when he'd been wistfully gazing at her, wondering how her hair was so flowy.

Sam picked up the piece-de-resistance. A big faux-gold badge on a red ribbon emblazoned with the words *Jim Fixed It For Me* in bold letters. He looped the ribbon over his head and settled the badge centrally on his chest.

In truth, he wasn't actually old enough to remember watching Jim'll Fix It on the telly; he was only about five years old when Savile died. But his step-dad Ron had shown him photos of this crazy-looking guy in a tracksuit from the 70s, and he'd assured Sam he'd be a great choice as he'd be instantly recognisable as the British TV institution. And Ron had taught him a few of his catchphrases too, so he was ready to do an impression at the drop of a hat if needed. Sam wondered if perhaps he should google Savile and do a bit of last-minute research on the guy himself. He glanced up at the Harry Potter clock on his bedroom wall. *Blimey, half seven! I've got to go*. He didn't want to turn up late and risk Veronica missing his grand entrance.

* * *

As he got on the bus, Sam felt a twinge of pride as the driver did a double-take of his outfit.

"Single to Beckenham, please."

"Are you looking to get your head kicked in tonight, son?" asked the bus driver.

Sam smiled politely, maybe this was a reference to Jimmy's TV show. "Now then, now then," he replied, before making a falsetto honking noise in an attempt to imitate Savile's annoying drone in the way his step-dad had shown him.

The driver shook his head despondently, took the money and then passed him a ticket stub. As the bus pulled away, Sam headed towards the back seats.

An old lady with a trolley bag sitting alongside the aisle glanced up towards him and screwed her face up. “Disgusting!”

Typical boomer, he smiled to himself. She obviously didn’t realise he was in fancy dress – she must’ve thought that’s how all the Gen Z’s dress these days. Bless her. As Sam settled on the bench at the back of the bus, he started to visualize how the conversations at the party would go. He figured he would probably walk in holding his oversized fake cigar, everybody would turn to look at his brilliant costume and burst out laughing. Then Veronica would sidle over to him and say something like ‘Oh Sam, I didn’t realise you were such a funny guy and that costume kind of suits you’.

Then he would say something funny, and Veronica would laugh at which point he’d follow it up with something insightful and deep and then she’d blush. He hadn’t quite worked out the details of what he would actually say, but in his head the scenario was rapidly developing into a full-blown relationship. Kids and everything.

Sam was snapped back into reality as the bus pulled over by Beckenham Green. He stepped off and started strutting down the high street in the direction of Veronica’s address.

* * *

As he neared her house, music pumped out across the street. Four turtles in ninja costumes were passing round a joint in the front garden as Sam headed up the path. He guessed they must be feeling pretty stupid right now, all coming in the same costume.

He gave them a cheery wave with his cigar, then pushed open Veronica's front door. He could hear people laughing and music blaring from within the lounge area. Was that Kim Wilde's *Kids In America?* He loved that song.

The lounge door swung wide open as Sam gave it a hefty push and all eyes immediately turned to look at him.

"We're the Kids in America, woah!" he sang jubilantly as he bowled through the door, cigar in one hand whilst performing a jaunty jazz hand with the other.

The excited chatter instantly died down and Kim Wilde suddenly fell silent. He looked around the room, waiting for a cheer, a laugh or even a solitary 'hey, there's Sam'. None of them came.

"What the fuck are you?" asked an Ewok.

"I'm Jimmy Savile," replied Sam, feeling a little crestfallen that no one seemed to recognise him. Veronica was standing by the window, with both of her parents.

"You've come to my birthday party dressed as a paedophile?" she clarified indignantly, removing her Batgirl mask.

"No of course not," he smiled awkwardly, "I'm Jimmy Savile!"

"You sick pervert!" spat the Ewok.

A girl dressed as Hermione silently walked up to Sam. "I suppose you think this is funny. You find paedophiles funny, do you? You laugh when children are abused, do you?"

"What? God no, why would I do that?" He felt everyone in the room glaring at him angrily.

Lion-O, the Leader of the Thundercats, put his beer down and stood alongside Hermione. "I think you and I should go have a little chat outside funny man, don't you?"

"No, I don't," retorted Sam indignantly, "I'm Jimmy Savile! What on earth is the matter with you lot? I don't abuse kids, I make their little dreams come true."

Sam's protest was met with a chorus of revolted groans from everyone in the lounge which were punctuated by Captain Kirk throwing an empty beer can towards him, which bounced off his head.

"Ouch! That hurt!" he snapped. "Why are you all being weird, I love kids!"

"Right, that's it," said Lion-O, putting Sam in a headlock. "Let's get you out of here."

"You're hurting my neck," he spluttered. "Let me go!" His sunglasses fell off his face and got trodden on by Lion-O's huge foot as he was manhandled back in the direction of the front door. As he struggled, Sam also became aware of Thor, grabbing him around the waist.

As they got to the front door, Lion-O released his grip on Sam and flung him unceremoniously towards the grass. A small crowd had gathered behind Lion-O and were jeering at Sam. Veronica forced her way through to the front garden, followed shortly after by her dad.

"Why would you ruin my party like this? Who the hell even are you, why are you even here?"

He felt the corners of his mouth tugging downwards and a lump in his throat as he stumbled up to his feet. "But I got an invitation. It was in the top of my locker last Friday."

Veronica's dad removed his Gandalf beard and puffed out his chest, guiding him away from his daughter. "Come now young man, it would appear that invitation clearly wasn't meant for you if Veronica doesn't know who you are. I think it's time you left, don't you?"

"Fine," sighed Sam, lifting off his medallion. An ironic cheer rippled around the garden as he trudged towards the pavement with his head down. Another empty can bounced off his head on the way out, which brought up another cheer and some cackling.

Sam didn't feel like getting the bus home, so he walked. All seven miles.

Alone.

* * *

The first thing to know about Sam Juniper, is that he was an excellent sleeper. That's not just to say he would sleep through a storm but, irrespective of how awful his day had been, he somehow had the uncanny ability to empty his brain of all nagging doubts and guilty feelings and fall into a deep and powerful sleep.

This in turn resulted in a newly birthed positivity when he woke up each morning, refreshed and invigorated. This positive start to the possibilities of each new dawn was embodied in his boundless, puppy-like enthusiasm – a built-in, spring-loaded determination that today would definitely be better than yesterday. After all, it was the first day of the rest of his life – college was over, and it was time to go out and make his way in the adult world.

His Transformers duvet was only just covering his gangly naked body when his mum walked in with a cup of tea.

"Morning petal! Somebody got home late last night, how was your party?"

"It was ok, Mum."

"That's good, you've got such nice friends. Now I'm making you a lovely breakfast downstairs, so I need you to start getting up. Me and Ron have got a special surprise for you downstairs."

Ron had been Sam's step-dad and his mum's boyfriend for the last two years. They got together shortly after his dad had died – a bit too soon if you asked Sam. Ron actually made him feel very uncomfortable most of the time, especially since he had taken it upon himself to move in with them and insisted on referring to himself as 'the man of the house'. Ugh, so cringe!

"A surprise? What sort of surprise Mum?"

"Well, I can't tell you that can I, my little cherub. It wouldn't be a surprise would it."

As soon as she toddled off out of the bedroom, Sam scrambled out from under his duvet and scanned out of the window. *Oh my God!* Sitting there on the driveway was a brand-new, denim blue Audi TT. He couldn't believe his luck. His mum knew he was desperate for a set of wheels so he wouldn't have to keep getting the bus, but this was the jackpot. It even had the roof folded down!

"Yesss!" Sam clenched his fists – he knew it was going to be a good day. He commando-rolled across his bed and whipped on his jogging bottoms. He pulled his T-shirt on both backwards and inside-out so had the label poking out the front but was too excited to notice. He ran to the bathroom, shuffled his toothbrush around his mouth at double-speed and then bounded down the stairs. He paused before he opened the kitchen door and told himself to take a breath. He didn't want to seem too excited as they'd know he'd looked out of the window, and it would spoil the surprise.

"Good morning, Ron, good morning Mother," he announced as he walked in, attempting to appear as dignified and casual as possible.

His mum was carrying a frying pan loaded with scrambled eggs in one hand and using tongs to share out sausages with the other. "'Ello dear, perfect timing. Come and sit down."

"And how are you on this fine morning, Ronald?"

"Fair to middling young man, fair to middling."

Sam was in such a good mood he was even willing to put up with Ron's stupid sayings. His mum finished ladling on the baked beans and added some fried bread to his plate.

"So, Ron and I have a surprise to tell you about, son."

"You have? How exciting, Mum."

She reached out and took Ron's hand across the table. "Now it might be a bit of a shock at first…"

"Sure Mum, I'll brace myself."

"But you're a good boy, so we know you're going to be pleased…"

"Absolutely."

"So, me and Ron have been talking, haven't we Ron...?"

"We have love," agreed Ron.

"Yes Mum?"

"And Ron has cashed in some of his pension…"

"Right..."

"And we've decided to spend some of it." Sam's mum took a bite of her sausage and looked excitedly towards Ron. "Do you want to tell him?"

"Mum, just tell me!"

"Okay, here goes," she grinned. "We're actually going to cash it all in. And we're renting out this house while we're gone…"

"What?" Sam felt a bit wrong-footed.

Ron butted in. "Me and your mother are moving out to Spain, Samuel."

"Spain? You're moving to Spain?"

"Yes, isn't that amazing? We've bought a villa in Alicante?"

"Alicante?"

"Yes dear. Alicante is in Spain," confirmed his mother, helpfully.

"But… when?"

"The villa's ours from this Thursday," chimed in Ron. "New tenant's will be moving into this old place on Friday."

"But what about the new car? The one in the driveway?"

"Ah that's my new TT," laughed Ron. "That's what we're using to get down to Spain."

Sam's mum let out a little whoop and then looked immediately embarrassed at the noise she'd just made.

"You're moving to Spain? With Ron? And an Audi TT?"

His mum nodded excitedly, grinning inanely.

"Am I coming?"

"Of course, dear…"

"Oh right, that's not so bad then."

"Oh darling, of course we want you to come out and visit," laughed his mum, "The villa has a sofa bed especially for when you come."

Ron looked thoughtful and then clarified. "Once or twice a year maybe, I mean not too often. The villa's quite small for three, Samuel."

"Oh right."

"Are you pleased for us, Sam? Say you're pleased for us."

"Now's not the time to be selfish Samuel. Me and your mother have been planning this for a long time. And we thought it would be a good chance for you to finally spread your wings. You know, grow up a little bit."

He looked at his mum's face. She seemed so excited, and her eyes were pleading for him to be overjoyed. "Sure

Mum. I'm pleased for you." Sam poked a sausage with his fork.

"Well tell that to your face then, Samuel. You've got the look of a spanked arse!" barked Ron.

"Well, I'm just not sure where I'm going to live. I haven't even got a job yet and you're talking about renting out the house I've lived in for 18 years?"

"Oh, we've thought of that already, darling," consoled his mum. "Ron's niece has a room off Lewisham High Street. It's a bit small but she said you can have it for free until you get a job."

Sam had met Ron's niece, Ruth, before. Ruth had the personality of a broken fridge and rumour had it she spent her weekends hunting wild boar with a baseball bat.

"Ruth?! I don't wanna live with Ruth. She's scary as fuck."

"Language darling!" scolded his mum, "Ruth's lovely… once you get to know her."

"Well, you can always go out and get yourself a job, Samuel," added Ron annoyingly. "Then you can live wherever you like."

Sam stared at his baked beans, despondently.

"Anyway sweetheart, we told her you'd be popping over this afternoon. You know, to have a look at the room. She said you can start sleeping there from tonight if you like."

He dropped his fork into the beans and got up to leave the table. As he left the room, he tried to slam the kitchen door behind him, but Ron had fitted it with a soft-closing device, so he just had to watch as it very slowly started to shut.

"By the way darling," his mum added as the door drew to a close at an excruciatingly sloth-like speed, "you've got your t-shirt on back to front."

Two Mules for Sister Sara

Sam sat on a bench in the park, staring at the joggers going round and round. The excitement he'd felt at the beginning of his new post-college life had quickly evaporated. They literally couldn't wait one week after he left college before making plans to pack up and slope off to Spain without him. He knew his Mum was just blinded by the excitement of it all, but this whole new scheme definitely had Ron's selfish pawprints all over it.

Sam knew he'd always had trouble fitting in. At school, he'd never really been into football or any of the other sports on offer, he wasn't coordinated enough to skateboard, he wasn't smart enough to be a nerd and he certainly wasn't cool enough to be popular. At his sixth form college, it had been a similar story. Those jerks at the party last night definitely weren't his friends and he'd obviously misread the signals from Veronica. And here Sam was homeless, penniless, car-less, mum-less and definitely Veronica-less.

He tossed half of his Wagon Wheel towards the pigeons congregated around the bench and watched them bicker over the chocolatey biscuit.

A boy on his bike whizzed past the bench, momentarily scattering the pigeons. "Morning paedo!" he laughed on his way past. It was one of the lads from Sam's college – obviously word from the party had spread quicker than expected.

“I’m not a paedo!” Sam shouted back. *Why was everyone calling him that?* He took out his phone and googled Jimmy Savile’s name. *Oh balls.* He sighed as he realised he had gone to Veronica’s party dressed as the most prolific sex offender in British history.

Why didn’t he check this before? He could have gone as one of the other British icons Ron had suggested from the TV – Rolf Harris maybe or even that pop singer Gary Glitter. Anyone would have gone down better than Jimmy bloody Savile?

The pigeons had all dispersed, but left the chunk of Wagon Wheel behind, obviously establishing it contained way too many E numbers for their liking. Sam decided to put it in the bin but as he picked it up, he noticed the chocolate had melted into the grass. He tried to wipe the mess up with the wrapper but then saw something unusual. At first, he wasn’t sure if he’d counted right – one, two, three, four – yes, he had! Right there in front of him, nestled in amongst the chocolatey grass, was a solitary four-leafed clover.

He got down close to examine the specimen and carefully counted the leaves again to be sure.

Satisfied his eyes weren’t deceiving him, he plucked the tiny clover and sat back to admire it. Having learnt from his previous mistake, he decided it was best to google *four-leaf clover* to make sure it was definitely lucky. The internet gods smiled on him, and he carefully placed his new lucky charm in his pocket. Looks like his luck was going to change at last. Oh yes, watch out world, Sam Juniper was back in the game.

With a sense that his new-found lucky forcefield was surrounding him, he headed off to Ruth’s house to claim her spare room.

* * *

When Ruth opened the front door, her first words were, "Oh, it's you."

"Hi Ruth," said Sam cheerfully, "I'm here for the spare room."

"You'd better come in I suppose."

He stepped warily into her hallway but was immediately halted in his tracks.

"Stop!" instructed Ruth, "We have house rules here. Shoes off at the front door."

"Oh sure," replied Sam, "Sorry." He started to undo his laces.

"Outside the front door." Ruth pointed back towards the step.

"You want me to step back out?"

"Yes. That's what shoes off at the front door means."

"Right. Of course it does." Sam stepped back out and continued undoing his laces. After taking them off, he stood back up, holding his shoes.

"Now put them down there." Ruth was pointing back at the step. "Are your socks dirty?"

He looked down at his socks. "Well, a little bit… from standing on the step, I guess?"

Ruth rolled her eyes and sighed. "Come in then but try not to mess up my carpet."

Sam tip-toed awkwardly into the hallway, trying not to press too hard on the carpet. A grey cat was sitting at the bottom of the stairs, looking back at him judgmentally.

"Right, other rules," started Ruth. "My cat is called Wordsworth. You need to tell him you like him each time you pass him, or he won't forgive you."

He looked at the cat. "Hello Wordsworth. I... like… you."

"Good. Also, please don't sit on any furniture. I'd prefer it if you sat on the floor."

"Right. No furniture."

"I've allowed for eight sheets of loo roll for you per day. If you need more then you'll have to buy your own."

"No problem, I'll buy my own."

"Wash your hands and feet before entering the lounge or kitchen."

He looked at his hands wondering if they somehow looked particularly offensive.

"Covid!" clarified Ruth. "I also lock the front door at 9.45pm. If you're not in by then, you'll have to stay outside."

"9.45, got it."

"Also, no non-vegan food, no sarcasm, no pop music and no guests."

"Well that all sounds very reasonable," he smiled, wanting to cry.

Ruth eyed him carefully, presumably scanning for sarcasm. "Okay, I'll show you the room." She headed up the stairs with Sam tip-toeing carefully after her.

"You're a nice cat," he whispered to Wordsworth as he went up the stairs.

* * *

Ruth opened the door halfway. "I'm afraid it doesn't open fully as the wardrobe's in the way. You'll have to squeeze past."

"Righto." Sam snaked his body around the door into the bedroom.

An ungainly wardrobe monopolised most of the space although there was a good two-foot square of scratched linoleum in the middle of the room. The single bed appeared to be around two-thirds the length of a normal single bed with a solitary chair optimistically presenting itself as the only other piece of furniture in the room. A bright orange shower curtain was draped across the tiny window and the tiled walls showed scars from where pipework had once been removed.

"Why's there a tap here?" he gestured towards a single fawcett sticking out of the wall, with no sink beneath it.

"Don't touch that, you'll get the floor all wet. This used to be the bathroom, but my uncle couldn't undo the nuts on that one, so we left it."

"Well, this all looks… lovely. I'm sure it'll be very cosy." Sam tried hard to smile, hoping he wouldn't register on Ruth's sarcasm detector.

"Good. Toilets are down the landing but don't forget what I said about the loo roll." With that, Ruth disappeared back downstairs, leaving Sam to explore his miniscule new home.

* * *

I need to get out of here, thought Sam.

He spent the next few hours slumped on his miniature bed, sulking that this was now where he was going to be living. He'd been quite happy at his mum's house for the last eighteen years – well, happy for sixteen of them maybe, until Ron had arrived on the scene after his dad had died. Why was everything suddenly changing so quickly?

Whatever it took, he knew he needed to get himself a job, any job, so he could relocate from this tiny sovereign dictator state ruled by the tyrannical Ruth. He pondered the quickest way to get a job so he could earn some money and find his own place.

He picked up his phone and typed in *Jobs Lewisham Anything*. He skipped through a series of adverts for professional recruitment agencies and came across a list of local job postings. Whatever the first one on the list was, he decided he would apply.

Table Dancers Wanted – South London – Training will be provided – £40p/h plus tips.

Okay, the money was great, but Sam figured he probably wasn't what they were looking for. Whatever the second one on the list was, he decided he would apply for that instead.

Junior Cat Litter Tray Emptier – Lewisham – No shoes in the house – Salary TBC.

He suspected that Ruth had probably posted that particular job and he had no wish to be Wordsworth's full-time poop scooper. Right, whatever the third one on the list was, he decided he would definitely apply.

Sandwich Board Salesman – New Cross – £6.80/hour

Jackpot, thought Sam. He loved sandwiches and he knew he would definitely be able to sell them to people. He checked the address and phoned them up to ask for an interview. Professional companies always love it when a random person just phones them up rather than going through the formal CV process.

"You want an interview? Uh, sure come on down about three this afternoon," said the confused voice on the other end of the line. "We're on Queen's Road. The blue shop with *Private* written above the door. I'll be here till seven tonight."

Sam was beside himself with excitement. Straight in there with a job interview, no messing around. The guy seemed a bit vague but that was fine, he was probably just taken aback by Sam's go-getter attitude. He wondered why a sandwich shop would have *Private* written across the top of the door. He guessed it must be very exclusive – maybe they only sold sandwiches to celebrities or something.

He ran back downstairs, paused to tell Wordsworth he liked him and then put his trainers on outside the front door. He had enough time to run back to his mum's house, take a quick shower and pick up his interview suit (in fact his only suit).

Maybe that four-leaf clover was bringing him a bit of luck after all.

* * *

Queen's Road wasn't the most salubrious part of New Cross. In fact, the part of it Sam was standing in consisted of a bookies with a broken sign, a greasy spoon and a dubious looking sex shop with blanked out windows. It was strange though because the address the man on the phone had given him should have been right where the sex shop was situated. Sam looked up and down the street, checking he was in the right place.

He looked at the shop again. The windows had all been covered over with blue paper on the inside and there was no shop name other than *Private* written above the door – *aah,* thought Sam. It seemed a strange place to sell sandwiches though. He tried to imagine an array of dirty old men in raincoats, nibbling on cucumber sandwiches whilst perusing the selection of pornographic videos available.

Oh well, he thought, *I'm here now – sure it'll make sense once I'm inside. Maybe there's a nice little café at the back?*

Once he was inside it was apparent there wasn't a nice little café out the back though there did appear to be a rather large dildo section towards the rear of the shop. The shop emanated a distinctive damp smell, a bit like a wet towel that had been left on the floor for a few too many days. There were several wobbly racks displaying magazines and DVDs and an array of cheap looking lingerie hung on plastic coat hangers.

"Can I help you?" came a gruff voice from the man behind the counter, who looked distinctly like Super Mario, only less pixelated. Sam stared in awe at the industrial-sized Black Mamba vibrator stood upright on the counter next to him.

"I said, can I help you?"

I mean, what the hell would someone even do with something that size? It looked like it was designed to break up concrete. It must have about three car batteries inside it.

"Look, we've got squish, slush, slosh, smash, scat, booty, nip-nops, foot fetish, furry, fuzzy, funny, hairy, hunky, monkey, manky, munter or, if you're a complete perv, we've got straight. How about you tell me what you're into?"

Sam felt a little stunned from the porn barrage. "Umm, nip-nops, I guess?" He had no idea what nip-nops meant, but it sounded like the most inoffensive thing on this pornographic menu.

"Right, nip-nops. You want big, small, jumbo, pointy, pokey, wonky or shonky?"

"Sorry, I'm not quite sure what shonky nip-nops are?"

Super Mario sighed, reached under the counter and pulled out a magazine called *Models with Shonky Nip-Nops*. "There you go sir – shonky nip-nops."

Sam looked at the cover, still not entirely sure which part of it could be described as a shonky nip-nop. "Who the hell is into that?!"

"Well, I thought you said you were, sir?"

"No! No, I'm not. I'm here for the interview. About the sandwich thing?"

Super Mario frowned for a moment and then his eyes lit up. "Oh! The sandwich thing, right."

"Yeah, the sandwich thing. You need to give me an interview, right?"

"Sure, sure. An interview." Super Mario then stared at Sam, blankly.

"So… have you got any questions for me?" asked Sam.

Super Mario looked around his store humming, then back at Sam. "So, when can you start?"

"Really?" exclaimed Sam, "You mean I've got the job?"

"Ah yeah, sure, you got the job. Congratulations."

"I can start straight away. The sooner the better."

"Ok, well the board's over there." The Mario brother pointed towards a timber A-frame with two straps sitting in the corner of the shop.

"What's that?"

"The board. It's the sandwich board. You just need to put it on and walk up and down New Cross High Street."

"Put it on?" Sam looked at the picture on the front of the board which looked suspiciously like a disembodied, plastic vagina. The image was accompanied by the words *The all-new Man-Gina, now only £24.95* followed by the address of Super Mario's sex shop.

"Sure, put it on. You did know what a sandwich board was, didn't you?"

"Yeah, course I did," lied Sam.

"Right then, here we go." Super Mario lifted up the A-frame, shuffled towards Sam with it and slowly placed it over him so the straps rested on his shoulders. Sam found himself appropriately sandwiched between the two heavy flaps; each side emblazoned with a brightly coloured Man-Gina.

"I don't even know what a Man-Gina is? What the hell is this thing."

"It's a stimulator, for men. You stick your thing in the hole and you're away." Super Mario was demonstrating by putting his forefinger repeatedly into the curled-up fist of his left hand, which made Sam feel very uncomfortable.

"Look," said Sam, "I'm really not sure I can do this."

"Sure you can." Super Mario leapt towards the front door and held it open. "Just walk up and down the high street. If anyone asks you about it, you send them here. And come back before 7pm or I'll be gone home. It's easy!"

Sam looked down at the Man-Gina in the picture, and then thought about the alternative of going back to Ruth's dingey room. "Okay. Let's get this over with."

* * *

Sam waddled up the High Street, banging his knees on the board with every step he took. The weight of the board was tugging the straps into his shoulders.

"What's a mangina?" asked an old lady standing by the bus stop.

"It's pronounced Man-Gina," replied Sam, "and please don't ask me to explain it."

"Is it for cleaning windows?"

He had no idea how the old lady had arrived at this particular conclusion but decided to go with it. "Yes. Yes, it's for cleaning windows." Sam waddled away as quickly as possible before she could ask any more questions. Then he heard a familiar voice from behind.

"Oh my god, Veronica look! It's the paedo from your party!"

He turned to see Veronica with three of her friends walking towards him. She had an entirely new look of disgust on her face, one Sam hadn't encountered before.

"Jesus, what are you wearing, paedo? Is that supposed to be a vagina?!"

He wanted the earth to swallow him up. Immediately. And then spit him out. And then stamp on him. "No, it's a Man-Gina. Look, I'm just trying to earn some money, that's all."

Veronica and her friends whooped with delight and derision at his explanation, and all simultaneously pointed their phones at him, recording his plight for TikTok. "You dirty pervert," said one. "Ugh, he's so disgusting," said another. Veronica walked up to Sam and looked him direct in the eye. "You are one disgusting little shit, Samuel Juniper."

Sam looked down at the pavement, feeling ashamed. He turned around and slowly waddled away like a sad penguin. In the background he heard the girls hurling insults at him and bursting into fits of giggles.

He kept walking to the far end of the high street where it was quieter, hoping to find somewhere no one else would see him. He eventually found a shaded spot around the corner, next to a public lavatory and wiped a small tear from the corner of his eye.

"Stupid bloody sandwich board," he muttered to himself. He reached into his pocket and felt around for his lucky four-leaf clover. He carefully grasped the stem with his thumb and forefinger and took it out to scrutinise it closer. He had to hold his arm out at full length in order to make eye contact with the clover around his sandwich board. "Well, you didn't help me much, did you?"

But then he noticed one of the leaves had fallen off in his pocket. His lucky four-leaf clover had now been relegated to the ranks of an ordinary three-leaf clover. No wonder it wasn't bringing him any luck. Sam placed it gently back in his pocket and wondered how much worse his luck was going to get now.

Three Amigos

Sam loitered out the way next to the public lavatory for about twenty minutes, trying to while away the time. Hopefully there would be much less chance of running into anybody else he knew.

Suddenly, seemingly out of nowhere, a girl with a skinhead came sprinting around the corner and smacked straight into him, knocking him and his sandwich board onto the pavement. Sam wriggled helplessly as he found himself pinned to the ground by the weight of the board.

The girl, who'd also tumbled to the floor, quickly picked herself up, then turned around to check behind her. Then she looked back at Sam, panting heavily.

"Quick. Hide this." The girl stuffed a screwed-up ball of brown paper into his hand. "Don't let anyone see it. Milquetoast will find you."

Sam was in no position to argue, as he found himself still pinned to the floor by his own sandwich board. He watched as the girl bolted towards the public toilets, opened the door to the Ladies and then quickly shut the door behind her.

She then poked her head back out the door, shouted, "I'm from MI-51," and then immediately slammed the door shut again.

Sam lay still for a moment, slightly baffled and wondering what had just happened. He could feel the ball of paper in his hand but couldn't crane his neck over the board to see what it was. He wriggled his body sideways, just enough to bend his knees, in order to try and heave himself up. He grabbed a railing next to the toilets and used it to lever himself back onto his feet. Having just got up, he became instantly aware of the sound of several more footsteps sprinting towards him, before two men charged around the same corner and then also clattered straight into him.

As they all tumbled to the floor, Sam once again found himself flat on his back on the pavement, flattened between the sandwich board. The two men angrily picked themselves up and dusted themselves down.

"Motherfu…" Sam looked up at the two men glaring down at him. They looked like they'd possibly just been hurrying home from a hitman convention.

"Did you see a girl come round this way? Looks like a tomboy, shaved head?" said one of the men.

Sam thought for a moment. "Umm… shaved head you say? Yeah, I think I might have."

One of the men reached out a hand to help Sam up, which he gratefully received. As he was hauled onto his feet, Sam looked around animatedly.

"Yeah, there was this girl. She had tattoos and a big, shaved head." he made an exaggerated circle gesture using both arms to fully clarify the roundness of her head, in case they doubted his statement. "I think she went up that way and over the bridge." Sam pointed vaguely up the street in the direction of Southwark.

The man looked at his colleague, they both nodded and then immediately started sprinting off up the pavement westwards. He watched them run into the distance, before stretching out his arm to see what the mysterious ball of paper in his hand was. Unfurling it in his palm with just one hand was tricky, but it looked to be some kind of map, albeit rather crinkled from being screwed up in his sweaty palm.

Sam waddled towards the Ladies toilet door, and gently tapped on it.

"Hello? Lady? You can come out now, they're gone." He listened but he didn't hear anything.

"Lady? Did you want your map back?" Still nothing. Sam wondered whether he should wait for her. She could be scared or injured, he thought, or just having a really long poop. But the map might be important, she might need it to get home or something. In Sam's head he was fairly sure people didn't use maps to find their way home anymore, at least not since Google Maps was invented but still, it might have been important to her.

He decided to take off his sandwich board and wait. It was nearly 5 o'clock now so that seemed like a reasonable time for him to knock off. He carefully lifted the sandwich board off his shoulders and placed it down against the wall. Then he tried knocking on the toilet door one more time.

"Lady, it's me. The guy you knocked over. It's okay to come out now if you wanted to." Again, no response. "Okay then, well I'm just going to wait out here for you. I'll be sitting over by the wall. No rush! You finish whatever you're doing in there and I'll wait here with your… er, map."

Sam went and sat on the pavement, next to his sandwich board. She probably wouldn't be long now.

* * *

It was about 9pm when Sam started to wonder if she was ever coming out. He was supposed to have returned the sandwich board two hours ago. It was rapidly getting dark, and his poor shoulders were in bits from carrying around the stupid sandwich board since this afternoon.

Surely girls didn't take that long in the toilet. He wondered if maybe he should go in and check on her. He'd never been into a Ladies toilet before so wasn't too sure what to expect. He nervously walked up to the door and tapped on it again.

"Hello lady? Are you ok in there? It's getting kind of late, and I was thinking about going home soon." He put his ear to the door to see if he could hear her response. Nothing.

"You know what lady, I think I'm going to come in. Just to check you're ok. I don't want you to be scared or anything – I'm not going to hurt you." He listened again but was just met with the same unnerving silence.

"Okay, I'm coming in now." He slowly pushed on the door, and then cautiously stuck his head through the gap. He couldn't see anything at first, so pushed the door a bit more. As he looked in further, he could see two cubicles adjacent to two wall-mounted sinks and a small plastic bin.

He was struck by how pleasant it smelt inside. Usually, public toilets wreaked of urine so much it made his eyes water, but this one had the scent of lemon sherbets. Sam wondered if all Ladies toilets smelt this nice.

He took a step inside and started searching for the woman. She wasn't in either of the cubicles, there were no windows she could have crawled out of, no roof light and no other doors. There was a small cabinet built into one of the walls but that was firmly locked shut. He scratched his head – *where the hell could she have gone?* He looked at the map scrunched up in his hand and figured he might as well just take it home with him, and investigate further in the extreme discomfort of his new, tiny bedroom.

As he opened the door and stepped out of the Ladies toilets, of course at that precise second his mum walked past arm-in-arm with Ron.

"What you doin' in the women's toilets, you dirty little pervert?" asked Ron.

"Oh, Samuel. I raised you better than that didn't I?" concurred his mum.

Sam just shook his head in defeat and accepted there was finally nobody left in South-East London who didn't somehow think he was a pervert or a paedophile. "It's been a long day, Mum. I'm not sure I can be bothered to explain anymore. I'm going back to Ruth's."

He picked up his sandwich board and trudged off towards Super Mario's shop. When he got there, the sex store was all locked up, so he left the board leaning against the front door. He took one last look at the picture of the Man-Gina and decided he wouldn't be coming back in the morning; nothing was worth this amount of humiliation.

When he finally got back to Ruth's house it was 9.44pm and all the lights were off. He took off his shoes, placed them on the step and rang the doorbell. Ruth opened the door in a matter of seconds but kept it on the chain.

"What do you want? I told you I lock the door at 9.45."

"It's 9.44 Ruth."

Ruth looked at her watch, waiting for the time to change. "Okay, now it's 9.45."

"Well, it is now because you just stood there staring at your watch."

"Don't take that tone with me, Samuel. Wordsworth doesn't like it when people take that tone with me."

Sam sighed. "Ruth… in the last twenty-four hours I've been put in a headlock, thrown out of a party, laughed at, made homeless, called names, mocked on social media, publicly humiliated, knocked over on my arse – twice, and now my mum thinks I'm a pervert. I really just need to come in and go to bed."

Ruth sucked her teeth for a few moments, rolled her eyes and then opened the door. "Fine… I don't need your life story."

"Thank you," he said indignantly, marching past her in his socks. As he stomped up the stairs he added in a cross voice, "I like you Wordsworth," just to make sure he wasn't transgressing any rules.

He got into his cot-sized bed, accepted that one of his legs would just have to hang out from the side of the mattress for the rest of the night, and went to sleep.

* * *

Sam woke up after an excellent night's sleep feeling re-motivated and utterly invigorated. A new day beckoned as the sun shone through the shower curtain covering the bedroom window.

Whatever went wrong yesterday was behind him, and today was officially the second attempt at the first day of his new life. And he had a map.

He sat up in his bed and fished the screwed-up paper out of his pocket. By the time he'd got home yesterday, he'd been too exhausted to peruse the map.

He unscrewed it and laid it out on his duvet. The map was about the size of Sam's laptop and was drawn on what appeared to be a piece of parchment – either that or it was so old it had just faded to brown. He studied it closely, noticing it had been carefully hand drawn. Very neat and precise, but definitely sketched with a fountain pen or something similar.

It didn't have the style of a pirate map – there were no X's marking the location of treasure. It was more like a detailed schematic, not dissimilar to a map of the London Tube, only none of the stations were marked. Instead, it seemed to consist of dozens and dozens of interconnected lines linked up to random points. Each of the points was labelled, not with a place name or a town but with a seemingly random building.

One of the lines started at a 'Ballroom' and then onto a 'Rabbit Warren'. Another was labelled 'Fast Food' and that one was connected to a random location labelled as 'Alleyway'. He scrutinized the rest of the map, looking for clues to understand its meaning. In the top corner it was stamped with the text *'MI51.co.uk – The Knowledge'.* Sam cast his mind back to the night before – *wasn't that what the skinhead girl shouted out to him just before she slammed the door shut? I'm from MI-51."*

Any sensible person might have googled *MI51.co.uk* on their phone right about now, but Sam didn't think of this. *What was that other thing she said? "Don't let anyone see it... something or other will find you."*

He racked his brains trying to think what the other word was. Was it Make-Toast? Milk-Toast? Something like that. Mick Toast maybe? Who the hell was Mick Toast? Shit, if only he could remember what it was that she said.

Sam folded the map carefully and placed it back in his pocket. He had bigger fish to fry today – his main priority was to get himself a new job. Ideally one that didn't involve him advertising sexual paraphernalia.

He took his phone out and pulled up the same list of jobs he was perusing the day before but decided to be a little more discriminating this time. He scrolled past the ads for table dancers, cat-poop cleaners and flipping sandwich board sales personnel and looked further down the list.

There was somebody looking for Saturday staff at a bread shop. There was another vacancy for a vacuum cleaner salesperson in Sidcup. Then he spotted something that interested him;

Sales Assistant required for Bike Shop – Full Time – £12/hour – Shadwell

That sounded great! Now, Shadwell was a bit of a trek, and Sam knew he'd have to travel north of the river, but it was only the other side of the Rotherhithe Tunnel, and the money was decent enough to make it worthwhile.

He looked up their number and decided to try his luck. After a few rings, a friendly sounding man answered the phone.

"BeeJay's Bikes, can I help you?"

Sam explained he was interested in the vacancy and told him a little bit about himself. The guy seemed quite interested and suggested that he come in for a formal interview.

"Wait a second," said Sam, suddenly getting suspicious after his previous interview. "This is a proper bike shop, isn't it? You're not going to tell me a bike is a euphemism for something else?"

"What are you talking about? Of course not. You know what a bike is, don't you?"

"Well, I thought I knew what a sandwich was, but I got caught out on that one. Are you talking about a bike with two wheels and a saddle? One that you can pedal and ring the bell?"

"Yes! A bike! What the hell else sort of bike is there?"

"Oh, sorry," replied Sam, feeling a little foolish. "I just needed to check this time."

"Right. Okay, so do you want to come in for an interview or what?"

"Hang on a second," said Sam as another thought popped into his head. "BeeJay Bikes?! Bee Jay, as in Blow-Job?! Are you sure this is legit?"

"No," said the man, "Bee Jay as in Brian Jennings. That's my name. Why the hell would I call my shop Blow-Job Bikes?"

"Oh. Sorry about that. I guess I'm just a bit over-sensitive to things like that at the moment."

"Look, do you want this interview or not?" said Brian.

"Yes, yes. I definitely would. I'm really sorry and I'd really like to come in for an interview."

Sam figured he'd blown it, but Brian agreed to let him come in for an interview that afternoon. They said goodbye and Sam set about trying to clean up his interview suit after yesterday's antics. He put the suit on first – an old trick his dad taught him. *Save you ironing it son, pop it on and let your body heat take out the creases. Thanks Dad*, thought Sam, *great little shortcut*.

As he stroked the creases out, he heard the sound of two rattly motorbike engines pulling up outside. He pulled back the shower curtain and peered through the tiny bedroom window. As he looked down, he could see the two guys from yesterday getting off the bikes and walking up the garden path – the ones who were chasing the girl with the skinhead.

Christ, how did they find him here? They must have figured out he had lied to them about the girl! Sam felt his heart immediately beat faster, and his legs instantly felt like jelly. As the doorbell rang, he squeezed his body past the bedroom door out onto the landing to peek down the stairs and listen to what they said.

He held his breath as Ruth clomped along the hallway to open the front door.

"Do you know this man?" asked one of the men holding a photo up towards Ruth.

Please say no, please say no, begged Sam in his head.

"Of course I do," replied Ruth, "the little runt lives upstairs."

Oh, you total twat Ruth, thought Sam.

"We would like to speak with him," said one of the men, "he has something that belongs to us."

The map, thought Sam, *they're after the map*. He tip-toed towards the bathroom at the end of the landing and silently locked the door behind him. He could hear Ruth stomping up the stairs with the footsteps of the men following behind her. Their footsteps were muffled, so he guessed Ruth must've made them take their shoes off.

He turned the shower on so that it wouldn't look like he was just hiding and listened through the door.

"Oh, sounds like he's in the shower," said Ruth. "You can wait till he comes out if you like?"

"We don't have time to wait," said one of the men, followed by some distinctive clicks.

"Bloody hell," screamed Ruth, "Is that a gun?! Why the hell have you brought a gun into my house?"

Jesus, they've got guns! What the hell is going on? thought Sam, panicking inside the bathroom.

"Stand aside lady," said one of the men. Realising the situation had spiraled to epic proportions, Sam instinctively clambered up on the toilet cistern and squeezed his body out the bathroom window. His arm reached around and grabbed a cast iron drainpipe. As he swung his body out, he heard two gunshots firing through the bathroom door and Ruth screaming at them to stop.

He half-slid and half-fell down the drainpipe, landing in a cat litter tray at the bottom. He picked himself straight up, ran to the bottom of Ruth's garden and threw himself over the fence. As he peeked back over, he saw the men cursing him through the bathroom window. Sam didn't stop to think, he just sprinted down the alleyway bordering the bottom of the gardens. He knew they'd have to get their shoes back on before they could chase after him.

He hadn't run this fast since they made him run the 400 metres back at school, but there was no way he was going to stop. He darted down side alleys, jumped over walls and did everything he could to get some distance between them.

Eventually he had to slow down and catch his breath. He crouched down behind an odd-looking church and listened out for the sound of motorbikes. They weren't racing bikes that had pulled up at Ruth's front door, he remembered, but more like off-roaders. Scramblers with chunky tyres and high-pitched engines – he felt sure he'd be able to hear them coming if they were chasing him down.

After hiding for twenty minutes or so, he figured he must have lost them. At this point, he decided to do what any sane person would do in this situation; He got his phone out, thought about calling the police but then decided to call his mum instead.

"Ello darling, what you up to? You're not sniffing around ladies' toilets again, are you?"

"What? No Mum, I wasn't sniffing around anything – look, forget that. I need you to come and pick me up."

"Oh, I can't deary, Ron's taking me shopping. He's going to buy me a bikini for Spain. Can you believe it? Me in a bikini after all these years?"

Sam shuddered at the thought of his mum in a bikini and Ron leering after her. "Look, it's important Mum, can you just do this last thing before you sod off to Spain?

“Well, what’s so blimmin’ important? Are you in trouble Samuel?”

Sam didn’t want to worry his mum, so he tried to think of something that she would consider important enough to replace bikini-shopping with Ron.

“Interview! I’ve got an interview Mum! In Shadwell, and I need you to take me across the River.”

“Ooh that sounds exciting love, well done you. Gimme a minute, I’ll ask Ron what time we’re leaving.”

He cringed as he heard his mum screaming up the stairs to Ron, and Ron repeatedly saying he couldn’t hear her because his sinuses were playing up again. After an extended interlude which, by all accounts, included a full rundown of each of Ron’s medical complaints, his mum came back on the phone.

“Okay darlin’, Ron says I can take you, but I can’t pick you up after. Whereabouts are you?”

Sam relayed his location round the back of the Kingdom Hall of Jehovah’s Witnesses, which took an inordinate amount of explaining to his mum, and then sat tight waiting for her Mini to turn up.

* * *

As they drove through the Rotherhithe Tunnel, Sam slunk down in his seat, wary of any motorbikes they passed. He didn’t know how they’d traced him to Ruth’s house but whatever the map in his pocket was, it was important. He had never had a gun fired at him before. Was that normal in the adult world? He was pretty sure it wasn’t.

“Sit up straight, darlin’. You’ll give yourself backache like that.”

“I’m ok Mum. It’s comfortable like this.” Sam’s knees were folded up against the dashboard and his head was just below the level of the windscreen.

“Is it your pants? Are they making you sit like that?”

“My pants are fine Mum. Leave me alone.”

“I bought you some nice pants from Marks & Spencer. Why don’t you wear them?”

“I do wear them. I’m just not wearing them today! It’s nothing to do with my pants Mum, it’s your stupid car that’s uncomfortable.”

His mum stroked the steering wheel of her Mini as they came out the north side of the tunnel. “Don’t you listen to him Minnie, I think you’re very comfortable.” She changed the subject away from her car.

“So, what sort of job is it?”

“It’s in a bike shop, as a sales assistant.”

“A bike shop? But you’ve never ridden a bicycle, Samuel.”

“I know,” he replied, glumly.

“You be careful, or you’ll have an accident.”

“I’ll be careful, Mum.”

“Especially if you’ve got your tight pants on. You could end up castigating yourself.”

“It’s castrating, Mum. And I’m not going to castrate myself.”

When they pulled up next to BJ’s Bike Shop in Shadwell, his mum leant across to peck him on the cheek. “Good luck son, try not to say anything stupid.”

Sam looked back at his mum, gave her a deflated half-smile and then slammed the car door shut.

* * *

BJ's Bikes looked impressive. Inside there was a shiny open showroom, with glazed partitions and modern lighting. There must have been around forty or fifty gleaming bicycles all neatly stowed in racks. He approached a smart looking woman standing behind the counter.

"Hi, I'm here for the interview at three o'clock. I'm a little bit early."

"No problem," said the woman, "you can wait in our coffee area if you like? Old Mac who fixes our bikes up is just having his lunch in there."

"Great, thanks." He followed the woman past the racks of bicycles, towards the back of the showroom. She opened a large glass door and gestured for Sam to go through.

"Take a seat, we'll give you a shout as soon as we're ready to start."

He went through and sat down on a plastic chair next to Old Mac who was busy tearing the crusts off his tuna sandwich.

He decided to be as friendly as possible. "Hi, my name's Sam."

"Hi Sam, I'm Old Mac," replied the man as he took a bite out of his sandwich.

"Have you worked here long, then?"

"About ten years," said Old Mac, "Bloody love fixing old bicycles. A chain here, a gear there – you can give them a new lease of life with a few spare parts. You want a sandwich? I made them myself."

Sam peered into Old Mac's tupperware box and examined his choice of damp sandwiches on offer. "I'm okay, I think. But thanks."

The two men sat in silence for a few moments, occasionally catching each other's eyes with sideways glances. Sam tried to think of some small talk to break the silence.

"So, were you nervous when you got interviewed for this job?

"Not really," replied Old Mac, "I'm pretty lucky with things like that."

"Oh," said Sam despondently. "I thought I was going to have a bit more luck, but then I broke my four-leaf clover." He took the little clover out of his pocket and held it up towards Old Mac to show him. Old Mac leant forward to examine the clover.

"So? What's the problem with that?"

"Well, it's lost a leaf. It's just a normal three-leaf clover now, isn't it?"

Old Mac frowned. "Of course not. If a person had an arm taken off, it doesn't mean they're not a person, does it? They're just a person with one less arm. Same with your lucky clover – that's very clearly a lucky four-leaf clover but with a leaf missing."

Sam looked down at his little clover and smiled. His lucky three-leaf clover. It had a nice ring to it.

"If I was you," added Old Mac dipping his sandwich into his tea, "I'd get it laminated and keep it safe forever."

The woman from the counter popped her head round the door. "Mr Juniper? We're ready for you now."

Sam said a cheerful goodbye to Old Mac and then followed the woman through the doorway. She led him through the maze of glass partitions and into a small meeting room. "This is Mr Jennings; he owns the bike shop. Brian, this is Samuel Juniper – he's here about the vacancy."

Mr Jennings stood up and extended his hand. "Aah yes, Mr Juniper. The one who wasn't sure what a bicycle was."

Sam felt his cheeks redden as he shook Mr Jennings' hand. He took a seat on the opposite side of the desk and attempted to look professional.

"So, by the sound of it you've only just left college, young man? You've not had a full-time job before then?"

"Well, I did have one job, briefly," replied Sam, "it was in marketing."

"Marketing?" I see, who was that for?"

"It was for a..." Sam paused, trying to think how best to describe his stint for a whole afternoon working for Super Mario's sex shop the day before. "... it was a leisure emporium."

Mr Jennings looked slightly taken aback. "A leisure emporium? What does that mean?"

"It sold equipment. For personal activities."

"You mean like... sports equipment?"

"Kind of. Yeah, sports equipment and magazines, that sort of thing."

"Well, that sounds like good experience. What sort of sports?"

"Solo sports, mainly."

Mr Jennings looked up at the ceiling, trying to decipher this coded language. "Like what? You mean gymnastics? Or horse riding? Or wrestling? Or maybe scuba diving?"

"Oh yes, all of those. Lots of riding, wrestling and diving. Quite a lot of gymnastics too."

Mr Jennings nodded approvingly and made a little scribble on his notepad. "So, have you done much cycling yourself, Mr Juniper? Mountain biking, road cycling – anything like that?" he asked.

"No, not really," said Sam, "actually I've never ridden a bike in my life. Just never had one as a kid. I was more into computer games."

"Well, that's no good is it," replied Mr Jennings, disappointed. "That's the trouble with young people these days, too much time in front of screens and not enough time out in the real world."

As he continued to pontificate, something caught Sam's eye over Mr Jennings' shoulder. As he looked through the glazed partition, he saw two men come into the front of the shop – it was the two men with the guns!

"Well let me tell you young man, it's not easy selling bicycles these days…"

Sam was now only half-listening as he kept his gaze locked firmly over Mr Jennings' shoulder at the two men.

"…So why don't you start by telling me the three key things that make for excellent customer service?" asked Mr Jennings.

Sam watched pensively as the two men talked to the woman at the counter. "Umm… yeah… customers… service… and, uh… guns…" he mumbled in response to Mr Jennings, unthinkingly.

"Well, you're right with the first two, customer service certainly includes *customers* and *service* but I'm afraid we very much frown on the use of guns here, young man…" Sam could hear Mr Jennings prattling on but was now slowly shifting out of his seat as he saw the men staring through towards the back of the shop.

"Perhaps you could tell me a little bit about your future career aspirations then, Mr Juniper?"

"My career what…?" Sam crouched lower behind the desk.

"Your career aspirations, Mr Juniper. Where do you see yourself in five years' time?"

"I… think... I'll just move over here." With just the top of his head poking up over the desk, Sam edged steadily away. The two men were now walking towards the back of the shop, clearly scanning each of the rooms through the glazed partitions.

"Of course, Mr Juniper, if that makes you more comfortable. But I would like to understand more about where you're headed in your career?"

Sam was now crouching and moving ever closer to the door, peering towards the shop as the men drew closer. "I'm just going to… head over this way…"

Mr Jennings rotated his chair towards Sam who was now fully squatting by the door. "Mr Juniper, I really think you'd be more comfortable if you came and sat back at the desk."

The men spotted him through the glass. "He's through there!" one of them shouted, drawing his pistol. Sam flung the meeting room door open and charged down the glass corridor in the opposite direction to the men, desperately hoping it would lead out of the building. He heard a gunshot and a fraction of a second later one of the glass partitions behind him shattered.

He glanced back to see the two men following after him, as they pushed Mr Jennings out the way. Sam bolted for the fire exit and clattered through it into a yard outside. He grabbed hold of a large trolley and pushed it on its side across the fire exit, in an attempt to slow them down.

Within seconds he heard them on the other side, pounding on the door, trying to force it open. Sam could see an exit gate on the far side of the yard, leading out onto the road. He sprinted towards it, hurdling over the tyres, old bikes and spare parts that were scattered across the yard. Then he spotted an old bike leaning against the wall. It was a small pink bicycle with white tyres and ribbons attached to the handlebars. He guessed it was designed for an eight-year-old girl, as it had stabilisers attached to either side of the rear wheel, but he didn't have time to be picky.

As the two men finally forced the building door open, Sam jumped onto the little bike and pedalled as hard as his legs would allow. He heard another gunshot fire, as a bullet ricocheted off a brick wall at the back of the yard as he sped out of the gate and onto the road. He swerved into the traffic causing cars to slam on their brakes and honk their horns, but Sam ignored them all, pedalling like a manic child high on E numbers. "I'm doing it, I'm doing it!" he yelled instinctively, wishing his dad was there to see him ride a bike for the first time.

Four Weddings and a Funeral

Sam didn't know where he was headed, but he just knew he had to keep going. He furiously pedalled up side streets and through alleyways until he eventually came to a stop next to a small café – a chance to catch his breath.

"Oh my god! The paedo is following us!"

Sam looked around and saw Veronica sitting with her friends outside the front of the café, drinking iced coffees.

"And he's nicked some little girl's bike! Oi, paedo, leave them kids alone!" Veronica's friends all broke into shrieks of laughter.

"I didn't steal it!" he protested, "I'm going to take it back… oh what's the point." Sam pedalled away, cursing his luck at running into them now, of all times.

"And stop following me around, you weirdo!" hollered Veronica in the distance.

* * *

Sam paused when he got to the end of the road to think for a moment. He knew he wasn't following Veronica around, but it did make him wonder how the two guys with guns kept managing to follow him. How did they know he was at Ruth's house? And then how did they track him all the way to BJ's bikes?

He took the map out of his pocket and examined it a little more closely – it was the only thing that was linking them to him. He held it up to the light and noticed there was one tiny part of the map that was opaque – a small, black, circular sticker. It looked out of place with the rest of the map as it was newer and obviously added on at a later date. He carefully peeled off the sticker and balanced it on his fingertip. He noticed that the underside had an adhesive coating as expected, but it also had a minute, metallic fragment within it, like a tiny microchip.

Maybe it was some sort of tracking device? There was no other way they could keep appearing the way they did. He squished the little sticker in his fingers and dropped it into the gutter. As he did so, he heard the distant, tinny rattle of motorbike engines steadily getting louder. He looked back towards the café and saw the two men on bikes racing up the road towards him. He stashed the map back in his pocket and frantically started pedalling again.

He pulled off the main road and headed down a slip road onto the pavement. He could hear the motorbikes getting closer by the second. He'd discovered the tracker a few seconds too late, so figured they must have spotted him pedalling away. He looked over his shoulder to see them both hurtling in his direction, swerving around traffic islands and narrowly missing cars. Sam wasn't watching where he was going and careered into a leafy bush, emerging on the other side down a sharp embankment.

The little bike bounced and juddered as he tried desperately to keep it under control. A railway line at the bottom of the slope rapidly loomed closer, causing Sam to instinctively squeeze hard on the handlebar brakes. As the bike squealed and skidded, he tumbled over the handlebars and crashed into the chunky gravel at the side of the rails.

Sam jumped straight to his feet and looked back up the embankment. He could see the two men looking down at him, but they had wisely decided against following his route through the bushes. He looked up and down the railway line, trying to figure out the quickest way to escape. The track led into a dark tunnel in one direction, but the other way it looked like there was a station platform. Sam grabbed the little bike and ran along the gravel towards the platform, stumbling and slipping as he went.

As he reached the platform's edge, he climbed up onto the concrete section and looked up towards the two men. They'd jumped off their motorbikes and were now running along the pavement towards the station entrance. He hoped they didn't have their Oyster cards with them.

Sam glanced quickly around the platform, trying to get his bearings. It was empty of people, but a large purple sign confirmed he was at Whitechapel Station on the Elizabeth Line. He knew they would be bursting onto the platform at any moment, and he couldn't see any way out other than the way he'd just come.

As he turned to look, he saw a train coming out of the tunnel, slowing as it pulled into the station. As soon as it settled next to the platform, he banged on the electronic push-pad until the sliding doors swooshed open. He dived on carrying his little bike, catching sight of the two men as they ran down the station stairs.

Sam realised they'd spotted him. He saw them unholster their weapons and jump onto the train at the other end of the platform. The inside of the carriages were connected all the way through the train, and he could see the two men about four carriages back, grimly marching towards him.

He jumped back on his bike and started pedalling through the train, hoping the little pink bike would be quicker than they were. It wasn't. Sam swerved between the strategically placed vertical bars and even found himself doing mini-wheelies each time he went over the ramps connecting each carriage, but the men were still gaining on him as the train surged into the underground tunnel.

Although the train was mercifully empty of passengers, the wheels of the tiny bike just weren't covering enough ground to help him get away. *Stupid bike,* thought Sam. Suddenly a bullet struck a seat close to his head, causing him to jolt and fall sideways. He jumped up and left the bike behind as he broke into a sprint through the train. He carried on running through the empty carriages until he found himself in the final one, at the very back of the train.

He ran past an old man reading a newspaper and cowered towards the furthest corner of the carriage, knowing he was trapped.

"No offence, but I think you better get yourself out of here, mister," warned Sam, "there's some bad people coming this way."

The old man briefly peered over the top of his newspaper. "Oh, tish and pish, old chap," he replied, "I'm trying to read my paper."

Please yourself, Boomer, thought Sam as he took the map out of his pocket and curled himself into a ball in the corner of the train. He wondered if maybe he should swallow the map to prevent them from getting it after they killed him. He tore a tiny corner off and put it in his mouth. He chewed it and swirled it around his mouth, trying to make himself swallow it but was surprised to find it unfeasibly difficult to eat paper. He looked at the rest of the map and decided it would take him a good twenty minutes to digest all of it.

The train sounded like it was speeding up as it hurtled through the tunnel, the rhythmic clatter of the rails underneath reverberating throughout.

The two men walked menacingly into the final carriage as they finally caught up with him. They could see Sam, curled up and defenceless in the corner, with nowhere else to run. They ignored the old man and strode up to Sam, cocking their weapons.

Sam lifted his head and peeked up to look at the two men pointing their guns at him, spurious questions bouncing around his head. *When is the next stop? Why does everybody think I'm a paedo? Why doesn't my lucky three-leaf clover work?*

Suddenly, and somewhat unexpectedly, all the lights on the train went out. This was followed momentarily by the train coming to a sharp, abrupt halt. The noisy train had been silenced and the whole carriage, both inside and out, was in complete and perfect darkness.

Sam looked around him, but could see nothing, not even his own hand. Then he heard a flurry of random noises. Scuffling on the floor, then there was the crack of gunfire followed by a brief shriek, muffled groans and then… then… nothing. Total silence again.

"Hello…?" he asked. "Is anybody there?"

There was an eery, lingering silence. *Perhaps this was what it feels like to be dead?* pondered Sam. *Maybe he'd been shot? He couldn't see anything or hear anything. Oh my god, was he a ghost now?*

Then he heard footsteps coming towards him and became aware of somebody breathing in his personal space.

“Perhaps I’d better take that for you now, old chap,” said a voice in the darkness. Sam felt a hand gently unclench his own fist and take the map from it.

“Who… who are you?” asked Sam, unsure if he wanted to hear the answer.

“I believe you already know my name,” said the voice. “But I’ll be keeping an eye on you from now on, young Samuel. From a distance.”

“I don’t understand. How do you know my name? What’s going on?”

“All in good time, old chap, all in good time.”

Sam sensed the man take a few steps back out of his personal space, then heard the sound of the carriage doors whooshing open.

“And don’t worry about these two gentlemen anymore,” said the voice, “They won’t be giving you any more bother.”

After a few moments the lights flickered on, the train groaned back to life and started moving off again. Sam blinked repeatedly as his eyes readjusted to the brightness. He nervously stood up and checked his surroundings. The old man with the newspaper was nowhere to be seen but the two men with guns were still in the carriage, only now they were both unconscious and handcuffed to the overhead rail.

An automated message played over the train speakers. ‘This is the Elizabeth Line. Apologies for the brief delay there. The next station will be London Liverpool Street. Please alight here for the Central, Circle, Metropolitan & District Lines and the Docklands Light Railway.’

Sam warily walked towards the two men, their bodies dangling helplessly from the handrail. He didn’t want to get too close in case they suddenly woke. Sam was too exhausted for any more surprises today. As the train pulled slowly into London Liverpool Street, he waited by the doors. He looked down the train to see if anybody else had witnessed what had happened, but it was still empty.

Sam looked up and noticed each of the CCTV cameras appeared to have black tape stuck over them. Surely the shadowy figure couldn't have gone around and masked over all the cameras before going full ninja on both of these guys in the darkness? He would have needed eyes everywhere to know that Sam would even be here with the mysterious map. How on earth could he have known Sam was on this particular train at this specific time?

The train doors opened and Sam jumped off, trying his best to pull his collar up over the sides of his face. As he walked out of the station, he heard a woman scream as she boarded the train, calling desperately for help from the railway staff. He guessed the police would soon be on their way to figure out who these two gun-toting lunatics were, and he didn't want to find himself trying to explain it all.

When he got out onto the street, he looked at his phone. Maybe he could give his mum a call for lift home. On second thoughts, she was probably walking around the garden in her bikini by now.

Sam started the long walk home back to Ruth's house.

Five Graves to Cairo

A month later, Sam's mum had finally emigrated to Spain with Ron, leaving him with a parting gift of an excessively large lasagna divided up into twenty Tupperware containers. After the incident on the train, Sam had resolved to keep a low profile in the hope that the police wouldn't be able to link him with the two men who had been chasing him.

He accomplished this primarily by staying in Ruth's tiny spare room, with only the occasional peek out of the curtains to see if anyone was approaching the front door. He checked his phone regularly to scan the news and lived off his mum's lasagna so that he wouldn't have to go shopping but other than Ruth shouting through the door to see if he was still alive, he didn't really hear much from anybody.

As time went on, Sam became more certain that nobody was looking for him at all. There was a brief story in the media about two criminals from Russia who were wanted by Interpol being captured on the Tube, but there was no CCTV released connecting Sam to the incident. The guy from the bike shop presumably never gave Sam's name to the police when they came to investigate the gunfire. It was like the whole incident had just evaporated and been forgotten about by the world.

With life seemingly returning to normal, Sam decided perhaps it was time for him to come out of hiding. If nothing else, he was rapidly running out of lasagna, so he knew he would have to recommence his quest for a job search soon.

* * *

The following morning, Sam ventured out for a walk to the park for some fresh air. He took with him his lucky three-leaf clover which was now safely laminated and had a permanent home in the watch-pocket of his jeans. He still wasn't convinced it carried much luck, but he felt happier he had it with him – just in case it *was* working. On his way, he stopped off at the newsagents to pick up a packet of Wagon Wheels and headed off towards his favorite bench.

Sam was in thoughtful mood, continuing to mull over the strange events that led up to him being chased onto the train four weeks earlier. He stared into the distance, trying to remember the name of the mysterious old man who took the map from him. Ever since he collided with the skinhead girl in the street, his brain had been going round in circles trying to recall the name that she had blurted out to him as she stuffed the map in his hand. *It was definitely milk-something. Milk-shake? Milky-milk? Milk-jugs? Milky-bars-are-on-me? Ah balls,* he thought, *I give up.*

He tossed a piece of his Wagon Wheel towards a gaggle of pigeons and watched them peck at it, all except one of them. This one pigeon, standing patiently at the back of the group, just casually stared at Sam, clearly not interested in the chocolate biscuit.

Reluctant to go back to BeeJay's Bikes to see if they would still offer him a position, Sam wondered if he would ever find a job that suited him. Maybe he should just go on *The X-Factor* and try and make it famous as a pop star. Everyone loved Michael Jackson when they were a kid, right? Deep down, even Sam knew he wasn't destined for pop super-stardom. Realistically, a depressing visit to the job centre was clearly beckoning.

Sam looked back at the lone pigeon, who was continuing to stare at him intently.

"Are you watching me?" he asked the pigeon.

The pigeon silently shook its head, turned around and flew off into the sky.

* * *

That afternoon, Sam got the bus to Lewisham High Street and headed towards the job centre. As he walked through entrance doors, he gazed around the uninspiring foyer. A gormless-looking security guard eating crisps instructed Sam to take a ticket from an adjacent machine and then wait for his number to be called.

Sam pulled out a printed ticket and dutifully sat on a wobbly plastic chair along the back wall. The soulless foyer consisted of a few more scattered chairs, a wire rack containing various government guidance leaflets and a solid floor-to-ceiling counter at the rear. The counter appeared to have a reinforced glass screen protecting the three members of staff sitting on the other side. Sam wondered what sort of aggression could possibly manifest itself in a job centre, that required the staff to be barricaded behind the counter – perhaps there were actually people who angrily objected to people giving them a job?

There certainly didn't appear to be an angry horde of eager job seekers on this particular day. There was a girl with a pushchair who was waiting to be called up next to Sam and an older scruffy man in a camouflage jacket who was already talking animatedly with one of the women on the other side of the counter.

After a few minutes, a digital display on the wall flashed up Sam's ticket number and he headed up towards one of the empty counter spaces. The chairs at the counter were a little more comfortable, with a cushioned seat and wheels on the bottom.

Sam scrutinised the woman on the other side of the reinforced glass screen. A plastic badge on her lapel read '*I'm Maureen - Can I help you?*'. She was busily filling in the sections of a printed form and occasionally tapping the keyboard of a computer on her desk.

"Name?" demanded Maureen, without looking up.

"Sam," obliged Sam, feeling very certain of this.

"Full name?" urged Maureen, already starting to sound irritable.

"Oh. Samuel Samuel Juniper."

"Two Samuel's?"

"That's correct. The first one is because I was named after my Grandad. The second one is because I was named after Samuel L Jackson."

Maureen slowly raised an eyebrow, glanced up over her horn-rimmed glasses and stared suspiciously at Sam through the glass screen. Sam smiled politely back.

"And for what reason did you leave your last employment?" mumbled Maureen, turning her attention back to the paperwork in front of her.

"Well, it was just a bit of a miscommunication really."

"A miscommunication?"

"Yes, could you just write that please?"

Maureen grunted and tapped some buttons on her keyboard. "And what sort of work are you looking for?"

"Well, I don't know. Anything really..."

"Doesn't... know... anything... really..." mumbled Maureen as she typed.

"Well don't put *that*. It makes it sound like I don't know anything at all!"

"I have to take your first answer. Do you like children?"

"I guess so. I couldn't eat a whole one though!" Sam hoped a little levity might crack Maureen's walnut façade.

"Wouldn't... eat... children..."

"Oh for god's sake, don't write *that* down!"

"Sorry, first answer." Maureen tapped her pen on her desk as if it were her imaginary judge's gavel.

Sam swivelled on his chair, haplessly gazing around the Employment Office. He wondered if anybody else was having better luck at their windows.

The teenage girl he spotted earlier had one hand on her pushchair and was arguing with her boyfriend on a mobile phone. On the other side of the waiting area, the scruffy man in the camouflage jacket was aggressively flailing his arms around and shouting at the woman filling in his forms. The disinterested security guard standing by the front entrance was now grazing on his second packet of crisps.

"Ok Mr Juniper," said Maureen abjectly, "try and tell me what your *dream* job would look like?"

Sam looked around for inspiration. A fire extinguisher was mounted on the wall to his left. "I could be a fireman? First answer, put me down as a firefighter."

Maureen stared at him blankly. "A firefighter. Have you put many fires out, Mr Juniper? Do you know anything about being a firefighter?"

"Sure I do." Sam reached out and grabbed the fire extinguisher, lifting it out of its wall bracket and plonked it on his lap. It was heavier than he expected.

"Mr Juniper, put the extinguisher back on the wall please."

"I wanted to show you what I know about putting out fires. Look, you put your finger in here to break the seal - oops!" Sam tugged a little too hard with his demonstration and the safety pin popped out the handle.

"Mr Juniper, please put the extinguisher back!" Maureen tapped her pen on the glass repeatedly.

"*Right, you motherfuckers! Everybody get your hands in the air!*" The scruffy man in the camouflage jacket had flipped his chair across the room and was suddenly brandishing a shotgun at the woman behind the glass counter. The other panicked staff behind the counter all immediately crouched down behind the desk or quickly fled into the back office.

The man swung his head round and looked towards the security guard. "You! Don't move! Hands in the air! No, get on the ground!" The security guard started to kneel down, while trying to hold his packet of crisps in the air, slightly confused how best to comply with all of the instructions simultaneously. The teenage girl with the pushchair bolted to the corner of the waiting area and clutched her baby tightly to her chest.

Sam was trying hard to look like he wasn't there. He was used to being ignored but had surprisingly never mastered full invisibility. He continued staring directly forward at the counter with the extinguisher cradled in his lap, hoping the shouty man wouldn't notice him.

He flinched as the irate man fired a shot into the ceiling tiles above, causing polystyrene to flutter downwards. "Nobody gets out of here until I get my fucking allowance!" The man picked up a charity collection box, shook it and then threw it on the floor in disgust.

Sam wondered how much the man's weekly allowance could be. Thirty quid? Fifty quid? Jesus, just give the bloke his money and then we can all go back to filling in pointless forms. He could see the top of Maureen's head bobbing around behind the other side of the counter and wondered if she was phoning the police down there.

Sam sensed he was being watched. Then out of the corner of his eye, something caught his attention. Trying not to attract the gunman's gaze, he strained his eyes to the left to see a pigeon sitting on the ledge, just outside the window. The pigeon was staring intently at Sam and seemed to be taking an unusual amount of interest in the events currently taking place inside Lewisham Employment Office.

"*You!* Why haven't you got your hands up?!"

Ah balls, thought Sam, *he's talking to me*. He saw the man's reflection looming closer towards him in the glass. Sam tensed up; he wasn't great in confrontations. He was okay in awkward situations, but confrontations; big nope.

"Are you fucking deaf?" said the man quietly, leaning close to the back of Sam's head.

The cold steel of the shotgun barrel lightly touched Sam's ear, making him shudder. Instinctively his grip on the fire extinguisher handle tensed and a loud rush of carbon dioxide gases surged out of the nozzle, thrusting him and his chair backwards.

As Sam and the chair tumbled into the crazed man, Sam rolled on top of him clumsily knocking the gun out of his hands. Sam panicked realizing he was now pointing the extinguisher directly at the angry man as it continued to emit torrents of chilling gas straight into his face.

"I'm sorry!" he shouted, "I can't turn it off!"

"*Turn it off!*" yelled the man.

"I can't, I can't!"

"Just let it go!"

Sam flung the extinguisher cylinder in panic, and as he released the handle the noisy jet of gas miraculously ceased.

"I'm sorry about that, I didn't mean to…" Sam looked at the man in the camouflage jacket. He was lying motionless on his back, with a trickle of blood coming out of his nostril and a large, extinguisher-shaped bruise starting to form on the side of his forehead. "Oh!"

A stunned silence echoed around the waiting area, which was shortly followed by a sudden burst of applause. All the staff behind the counter were clapping enthusiastically.

The teenage girl with the baby was smiling through her snotty tears whilst the security guard rushed up to put handcuffs on the man whilst he remained unconscious.

Seconds later, three police cars screeched to a halt outside the building with their sirens wailing. Two police officers barged through the entrance doors, followed shortly after by another two. "Blimey, what's gone on here then?" said the sergeant.

Maureen tapped on the glass with her pen again. "Fireman was it, Mr Juniper?"

The pigeon was still sitting on the window ledge outside, watching with interest.

* * *

That afternoon, Sam found himself sitting in the Interview Room at Catford Police Station, getting irritated by a policeman.

"So let me get this right," said Sam. "I've had a shotgun pointed at me, I've disarmed an armed raider, potentially saved the lives of a dozen people and you're seriously telling me I'm now the one under arrest?!"

Constable Sullivan tried his absolute best to be sympathetic. "Yep! His lawyer is claiming for assault with a deadly weapon. How's your luck?"

"A fire extinguisher?! That's *not* a deadly weapon!"

"Depends where you put it, ma'am!" grinned Sullivan, doing his best Groucho Marx impression. "Wagga, wagga, wagga!"

"I don't understand. This is ridiculous. Can't your lot put a word in for me or something?"

"My lot? What are you saying? You mean Freemasons?"

"What? No, of course not. Your lot - the police, I meant!"

"Oh yes, I see. That does make more sense."

Sam studied Constable Sullivan carefully, just to make sure he was a real policeman.

"So how long is this all going to take then?" he asked.

"Well let's see now. We'll have to sort out the paperwork, make some phone calls, have a coffee and then we should be able to get you a solicitor."

"How long will that be?"

"That's what she said!" grinned Sullivan.

"How long?"

"About four days."

"Four days?! Are you kidding me?"

"At least it's not a week?"

"Thanks Columbo. So, I've got to sit here in a cell for four days?"

"No."

"What do you mean *no*? You just said four days."

"Well, we don't have a spare cell at Catford for four days. We'll have to send you somewhere with fewer criminals. Tunbridge Wells maybe? It's nice there, they hardly arrest anyone."

"Tunbridge Wells. So, when are we going to fucking Tunbridge Wells?"

* * *

Around ten minutes later, Sam found himself inside a police car parked in the yard at the rear of the police station. Constable Sullivan sat in the driver's seat and his partner Constable Gilbert had turned up and sat on the passenger side. Sam was handcuffed and plonked in the back.

"Shall we put the sirens on?" grinned Sullivan.

"Yeah, go on!" replied Gilbert.

Sam winced as the shrill whoops of the sirens sounded out around the police yard.

"Breaker, Breaker, this is one-zero-five about to break the sound barrier!" Sullivan and Gilbert both laughed hysterically.

"Let me have a go!" said Gilbert, grabbing the microphone. "Ground Control, this is Major Tom, permission for a low pass!" More hysterical laughter followed.

Christ almighty, there's two of them, thought Sam.

A voice came back on the radio. "*One, Zero, Five, can you stop pissing about with the radio. And Sarge says turn your bloody sirens off.*"

The gates to the yard opened and they headed out.

They had been driving approximately forty-five seconds, when Sullivan decided he was hungry.

"So what you thinking, Gilbert? Quarter pounder? Tacos? Kentucky?"

"Oooh Kentucky! Get in!"

"Get in my son!"

"Yes!"

"Kentucky it is!"

After a brief diversion, they quickly spotted a KFC. Sullivan pulled the car up onto a kerb which was broadly in the vicinity of a parking space and turned round to look at Sam.

"Right, you stay *there.* No funny stuff and maybe I'll bring you back a piece of chicken. I'm locking the doors anyway."

Sam looked down at his handcuffs as the cops slammed their doors and the automatic locking clunked into place. He forlornly stared out of the front windscreen at the two uniformed clowns heading inside the fast-food joint and sighed. Then he noticed a pigeon sitting on the bonnet, staring back at him. Sam wondered if it was the same pigeon that was staring at him earlier, outside the job centre.

The offside rear door unexpectedly opened, and an elderly man climbed into the back seat next to Sam.

"Hello Samuel," he said.

"Uh… hi," Sam mumbled back. "Sorry, who are you? How do you know my name? How did you do that? I thought the doors were locked?"

"Let me ask you a question instead, Samuel," said the old man.

"Ok, I guess," replied Sam, confused.

"After you discharged that Co2 extinguisher and knocked out that awful ruffian, how did it make you feel?"

"I'm sorry, who are you? How did you know my name?" The specificity of the question from the stranger led Sam to conclude this wasn't the idle chit-chat he might have expected from a passer-by in the back of a police car.

"I mean, having heroically rescued multiple innocent people and yet subsequently finding yourself being the one arrested… how does that actually make you feel?"

"I guess kind of shitty," resigned Sam, "but I'm not sure I could have done much differently. I mean, I didn't exactly plan on taking that dude out. It just kinda happened. I guess in the same situation again, I'd do pretty much the same thing."

"I've been watching you for some time Samuel. Luck appears to follow you around, doesn't it?"

"Like that pigeon, I guess." Sam pointed towards the bonnet where his feathery stalker was still eyeing him suspiciously.

"Ah yes," smiled the man. "Like the pigeon." The stranger had a boney face, neatly combed grey hair and delicate half-moon spectacles perched on his beaky nose. "Some may call it luck. Other people might suggest you are… *charmed*."

"Sorry, who exactly are you?"

"My name is Mr Milquetoast," said Mr Milquetoast.

"Milktoast?! You're Milktoast? That's the name that the girl with the map said!" Sam excitedly rotated his body so he could look more directly at the stranger. "So were you the old guy on the train? The one that took the map out my hand?"

"The name is *Milque*-Toast," clarified Milquetoast, correcting Sam's pronunciation.

"Oh. I see, *Milque*. Like French, I guess?" asked Sam, clutching.

"Certainly not," said Milquetoast indignantly. "I am an Englishman, a most loyal subject of His Majesty."

Milquetoast was dressed quite immaculately. His hands were rested on the handle of a carved mahogany walking cane and his right arm was adorned with an ornate gold wristwatch.

"Mr Milquetoast. Sorry, won't those two policemen go nuts when they come back and find you sitting in the back here with me? You realise I'm on my way to a jail cell, right?"

"Jail cell, dear boy?" smiled Milquetoast. "We will not be heading to any such establishment today, Samuel. A gentleman displaying your natural aptitude for luck, chicanery and artifice is much too valuable an asset to languish in such an institution for any length of time…"

Sam could see Sullivan and Gilbert leaving the restaurant each carrying a large bucket of chicken and already tucking into it.

"You are coming with me, Mr Juniper. I have need of your prodigious talents," declared Milquetoast, assuredly.

Sam had the uncomfortable feeling he may shortly be offered either a blue pill or a red pill. Sullivan and Gilbert climbed back in and started divvying up napkins and straws. Sullivan turned around to pass a chicken drumstick to Sam. "Here you go fella- *WOAH! Who the fuck are you old man*?!"

Gilbert reacted instinctively by whipping the Taser out of his pouch, juggling it briefly and dropping it down the gap between the seats.

"Gentlemen, no need for alarm," calmed Milquetoast. "Your Superintendent asked me to pop by. I'll be needing you to escort myself and this young prisoner to this address. Here, this memorandum will explain everything." Milquetoast passed a note across to Sullivan with an address on it.

Sullivan scanned through the note and then passed it to Gilbert.

"And you're saying *our* Superintendent wrote this?"

"Absolutely," confirmed Milquetoast.

"You're not lying to us?"

"Scouts honour, gentlemen."

"Well okay then, let's go." Satisfied with this explanation, Sullivan bit into another leg of chicken, swung the car around and headed off towards their new destination on the Old Kent Road.

Sam was bemused. As they drove off through South London, he played the conversation back in his head and wondered just how gullible these police officers could be. I mean they were dumb sure, and definitely unfunny. But did this old guy have Jedi powers or something?

He leant across towards the old man and whispered. "How did you do that?"

Milquetoast smiled mischievously and whispered back to Sam. "Sodium Pentothal. I wouldn't eat too much of that chicken, old chap."

"You put drugs in their chicken? When did you do that?"

"My organisation has contacts everywhere Samuel. Even in fast food restaurants. It certainly makes life, aah what's the word… simple!"

"But they're driving!! Is that safe?"

"Oh, quite safe, dear boy. This chap only thinks he's driving. Be assured this vehicle is operating under remote instruction from our Control Room."

"Control Room?"

"All in good time, old bean. All in good time."

* * *

Meanwhile, some distance away in central London, Florence Lawrence stood halfway across Tower Bridge, smoking a cigarette. She looked down at the muddy waters swirling below and exhaled.

This was where they both used to go for a cigarette break, one of the few places in Central London where you could see someone approaching from almost any direction. Not just in front and behind you, but left and right, above, below — pretty much anywhere you looked you had line of sight for the best part of half a mile. Cornelius had taught Florence lots of little tricks like that. He'd been a good mentor. And a great partner.

She stroked her finger across the inscription on her zippo lighter. 'No Fraternising.' He had given it to her as a gift when she had been inducted into the department as a full agent seven years ago.

It had been their little joke, but it had new meaning to her these days. They both knew the rules when they had signed up and in spite of their baser instincts, they'd always both tried to resist.

But now he was gone, she realised exactly why that rule was in place. It hurts more if you care too much.

* * *

It took about fifteen minutes to get to the Old Kent Road. The two police officers were now blissfully snoring in the front seats as the car sped along.

"Where are we going exactly, Mr Milquetoast?"

"I am taking you to where I work Samuel, the Brigadier would like to meet you. If he likes you, he may offer you a 'trainee position.' If he doesn't like you, then we'll drop you back off at a cell in Tunbridge Wells and save these good officers the bother."

Sam tried to visualize at what sort of place the enigmatic Milquetoast might work. An ultramodern headquarters maybe, or an underground nuclear bunker perhaps?

Milquetoast tapped his walking cane on the floor of the car to signal it to stop. Within seconds, the vehicle obediently pulled to the side of the road and stopped.

"We are here, Samuel," declared Milquetoast as he swung the door open. Milquetoast stepped jauntily out of the car and started to fiddle with his watch. Sam clambered out the other side, struggling with his handcuffs.

Milquetoast walked around the back of the car towards Sam and extracted an inch long metallic key from the face of his wristwatch. He took Sam by the wrists and gently inserted the key into the handcuffs. As the cuffs fell away, Sam took in his surroundings.

He looked up at the building next to which the car had pulled up. He gazed up, and then up some more, and then continued to look up further trying to fathom the sheer scale of the building. It was a colossal structure of steel and glass that appeared to extend up to thirty storeys, maybe more. It reached towards the heavens like some divine, monumental, superstructure heralding the modern age of architecture. Whatever it was that Milquetoast did for a job, Sam decided he wanted in.

"Right then Samuel," said Milquetoast, "When I take you in, please do not touch anything. And I mean *anything*. Just follow me, not touching anything and please do not attempt to take any souvenirs. But most of all, do not touch anything."

"Understood, Mr Milquetoast, don't touch anything."

"Splendid!" said Milquetoast, who abruptly turned around on his heels and strode across the Old Kent Road towards a rather dilapidated video rental shop.

Sam stood rather still for a moment. A quick double-take confirmed that Milquetoast was most definitely not taking him to the 21st century equivalent of the NASA space centre and was most definitely skipping jauntily towards what could only be described as a shithole. A 1990s shithole of a shop built by the Acme shithole shop building company back in the era when utter shittiness was considered to be far more acceptable.

* * *

Sam followed Milquetoast towards the entrance of the video rental store. A flickering sign above the doors declared 'VIDEODROME – HIRE OR BUY!'

The windows across the front were filled with oversized posters of movies starring Jackie Chan, Steven Seagal or other action heroes from a bygone era. It was without doubt an astonishingly below-average shop front, amongst a row of neighbouring ramshackle properties. Several tiles appeared to be missing off the pitched roof, and a blocked drainage pipe running down the left flank overflowed with green and black gunk.

As they walked into the store, Sam was equally underwhelmed to find the interior matched the shabby frontage. It was clear that he had entirely underestimated the full extent of the shitivocity that this video store truly possessed. The peeling walls were interspersed with movie posters held on with blu-tack and the threadbare carpet had a spectacular faecal brown-ness to it.

The shopfloor was lined with dozens of racks containing VCR cassette covers; Porky's, The Breakfast Club, Beverley Hills Cop. All of the ancient, corny movies Sam had vaguely heard about from the 1980s but never actually been bothered enough to watch. The oppressively repellent atmosphere of the store was punctuated by the unmistakable aroma of damp (and possibly deceased) old person.

Sitting towards one side of the store was an unimaginative formica desk with an anaemic looking teenager flopped in a chair behind it, feet comfortably up on the counter.

The teenager sported what appeared to be a mandatory Videodrome t-shirt which was conceivably three sizes too large. In all likelihood, Sam considered, the damp-old-person-smell was most likely a damp-young-person-smell.

"Krueger!" declared Milquetoast loudly and proudly as he bounded purposefully towards a curtain at the far end of the shop.

"Afternoon Mr M," drawled the disinterested teenager without looking up.

Sam quickly followed Milquetoast to the rear of the shop. "You actually work *here*? In a video shop?"

"It's a video rental store, Samuel. And yes, this is my place of work. Well, one of them."

Sam paused, picked up a plastic case from the rack next to him and held it up. "The Goonies! Who on earth is going to watch *The Goonies*? On fucking VHS?! Nobody even has videos anymore, have you not heard of Netflix? You people do know the internet has been invented don't you?"

Milquetoast stopped at the curtain and turned. "Quite so, old chap. It's almost as if we don't want to encourage people to come in here, isn't it?" He looked across to the shop assistant. "We're going to peruse the Betamax section, Mr Krueger."

"Right you are, Mr M," replied the teenager.

Milquetoast drew back the curtain, waited for Sam to walk through and then pulled it firmly back into place behind him.

"What's a… Beater Macks section?" asked Sam.

"Oh my, you have led a sheltered life haven't you, Samuel. *This is*, of course." Milquetoast gestured around at the smaller, danker backroom they were now standing in. The room contained further racks full of similar video cassette cases, only these cases appeared to be slightly smaller.

"Is that shop assistant on some sort of work experience or something?" whispered Sam, conscious that he could be overheard through the curtain.

"Work experience? Goodness no. Why on earth would you think that?" retorted Milquetoast indignantly.

"Oh. He just seemed…" Sam pondered the right words "…um, kinda bored. I mean, he barely looked at us?"

Milquetoast tucked his cane underneath his arm and turned to face Sam, leaning his body against a rack of romantic comedies. "Let me tell you Samuel, that *shop assistant* is a highly-trained and proficient, specialist killing machine. The mere suggestion that Agent Krueger is simply bored is quite frankly ludicrous, old chap."

Sam pulled the curtain to one side and peered back at the shop assistant. Agent Krueger had his hand down the front of his jeans and was apparently engaged in a specialist ballbag-scratching mission at that precise moment.

Sam looked around him. The movies appeared to be from the same era as the ones displayed out on the shop floor and were all neatly arranged by genre. Sam reached up to the Sci-fi section to grab a copy of a movie called *Labyrinth*, one he remembered watching as a child.

Milquetoast rapped Sam sharply across the knuckles with his cane. "What did I say? Don't touch!"

"Sorry." Sam petted his knuckles defensively. "So what's so special about these Beater Macks?"

"Betamax was just another format of video tape Samuel. It was rather less successful than its cousin the VHS tape. Hence there is even less reason for anybody to venture out the back here."

The flickering fluorescent tube lights fixed on the ceiling hummed like broken fly-catchers giving the Betamax section an unwelcoming electric blue hue.

At the back of the room there was an old-fashioned lift. Adjacent to the lift stood an old Victorian desk with a dilapidated video player on it. The lift-shaft doors were wound fully open, along with the provision of a yellow and black cone and a faded handwritten sign stating: 'THIS LIFT IS KNACKERED – DON'T FALL DOWN THE SHAFT!' In somebody's opinion, this was evidently more than adequate to prevent any passing employee from accidentally plunging to their death down a dark and lonely lift shaft.

"So what are *we* doing here?" asked Sam, definitely not touching anything.

Milquetoast was running his finger along the different cassette covers, clearly scanning for a particular title. "Ah, here we are. *Journey to the Centre of the Earth*. I always rather liked James Mason." Milquetoast pulled the cassette out of the cover and slotted it into the video player.

Sam looked around, expecting the video to start playing on a screen. But there was no screen.

Instead, the unserviceable lift shaft slowly groaned to life. Pulleys, cranks and cogs within the shaft clunked and whirred and, after a few moments, a large and cumbersome lift car strained itself upwards and into position at the opening. Milquetoast daintily sidestepped around the yellow and black cone and took up position inside the lift car.

Sam stood motionless, feeling somewhat perplexed. "So we're not watching a movie?"

"Good grief, no man. We've got work to do. Get in."

Sam stepped over the cone and into the lift. Milquetoast tapped his cane gently on the lift car floor causing it to immediately begin shunting downwards, into darkness.

* * *

The lift car was uncomfortably dim, smelt of engine oil and was incredibly noisy. The juddering components scraped together, causing a ghostly metallic wail to continually echo up the shaft, like the building was somehow screaming in pain at this unwanted activity within it. Every few seconds there was a loud clunk as gears shifted into place, causing Sam to twitch nervously.

The momentum of the lift car movement caused Sam and Milquetoast to sway back and forth. It wasn't altogether obvious to Sam if he was going up or down, or perhaps a bit of both.

Sam winced as the lift continued to growl and grind so decided it would be safest to put his fingers in his ears before his ear drums popped out onto the floor. He surreptitiously eyed Milquetoast, who appeared entirely unperturbed by the noise. The elderly man's expression remained blank as he impassively awaited the lift to complete its journey.

Sam felt the overwhelming urge to say something and start a conversation. Surely Milquetoast was thinking the *exact* same thing? Sensibly, Sam decided this would absolutely be the worst place to try and strike up a conversation. He could barely hear his own thoughts amongst the din of this vibrating mechanical monstrosity

- trying to start some chit-chat or elicit any further useful information out of the enigmatic Milquetoast would surely be utterly fruitless. It would make no sense at all. Any sane person would simply stand still, wait patiently and say nothing.

"MR MILQUETOAST," shouted Sam. "WHAT SORT OF ORGANISATION IS THIS?"

"Eh?" asked Milquetoast, looking quizzically back at him.

"I SAID..." shouted Sam even louder, "WHAT SORT OF ORGANISATION IS THIS? WHERE ARE WE GOING??"

"Oh, I see," said Milquetoast nodding helpfully. He went on to explain exactly what sort of organisation it was that he worked for and was careful to include thorough details of how he came to be involved with the organisation, how long he'd worked there and what he thought was particularly good or bad about it. He then went on to explain a little about the history of the organisation and the nature of the industry they worked in before clarifying exactly how he thought Sam could be useful to the team going forward. Milquetoast actually felt very satisfied with the clear, concise and comprehensive explanation he had given Sam.

Unfortunately, Sam didn't hear any of it.

He'd tried to carefully watch Milquetoast's lips and occasionally caught the odd word but on the whole Sam was fairly sure he'd missed approximately 97% of what Milquetoast had said. And it felt kind of awkward to ask him to say it all again.

The cacophony of metal scraping, chains pulling, and motors groaning continued to drown out his senses. He decided that he had been absolutely right that it was definitely a really dumb time to ask questions. What would be even dumber would be to try and ask another question.

"SO WHY DOES YOUR COMPANY HAVE SUCH A CRAPPY OLD BUILDING?!" Sam yelled at the top of his voice. Just as he stopped shouting the lift crunched to an abrupt and thundering halt.

Milquetoast looked thoughtful. "Well, that's quite simple, old chap. We could erect barbed wire and enormous fences to keep out prying eyes if we wanted to. We could even arm ourselves with gun turrets and laser beams. But the thing is Samuel, what you like to refer to as a *crappy old building...*"

With the lift now at a standstill and the thunderous noise suddenly ceased, Milquetoast clasped the metal handle on the lift shaft door and concertinaed the iron shutter sideways. He looked at Sam directly in the eye.

"… We like to call *security through obscurity*!"

* * *

Florence held her silver plated hip flask out over the Thames and tipped it.

"Here's to you Cornelius, you grouchy old bastard. Here's to *No Fraternising*."

It was her fault he was gone. Everybody had assured her that there was nothing she could have done but that did little to console her.

She had replayed those moments over in her mind a thousand times. Seeing his face for the last time as the lift doors trapped her inside. The helplessness of hearing the gunfire on the other side of the doors and hearing his lifeless body thud to the floor. The pain of identifying his lifeless body in the morgue, hours later.

She had resolved a long time ago that it wouldn't happen again. Florence would make sure of it. She'd learnt from her mistakes four years ago. She only worked solo these days.

No partners.

The *Sixth* Sense

Sam stepped cautiously out of the lift and looked around.

"Welcome to the HR department," declared Milquetoast.

"HR?"

Milquetoast blinked. "Human Resources, Samuel. Tell me you are familiar with the concept of a Human Resources department?"

"Oh. Yeah. Human Resources, sure. Resources for all the… humans. Makes sense." There was only one human evident in the Human Resources department at that moment.

The lift had opened into a brightly lit, open plan space. A single white desk was positioned in the centre of the white room.

Behind the desk sat a prim, immaculately-dressed female, typing keenly on a keyboard. She looked up, paused typing momentarily, and eyed Sam suspiciously as he entered.

Milquetoast gestured Sam forward and formally introduced him.

"Samuel, this is Foxfire."

"Ooh, hello," said Sam politely. He turned to Milquetoast and whispered, "I guess she's a highly-trained, specialist killing-machine in disguise too, right?"

Milquetoast looked at him, and then looked at Foxfire.

"Good god man, what are you talking about? She's the HR Receptionist. Why on earth would she be a *killing machine*?!"

Sam looked bemused. "I just thought maybe… you know, like the shop guy upstairs?"

"Didn't you listen to anything I told you in the lift, Samuel? Ms Foxfire here will be able to arrange your personal expenses, coordinate your payroll and ensure you are issued with a temporary contract." Milquetoast held his palm out towards Foxfire's desk.

Foxfire smiled sweetly at Sam.

"Please ensure any claims are submitted on the 3rd Wednesday of each month," she said, twirling a particularly long, sharp and lethal looking letter-opener somewhat menacingly.

"Right. 3rd Wednesday of each month. Got it. What do we do for lunch round here?"

"We have a staff canteen, a staff breakout area and a staff banqueting suite. We can provide proprietary nutrition pills, access to all vending machines globally as well as vitamin injections. We have all-access passes for a variety of chain restaurants and gold cards for most Michelin starred restaurants worldwide. We can deliver all vegan, vegetarian, non-vegetarian, lacto-ovo vegetarian, pescatarian, flexitarian and macro-biotic food types to your location. If you require kosher, freeze-dried or pan-continental variations please allow two hours' notice. We also supply luncheon vouchers."

Sam had zoned out somewhere around nutrition pills, but cautiously approached her desk. "So your name is *actually* Foxfire. It's not like some kind of secret agent codename?"

Foxfire fixed her stare at Sam. "You think everyone's got a boring name like *Samuel*?!"

Sam found the mocking emphasis, as well as the face Foxfire pulled as she said it, to be a little hurtful.

"We have an appointment with the Brigadier, Ms Foxfire. Follow me Samuel, we have places to be!" instructed Milquetoast. He flamboyantly spun his cane a few times and strode in the direction of two swing doors towards the rear of the office.

Sam looked briefly at the secretary who was still eyeing him with some degree of considered contempt. He decided against attempting any further pleasantries and quickly followed on after Milquetoast.

* * *

Milquetoast continued to twirl his cane ostentatiously as his heels click-clacked down the corridor. The corridor was bright and tidy with polished marble flooring. The walls were sporadically adorned with framed pictures accompanied by small brass plaques beneath.

Sam vaguely recognised some of the pictures on the walls and tried to quickly scan the descriptive text below.

"Don't dawdle, Samuel. Chop, chop," commanded Milquetoast.

Sam hurried to keep up with him, whilst continuing to randomly try and pick out the wording on the passing plaques. He managed to focus on one that read '7th Earl of Lucan' accompanying a black and white photo of a heavily moustachioed gentleman in a three-piece suit. He also spotted another one entitled 'D.B.Cooper', again accompanying a black and white photo above.

Sam skipped to catch up. "Who are these people?" he asked.

"Hmmm? Oh, the pictures you mean. Ancient history, most of them Samuel. Let's just say sometimes we require certain people to, hmmm how should I say it..." Milquetoast pondered his choice of words, "...*Disappear!*"

Sam felt the eyes of the pictures now following him, accusingly. He wondered if perhaps his own picture might one day be hanging up alongside them in this odd gallery — *was he destined to also 'disappear'? What sort of rogue's gallery was this?*

"So are we deep underground now, Milquetoast?"

"I suppose we are in deep, in a manner of speaking," confirmed Milquetoast.

"Are we in the building's basement?"

"Well, that we are my observant friend. But perhaps not the building you are thinking of."

"The lift ride seemed to go on forever, how far down did we go?" asked Sam, confused.

"Well we went down a few levels, I believe. And then we went East a few blocks. Then up a bit. Then we went down some more and then... west for a bit, I think."

"Oh."

"Think of the Betamax store as our reception foyer. Call the lift with the correct video tape and it'll take you to whichever department you require. Right, here we are, young man," declared Milquetoast turning a corner.

He knocked loudly on a glass door three times and then marched jubilantly into the office.

"Salutations of the day, Pip old chap! I have brought to you the new candidate for your consideration, this here fellow is the one and only Mister Samuel S. Juniper!"

Milquetoast held his arms aloft triumphantly as if to herald the immaculate arrival of Sam into the room.

"Samuel, may I introduce you to our illustrious HR manager, the most venerable and esteemed Brigadier Longstocking."

* * *

"Juniper! Yes Juniper! Come in, come in!"

Brigadier Longstocking was a big man sitting in a big chair behind a big desk. His big, pink face was punctuated with a big, ginger, extraordinarily-bushy moustache. He wore a classic olive green military-dress uniform decorated with an array of ribbons, rank badges and medals. On his head perched a peaked cap with a gleaming brass army badge situated front and centre.

The Brigadier animatedly welcomed in his guests, his bulging arms flailing around, flapping the paperwork off his desk.

"Come in and sit down here, son! Milky-bar, grab that chair in the corner and take a load off too," he boomed, gesticulating towards variously scattered furniture.

The Brigadier's desk was, to all intents and purposes, likely to be large enough to be utilised as a full scale aircraft carrier in times of war. However, Sam noticed it also somehow managed to be entirely swamped with precariously balanced stacks of books, trophies, stationery, notes and general paraphernalia.

Pictures were hung covering almost all wall surfaces of the Brigadier's office. The general theme of the pictures appeared to be the Brigadier being awarded commendations, the Brigadier posing with guns or tanks and the Brigadier with his arm around the shoulders of various celebrities from a bygone era. *Was that Elvis in one of the pictures*, wondered Sam?

"Well then Juniper m'lad," began the Brigadier, "My friend Mister Milkfloat here tells me you might just have some serious lead in your pencil and some fire in your belly and that we can make some old fashioned sausages - is he right?"

Sam literally had no clue what the Brigadier was saying.

"Sure. Belly sausages. And pencils."

"YES YOU BLOODY HAVE MY SON!!" roared the Brigadier banging his elephant-sized fist on the desk, as a rugby trophy toppled off in submission. "I've eaten lots of sausages in my life and, let me tell you, you my son have Belly Fire!"

Sam had no doubt that the Brigadier had certainly enjoyed lots of sausages in his life. The fact that the fabric on his uniform was up to the task of contending with the massive bulk of the Brigadier's arms, shoulders and chest was a testament to the robust stitching of the British Army's seamstress department.

The Brigadier reached under his desk, pulled open a draw and whipped out a printed sheet of paper.

"Right you bloody warrior, first things first. I need you to complete this questionnaire. Nothing important, just a formality. Bloody pen-pushers are getting everywhere these days." The Brigadier slammed the draw shut and off toppled another trophy. "Here you go, use my pen."

The Brigadier swept his hairy forearm across the desk surface nearest to Sam to make some writing space for him and plonked down the pen and paper. "Right, ten questions, you've got five minutes, go."

The Brigadier rocked back in his chair twiddling the tips of his moustache in his fingers. Milquetoast nodded politely at him from the corner of the room and then carefully watched Sam.

Sam looked at the paper and then slowly picked up the pen.

* * *

Sam read the summarised instructions at the top of the paper and then scanned through the questions.

Please read all instructions carefully. This questionnaire is designed to identify the appropriate MI:51 departments that you may display suitable aptitude for employment within. All multiple choice questions should be answered in black ink. If there is any question which you are unsure about, you should leave all answers blank.

1. Who are you, and why?
2. Is your morality objective or subjective?
3. Do you hold beliefs that cannot be scientifically justified?
4. Are you replaceable, and if so by what?
5. What is a harsh truth about yourself that you choose to ignore?
6. If your happiness has a flavour, what does it taste like?
7. Is your worldview based on consequentialism or deontology?
8. What is the worst piece of advice you have ever given someone?
9. What does a feeling feel like?
10. In a fictional world, could a four-sided triangle exist?

What sort of questions were these? Sam tapped the pen on his head several times, as if to try and jumpstart his brain. *What the hell sort of crazy questions were these??*

Sam looked at the Brigadier who had produced a miniature comb from his drawer and was happily stroking it across his moustache. Milquetoast was winding the mechanism on his ornate gold wristwatch.

Sam re-read the questions. He knew he could take a stab at some of them, but what kind of answers were they looking for? Did they want him to be insightful, was it stuff he should really know or was it just some sort of joke?

He re-read the paragraph of instructions at the top of the page, then scrutinised the last clause.

'If there is any question which you are unsure about, you should leave all answers blank.'

Sam left all of his answers blank and handed the paper back to the Brigadier.

* * *

The Brigadier put on his spectacles and scrutinised Sam's paper closely. He appeared to be going through each question one by one and was actually marking Sam's answers, or rather his total lack of answers, individually. Occasionally he stopped, rubbed his chin and looked skyward as if in deep thought about the complexity of Sam's complete lack of response.

"I like your answer to number 5. Interesting. Veeeerrry interesting."

Sam screwed up his face, bewildered at what could be even vaguely revealing about an entirely blank answer sheet.

The Brigadier picked up a notebook from his desk and ran his finger along the charts, cross-checking it with Sam's answer sheet. He started to scribble notes on Sam's sheet and wrote on the bottom in letters large enough for Sam to read from across the desk *'PASS - 10/10'*.

"Excellent work Mr Juniper. It's been a long time since anybody scored 10/10 on the selection questionnaire," the Brigadier beamed. He looked across to Milquetoast and passed across Sam's answer sheet. "Here Milkfart, take a look."

Sam was bemused and unable to fathom how his blank answer sheet had elicited such elated satisfaction in the Brigadier.

"Your answers are most perceptive Samuel," nodded Milquetoast approvingly. "You have demonstrated both your attention to detail and your capacity to follow instructions carefully. Most candidates feel obliged to commit themselves to an answer, regardless of their understanding of the question."

Milquetoast peered at Sam above his half-moon spectacles. "When we were children, Samuel, we were encouraged to ask questions and to put our hands in the air when we didn't understand. Unfortunately, as we get older and more jaded, the emphasis becomes more about reinforcing our own predisposed beliefs and proving our own point of view regardless of any evidence to the contrary. To quote the great Bertrand Russell - *One of the painful things of our time is that those that feel certainty are often very stupid, and those with any imagination and understanding are often filled with doubt and indecision."*

Sam pondered this quote, wondering who Bertrand Russell was. "So, you're saying it's better *not* to know things?"

"What I'm saying is the more we understand, the less we know, Samuel. Therefore, the curious mind is far more valuable than one filled with abject certainty of their own opinions. Let your doubts prevail, my good man."

The Brigadier reached into his drawer again and pulled out another piece of paper with a printed list on it. "Do you know what this is boy? It's a list of current trainee vacancies in our organisation. With your smasheroo score of ten out of ten, you'd be suitable for working in any of the departments listed on *here*?"

The Brigadier excitedly passed Sam the list with a dramatic flourish, much like a magician revealing a bunch of plastic flowers.

Sam's jaw slowly dropped open as he studied the variety of job descriptions listed.

MI:51 – Current Trainee Vacancies

Department of Propaganda *– Trainee inspirer / de-inspirer required. Must be capable of motivating and / or demotivating citizens in order to promote and / or marginalise relevant demographics within society.*

Department of Interrogation *– Nice guy trainee required for Mr Nice / Mr Nasty interview partnership.*

Department of Manipulation *– Weaselly trainee required for part-time role editing the wording of party political broadcasts (Tory background an advantage).*

Department of Superstition – *Virgin trainee required for participation in various nefarious ceremonies and / or Church of England regional meetings.*

Department of Addiction – *Trainee test pilot for innovative new recreational drugs required. Previous experience of heroin, ecstasy or cocaine an advantage. Non-smoker preferred.*

Department of Confrontation – *Trainee conflict escalator required to assist department head in high volume meetings. Must get very angry, very quickly, unnecessarily and without warning.*

Department of Bureaucracy – *Loquacious expert required to write small print, disclaimers, provisos, prerequisites, minutiae, restrictions, escape clauses, terms, conditions, stipulations and other specified particulars.*

Department of Subversive Toys – *Ideas person wanted. Must like manipulating tiny children's tiny minds.*

Sam read through the list of job descriptions three times and then stared at the Brigadier. "Is this for real? Department of Subversive Toys? Department of Interrogation?? What is this place, the job centre for sado-masochists?!"

"Ooh yes!" enthused the Brigadier getting out of his seat. "The Department of Subversive Toys, that'd be a great place for you to work. So many opportunities for a bright young man like you. You my son, are Subversive Toys material, without a doubt!"

"But… what do you mean? What do they do?"

The Brigadier looked confused. "Milquetoast, didn't you explain?"

"Of course I did," replied Milquetoast, who in turn looked annoyed at Sam. "I told him all about the different departments in the lift on the way down here."

The Brigadier seemed irritated by the lack of effective, military-grade communication between them but opted to fill in the gaps himself. He loved an opportunity to grandstand his historical knowledge about the various sections within MI-51.

"The Department of Subversive Toys has been instrumental in the creation of some of the world's most incredible inventions and plans. Transport yourself back to the start of the century, a somewhat more innocent time. You remember 9/11, Samuel?"

Sam was born shortly after the millennium, so remembered it—not very well at all. But he had seen all the clips on the internet. "Not really. You're not going to tell me you helped blow up the Twin Towers, are you?"

The Brigadier snorted. "Don't be ridiculous, boy. But our Subversive Toys team were assigned to help the CIA in the years following it."

"Help them how?"

"Oh, all sorts, absolutely everything! Ever heard of *Operation Devil-Eyes*? Look that up on your fangled twitternet. Then you'll see what those chaps can do."

Devil eyes? What fresh nonsense was this? Sam looked across at Milquetoast to see if he was having his leg pulled.

"The Brigadier is quite correct, Samuel," confirmed Milquetoast. "You can look it up for yourself if you don't believe us. Operation Devil-Eyes was a highly classified project from around 2005, where we helped the CIA concoct a design for an *Osama Bin Laden* action figure. One of our most interesting *subversive toys*."

"Well, that sounds like an excellent use of your time." Sam rolled his eyes. "Why would you want to do that?"

"To give to all the little children of course! The project involved mass-producing thousands of *Action Man* dolls in the blighter's likeness and giving them out to tiny children up and down Pakistan."

"But he was the bad guy. Why would you and the CIA make dolls of him? And why the fuck were you giving them to kids in Pakistan?"

"Well that's the clever bit!" butted in the Brigadier. "The face was designed with heat-dissolving material, so the paint would peel off after a few weeks and it would reveal Bin Laden as having the face of the devil!"

"The devil?"

"Absolutely! A red-faced demon with horrific green eyes! Gives me the woollies just thinking about him." The Brigadier shuddered in his seat.

"I can't believe you people would concoct such a ridiculous scheme."

"Our job Sam is to make things happen!" clarified the Brigadier. "Or sometimes, make things not happen. Or maybe even to make things up. It really depends."

"So did the *kids* like them?"

"Oh God no, they thought it was monstrous! Gave half of them nightmares I'd imagine. But that was the idea, young man. Hearts and minds! Subvert their little minds and help them to see Bin Laden for what he really was. So, I'll stick you down for the Department of Subversive Toys, yes?"

The Brigadier had an excited smile on his face, obscured by his big, bushy moustache, as if the excitement of this opportunity would be just too much for Sam to take.

"Hmm. I'm not sure. I mean it all sounds kinda crazy in this Department of Subversive Toys. Isn't there anything else I could do? Maybe, the Department of Interrogation, that sounds interesting?" asked Sam, pointing back at the list.

"Ohhh yes, the Department of Interrogation!" grinned the Brigadier, clapping his hands together excitedly. "Some of my best friends are interrogators and you, my son, are most definitely interrogator material!" The level of enthusiasm the Brigadier was once again displaying instantly made Sam grow suspicious.

"There are so many techniques for you to learn." The Brigadier started to list them on his fingers, "Sensory deprivation, disorientation, isolation, falsified documents, stress positions, dietary manipulation…" His brow started to furrow as he racked his big ginger brain, reminiscing about the vast array of interrogation techniques he had encountered. "…rapid-fire questions, repetition, sleep deprivation, ego boosting, ego reduction, phobia persuasion, environment manipulation…"

Milquetoast clearly wanted in on some of the sadism. "Not forgetting the verboten techniques like waterboarding, bloodletting, scolding and fingernail removal!"

"And ball-spanking!!" beamed the Brigadier.

Sam looked at the Brigadier and Milquetoast who were gleefully adding to each other's lists with the comparative excitement of two schoolboys enthusing over insects in a jar.

"I really don't think that the Department of Interrogation is the one for me after all."

The Brigadier and Milquetoast both looked a little crestfallen. "Right-o," said the Brigadier, "let's see what else we have." Suddenly, he turned and slammed both fists hard down on the desk.

"What about the Department of Confrontation? SHOW ME YOUR ANGRY-FACE, BOY!!"

Sam ran through the repertoire of facial expressions he had in his head and tried to summon up a suitable angry face. He grimaced hard, lowered his brow and tried to look as wild-eyed as possible.

The Brigadier looked back at him, somewhat confused.

Sam supplemented his performance by swirling his head around and clenching his fists. He could feel the veins straining in his neck as his cheeks flushed.

"What *are* you doing?" asked Milquetoast looking slightly revolted.

"My angry face."

"You look like you're having a stroke."

Sam untensed the muscles in his face. "I guess I'm just not really an angry person. I'm not sure I have an angry face?"

"SURE YOU DO, SON! GRRRRR! SHOW ME YOUR ANGRY FACE!" yelled the Brigadier.

Sam went full banshee, waving his fists in the air and screaming. "RAAAAARGHH!"

"Good God, stop man," insisted Milquetoast, "you're like a wailing toddler."

"Well, I said I didn't have an angry face."

The Brigadier put a cross against that vacancy. "Hmm. Okay then. Test pilot for recreational drugs? Any 'experience' in that area?" He held up two fingers on each of his hands to indicate his imaginary quotation marks around the word 'experience'.

"Not unless you count Haribo. And possibly Pornhub?"

The Brigadier shook his head, disappointed. "What about the Department of Superstition, they need a virgin?"

"Sorry," Sam stared blankly, "I'm not taking a job based on me proving my virginity."

"Oh. That's disappointing."

"Mr Juniper," interrupted Milquetoast. "If we're not able to place you in a suitable position, I'm afraid we're going to have to pop you back in that police car and ship you off to Tunbridge Wells."

"Good God man, there must be something here that you can do." The Brigadier flopped heavily back into his chair, with his flopping resulting in a magnificent flurry of paperwork cascading off of his desk. Sam looked down at the dispersed papers, one of which was the job description list they were discussing. He helpfully picked it back up, and in doing so noticed the list continued on the reverse side.

Department of Conspiracy *– Multi-skilled trainee agent required. Ideal candidate will be anfractuous, pernicious and capable of considerable artifice.*

Sam wasn't sure what any of these words meant. "How about that then? How about the Department of Conspiracy?"

The Brigadier's face lit up again. "You would bloody shine in the Department of Conspiracy, my lad!" he roared with relish. "Some of my best friends have worked in the Department of Conspiracy and let me tell you, you are Conspiracy material, my lad!"

Milquetoast rolled his eyes at the Brigadier's glee. "There's only one problem though. It might be problematic for Samuel to integrate effectively within the Department of Conspiracy."

"Integrate?" asked Sam.

"Ah yes," admitted the Brigadier. "We have had some HR issues with that particular department."

"What sort of HR issues? What sort of people work in that department?"

"Well, umm, hmm. Just one person actually. But they haven't worked with a partner for quite a long time."

"Indeed," concurred Milquetoast. "A very long time. Let's just say they don't necessarily play well with others."

* * *

Milquetoast led Sam back down the corridor lined with pictures.

"Mr Milquetoast," Sam coughed to clear his throat. "The Brigadier said that your organisation exists to make things happen… and to make things not happen? What exactly is your organisation called?"

Milquetoast looked a little puzzled.

"We went through this in the lift, Samuel. Have you not been paying attention? You remember the map? We're MI-51."

"Right, M… I… 51. But what is that? Is it part of the government?"

Milquetoast stopped mid-corridor by a framed picture of famous aviator Amelia Earhart.

"You've heard of MI-5, yes? And MI-6, I presume? The so-called *secret* intelligence services." Milquetoast rolled his eyes with the word *secret*. "MI-5 are the oh-so-secret governmental agency responsible for dealing with internal security and counter-intelligence on British soil. MI-6 pretty much have the same scope, but they do their showboating overseas."

"Sure, James Bond, Judi Dench and unstirred martinis, right?"

"Hmm, quite. But has it ever occurred to you that our *secret intelligence services* are actually very well known about? I mean, good grief man they advertise in *The*

Spectator and on university campuses. Does that not seem a little odd to you?"

"Well I guess, when you say it like that." Sam scratched his head.

"That's because they are *our* cover. Our decoys. Our stooges. Our public veneer if you will. Have you ever wondered why you've never heard of MI-1, or MI-2 or even MI-19 for that matter? Why is it you only ever hear about MI-5 and MI-6?"

"Is there an MI-1?"

"Of course! Well, at least there used to be many years ago." Milquetoast continued walking. "MI, or *Military Intelligence* as it is called, had agencies numbered all the way up to MI-19 until the 1960s. MI-1 was Codebreaking, MI-2 was Russia and Scandinavia, MI-3 was Eastern Europe and so on."

"There were more?"

"Certainly. I'm rusty now Samuel, but I do remember MI-4 was for aerial reconnaissance, MI-8 was communication interception, MI-10 was weapons analysis, MI-14 & 15 both concentrated on the Germans and MI-19 was prisoner of war debriefing. We really were quite the conglomerate."

"So what happened? Where are they now?"

"Well distrust kicked in and then bloody NATO happened, didn't it? No need for all that investment in diversified national security when the CIA pretty much had everyone on lockdown anyway. So they bundled them all up into MI-5 and MI-6 and put the rest out to pasture. It was a mass euthanasia of all our security specialists and the newly sterilised American-led global structure took its place."

Milquetoast came to a stop as they walked into the foyer where the ninja secretary resided. Foxfire nodded politely at Milquetoast, who continued on into the waiting lift-car.

Sam followed close behind, being careful not to make eye contact with Foxfire. “So, I don’t understand. Where do you come in? Who the hell are MI-51?”

“Well, the problem with any mass euthanasia is that new viruses will emerge. And emerge they did, young Samuel.”

“You mean the IRA? Or Al Qaeda? Or… the Russians??!”

“Oh all of those Samuel, and many far more insidious organisations as well. We’ve certainly had our games of cat and mouse with our traditional enemies over the years. But you have to remember many of our allies have also been motivated to tinker in our affairs over previous decades, as well as our enemies.”

“Really? Like who? Why?”

“Well, the Americans certainly. Global policemen and all that. But the Israeli’s had—”

“Mossad!” Sam interjected, trying to demonstrate his own world affairs knowledge.

“No, not Mossad, they’re not so bad, old chap. The Israelis had a group called the *Irgun* — they were an underground secret society formed to resist British occupation of Palestine. Far more terrifying if you ask me.”

“Oh, I see.”

Milquetoast tapped his cane firmly on the floor apparently instructing the lift to begin its cacophonous journey back up. Sam didn’t ask any more questions on the way up but Milquetoast was still happily jabbering away. After a minute or two the ear-splitting noise ceased again as the lift came to a stop back at the Betamax section at the rear of the video store.

Milquetoast was still talking, "Then you had others like the Brotherhood of Imhotep, they were an ancient secret society from Egypt. And yes the IRA, but certainly not the ones you're thinking of. The Internet Research Agency are part of the KGB, they're the lovely chaps that like to influence our discerning electorate every four years or so. Bloody nuisance I call them."

"So you mean MI-51 was set up to fight them? All these hidden spies that are working for our allies?"

"Well, in a manner of speaking. But these little collectives do not fight by traditional methods Samuel. These people do not just use guns and bombs like a conventional enemy. They operate on the periphery, they operate deep in the shadows. They will undermine a nation from the inside without a nation's government even knowing there has been an attack, sometimes until decades later."

"So how do you fight someone like that. What is it you do? What is MI-51?"

"Please try and pay attention, Samuel, we've been through this. MI-51 specialise in *black propaganda.* We operate in the world of fabricated evidence, fake news, disguised motivations and staged media events. Our mission is to counter all forms of misinformation, disinformation and malinformation."

Sam watched Milquetoast as he leafed through the video cassettes again.

"Which tape are you looking for now?"

"Hmm? Oh, well, we're heading for the Department of Conspiracy to introduce you to your new colleague, young Samuel. So that means we need… Ah! Here we are!" Milquetoast pulled out a box set of the original 1979 *Tinker, Tailor, Soldier, Spy* starring the veteran actor Alec Guinness and waved it at Sam.

"Welcome to the rabbit hole, Samuel."

Se7en

Jeffrey Braithwaite was sitting at his breakfast table, eating a slice of marmalade on toast, when a small article in *The Times* caught his eye.

'Home Office Implicated in Unorthodox Research'

The two paragraphs that followed summarised an internet rumour that was circulating which suggested members of his own department were implicated in commissioning unconventional research on animals. Jeffrey pondered the story briefly. He was fairly sure, as the Minister for the Home Office that he had most definitely *not* authorised any such research. *What an odd story* he pondered. Jeffrey buttered another piece of toast and figured he would probably look into it once he was at work. He promptly turned over to the sports pages. Looks like England were off to a flying start in the First Test at Headingly. Lovely stuff. He finished his last sip of tea and untucked the napkin from his collar.

"Right, I'm off to the office, darling."

"Ok, hold on!" Jeffrey's wife Sarah skipped through to the dining room and placed a loving kiss on her husband's cheek. "Goodbye, sweetheart."

As the Conservative MP for Twyford, Jeffrey was proud to fulfil his role as the Head of the Home Office. He also felt blessed in his homelife. Sarah was everything he had wanted in a wife; sweet, caring, intelligent and loyal. His daughter was happily away at university studying botany and his kind-hearted younger son regularly volunteered at the local animal shelter. His picturesque home in Berkshire was paid off and he delighted in driving to the office in Westminster in his new Nissan Leaf.

Jeffrey had strived his whole career to get where he was today, and he was pleased to say he'd done it the tough way. By working hard, being honest and being kind to people. He'd never succumbed to bribes, he never got involved in the dirty tricks some of his colleagues had indulged in and he was always careful that his private life could not result in some embarrassing scandal.

Life was good, Jeffrey thought. Sometimes the nice guys can win.

* * *

Milquetoast and Sam stepped out of the lift into a small, tidy lobby. In front of them was the entrance door to the Department of Conspiracy office which was helpfully identified with the words 'Fuck Off!'

Florence Lawrence was stood talking into a mobile phone as Samuel and Milquetoast walked into her studio. She did not look at them as they entered.

"I'm not interested in your excuses Nathan. I'm telling you to get your arse back into the restaurant and relieve the acquisition of that suitcase now. Alternatively, I will turn up there, retrieve the suitcase myself, lightly coat it in olive oil, wrap it in tinfoil, bake it in the oven, sprinkle it with salt and pepper and then shove it so far up your fucking dick-hole that your balls will pop out of your ears. Is that a copy?"

Florence turned the mobile phone off and then abruptly threw it at the wall. It bounced off with a clunk and landed in a wastepaper basket.

"Oh God, Milquetoast. What the fuck brings you skulking down to my office?"

"How delightful to see you too, Ms Lawrence." Milquetoast gulped but otherwise appeared unflustered. "Orders from the Brigadier. You've been assigned a new trainee — this here is Mr Juniper. Samuel Juniper. He is to shadow you for stage 1 of his probationary process, he'll be with you on light duties for a period of four weeks. You're going to need to…"

Milquetoast ceased speaking at the moment he noticed Florence Lawrence had her fingers in her ears.

"Blah, blah, blah," said Florence, contorting her face. "You *know* I'm a one-woman operation down here Milquetoast. I don't need you prancing into my office as head pencil-pusher with your corporate agenda bullshit. Unless you want me to push your pencil somewhere up your crusty old agenda."

"As always Ms Lawrence, you paint quite the colourful picture. Alas, these orders do not come from me but directly from the HR department and the Brigadier himself."

"Milquetoast. You tell that fat, beetroot, cross-dressing, fuck-biscuit that I don't need a trainee. I don't want a trainee and if he sends me any more trainees I'll be marching back round to his spunk-ridden splaff-hole, and I'll take that ridiculous minge of a moustache and shove it so far down his throat that he'll be coughing ginger furballs for a week."

Florence's studio-style office maintained a spectacularly different vibe in comparison to Brigadier Longstocking's disorganised workspace. The walls were fitted with whiteboards displaying handwritten notes, mugshots and post-it labels. Information had been annotated with red marker pen and strings that stretched between them were held in place by drawing pins, marking connections between seemingly random sets of data.

There were two desks, both neatly stacked with manuals and reference sheets and a single, black leather seat behind each one. A multitude of laptops, radios, charging equipment and other electronic gizmos provided an ambient, artificial hum. The room emanated a confusingly sterile intensity that seemed to simultaneously combine the aura of a surgical operating theatre mixed with an IT helpdesk manned by the Nazi party. Or perhaps that was just Florence's demeanour.

"Of course, Ms Lawrence, I'll be sure to notify the Brigadier of your considered opinion for his hairy facial appendages," said Milquetoast, adjusting his spectacles. "However, I should make you aware that the Department of Logistics has also given me notice regarding your under-utilised office space down here…"

Florence folded her arms, anticipating a classic Milquetoast manoeuvre.

"…The two desks you've had allocated all to yourself in this office for some considerable time, both require to be occupied. As such this office is scheduled to be re-allocated to the Department of Procurement who are in need of additional office space…"

Florence's eyes narrowed and her top lip furled upwards. She was well aware that she suffered from undiagnosed, acute, constant angry bitch-face whenever she was being given information she disagreed with.

"…Regrettably," Milquetoast continued, "if we cannot confirm two personnel to be assigned to your sizeable studio here, you are to be relocated to the mezzanine."

The mezzanine was most definitely not a place that Florence wanted to be relocated to. It wasn't so much the open-plan nature of the mezzanine which encouraged social engagement that Florence despised. It was more the fact that the Department of Bureaucracy occupied the vast majority of this area and frankly they were, in Florence's considered opinion, the most pretentious bunch of chinless fucktards that existed within the whole of MI-51. With the possible exception of the Department of Logistics.

"Four weeks, Ms Lawrence."

Florence eyed Sam with visible disgust and then turned her back on the pair of them whilst she mulled over her options.

"Hear me now, Milquetoast. Four weeks and then he's your problem, not mine. If Jennifer here so much as farts in the wrong direction I'll have him minced, folded into a burrito and put on the first flight to Acapulco."

Sam wasn't sure whether he should be more offended about being referred to as Jennifer or being threatened with being made into Mexican food.

"Excellent. Your cooperation is very much obliged, Ms Lawrence." Milquetoast started to shuffle backwards towards the door. "Samuel do enjoy your initial placement. I'm sure you'll find Ms Lawrence most obliging and supportive during your induction. I'll have Ms Foxfire dispatch your contractual documentation shortly. And Ms Lawrence..."

Milquetoast's body had reversed completely out of the doorway so only his head was left peeking into the room.

"...I'll get you a desk prepared on the mezzanine, just in case this doesn't quite work out!"

He swiftly shut the door behind him.

* * *

Florence was sitting at one of her two desks, engrossed in one of the three computer screens placed upon it. Sam hadn't moved for approximately twenty-five minutes and was continuing to stand by the door. Intermittently, Florence would pick up one of a variety of mobile phones, tap in a text message and then avidly return to her computer screen.

"Shall I perhaps sit over there?" offered Sam, meekly gesturing towards the only other empty desk in the room.

"You shall not," replied Florence. "That is my *other* desk and I need it."

"Sure, sure." Sam decided it would be best to leave it for a good fifteen minutes before attempting any further polite conversation. Sam spotted a couple of footstools folded up behind a grey filing cabinet. He slowly shuffled sideways towards them, trying hard not to make any direct eye contact with Florence.

Florence eyed him suspiciously over the top of her monitor. Sam paused and looked down at his feet until he felt her gaze had shifted. He then continued to slowly shuffle sideways. Once he was within tantalizing touching distance, he slowly and cautiously reached out towards one of the footstools, and gently lifted it out from behind the cabinet.

Florence sat upright and motionless, focusing her full bitch-stare at the side of Sam's head. Sam was not only uncomfortably aware that he was being intently scrutinised, but he also fully anticipated a sniper rifle was going to take him out from behind the computer monitors at any moment.

Feeling much like a proverbial deer in the headlights of a Sherman tank, Sam proceeded to unfold the footstool and very carefully set it down in the precise location that he calculated to be the most geographically distant part of the floor away from where Florence was seated. The footstool consisted of a rickety metal frame with two narrow steps - the sort of mini-ladder normally used by short people to help them reach the biscuits on the top shelf.

Florence remained impassive and entirely motionless with just her eyes following his every move, the embodiment of a cobra poised and ready to strike at a cowering fieldmouse.

When the footstool was folded out, Sam couldn't help but feel slightly underwhelmed at its overall dimensions. With just two steps, it was approximately knee height at best. Nevertheless, Sam attempted to carefully sit himself down onto it as if it was an entirely normal item of office equipment to sit on.

He folded his knees up so that his feet were perched on the lower step and leant back slightly in order to appear as nonchalant and relaxed as possible. He felt determined not to let his own lack of comfort create some sort of awkward atmosphere within the room.

Florence continued to glare directly at him, wondering how the hell she'd managed to end up with this spectacularly ridiculous-looking moron perching like some sort of oversized office gnome in her studio.

She looked back down at her computer and continued with her work.

Sam was fairly sure he had entirely maintained both his professionalism and dignity in a difficult situation.

* * *

Over the course of the next four hours, Sam had discovered there were only a finite number of positions by which a fully grown human male could practically sit on a two-step footstool without either his spinal column cramping up or his butt cheeks going into zombie spasms.

He had however found that he was remarkably adept at leaning on his own thigh to create a makeshift desk while he filled in his HR paperwork. He had even formulated a system for storing his stationery, with two biros behind his left ear, one in his right hand and a pencil gripped in his teeth.

But overall, his footstool-workstation was proving somewhat challenging.

He looked at the clock on the wall behind Florence's second desk. He was fairly sure he hadn't seen it change since he'd arrived in the room. It indicated nine o'clock, but without any windows in this mysterious sub-terranean office, Sam really couldn't hazard a guess if that meant it was morning or evening.

"Is it likely that we'll be finishing work at any point today? Or is this a kind of twenty-four-hour gig?"

Florence did not answer Sam. Instead she was busy tapping buttons on a calculator with one hand and jotting notes on a pad with the other whilst simultaneously listening to dictation through a set of headphones.

The long, stony silence continued to make Sam feel uncomfortable. Sam weighed up his options, perhaps he should try a different tack in an attempt to break the silence? He ran through all the suitable conversation starters he could think of in his mind. He needed something sensible. Something interesting. Something that Florence would be undeniably curious to know more about.

Ok, here goes.

"Did you know vending machines are a bigger threat to humanity than sharks?"

Florence stopped tapping her calculator, and looked disdainfully in Sam's direction, although she didn't remove her headphones.

"No, really. You're actually twice as likely to be killed by a vending machine than a shark!" he followed up helpfully.

Florence turned her attention back to the calculator and continued with what she was doing. Okay, thought Sam, that nearly worked. Maybe she's just not a shark kind of girl. Hmmm. What would be a more interesting fact to entice a hostile woman into a conversation.

"Fun factoid for you! Did you know hunting unicorns is legal in Michigan? Interestingly, Lake Superior State University actually offers a Unicorn Hunting Licence!"

This time Florence didn't even look up, she just shook her head and continued to make written notes from her recordings and tap away on her calculator. Maybe that wasn't such a fun factoid after all thought Sam. Perhaps he should try and demonstrate his intellect. Who's not impressed by long words?

"So something I found interesting, is that the technical name for having an irrational fear of long words is hippopotomonstrosesquippedaliophobia."

Florence grasped her headphones and slammed them down on the desk, glaring angrily at Sam.

"What the fuck is wrong with you?!"

Sam bit his bottom lip. "I was just saying, did you know hippo—"

"Listen you irritating twat-waffle, just stop talking to me. I'm in the middle of an extremely sensitive investigation concerning the Italian prime minister so no, you can't help me. You can't even help me a little bit. Think of it like this; everything you know is wrong. There is nothing you can say that is in any way going to be helpful to me. I do not give a shit about sharks, unicorns or hippos. Please just stop talking to me."

Sam smiled politely and nodded. He didn't want the situation to seem awkward by her thinking he had somehow taken offence.

"I'm not sure it's true to say that *everything* I know is wrong," he said quietly.

Florence paused, composed herself, and then stood up.

"Actually Jennifer, it is. Everything you know is wrong. Absolutely everything you think you know up until this moment in time is incorrect. It's all wrong. Uber-wrong. Post-wrong. Trans-wrong. Ultra-wrong. Meta-wrong and so wrong that it cannot even be proved wrong."

Sam continued to smile politely, stroked his stubble and tried his best to look like he was partially agreeing with her. He figured perhaps she sometimes just struggled to get her actual point across.

"I have other factoids. Maybe if—"

"No. Just no. No fucking factoids. Ever. What are you, like eight years old?" She walked round to the front of her desk and put her clenched fists on her hips. "Let me be clear. The Great Wall of China is *not* visible from the moon. Eskimos do *not* have a hundred words for snow. If you swallow chewing gum, it *doesn't* take seven years to digest. Bulls do *not* hate the colour red."

Florence leant forward, focusing the culmination of her tirade directly at Sam with laser-guided accuracy.

"Lemmings *don't* commit mass suicide by jumping off cliffs, bats are *not* blind, Einstein *didn't* fail maths, the Earth *isn't* flat and the moon is *not* made of cheese. It's all wrong, Jennifer. It's all bullshit. All of it."

Florence stared intently at Sam. He couldn't help noticing her nostrils were flaring a little bit like a horse.

He wondered if she might be interested in a horse factoid. Horses can't breathe through their mouths, that's why their nostrils flare. Maybe that would be a good one? Maybe she only breathed through her nose?

Sam decided against a horse factoid and gave Florence an amiable nod instead. "Alrighty then."

She walked back round to her own side of the desk, watching Sam warily as she went. She slowly sat down, placed her headphones back over her ears and then picked her pen back up.

"Just to clarify," added Sam, "I never actually thought the moon was made of cheese, you know."

* * *

As a further two hours crawled by, Sam remained perching on his footstool trying to fill in his next of kin details on a P14E form, utilising his makeshift thigh-desk system.

Meanwhile, Florence now had a mobile phone wedged between her ear and her shoulder and she was standing at one of the whiteboards transcribing notes at the same time as reading an email from a second phone. She was clearly getting irritated with the caller on the other end as well as becoming extremely frustrated with the limited number of usable hands she had available (two in total) to hold things.

"Nathan, who the hell is Icy Mike?? Why have we not heard of him before? Is he KGB?"

Sam had stopped filling in his P14E form and was curious to try and fathom the context of the conversation. It looked like a list of names Florence was writing on the whiteboard.

"Ok, so Icy Mike, then Hot Karl and then the mysterious Angry Pirate, yes? They're all on the Italian prime minister's list, right? None of this makes any sense. Why don't we have any intel on any of these names — are you sure the wiretap was transcribed correctly?"

Sam could hear Nathan's muffled voice on the other end of the line sounding equally confused.

"And the Flying Camel and the Cowgirl are on the list too? That sounds like it could mean the Arabs and the Americans are involved? Who the hell does the Walrus work for??" Florence continued to add the codenames to the whiteboard as she spoke;

Icy Mike
The Angry Pirate
Walrus
Hot Karl
The Flying Camel
The Cowgirl

"Hmmm. Okay, I'll run those all through the computer but if this is a multi-national operation, we could be in serious trouble, this must be an entirely new cartel."

Florence turned the phone off and studied the list of names on her board. Sam looked on impassively as she annotated further queries to her whiteboard. *Shipment of drugs? Gun smugglers? People trafficking?*

"Can I help?" asked Sam, from his footstool desk.

Florence ignored him and instead tried tapping the code names into the MI-51 database.

"Maybe I could help?" asked Sam again since Florence mustn't have heard him the first time.

Florence underlined The Angry Pirate in red ink and seemed to be muttering to herself under her breath.

"Maybe he's from one of the Somalian contingents? They can be pretty brutal out in the Indian Ocean?"

"Y'know, I really think I might be able to help you," insisted Sam.

"Christ Jennifer, can you shut your noise, I'm trying to think!!" Florence glowered at Sam, daring him to utter another word.

"I just… I figured maybe I could help you with your list?"

"Listen cock-nostril. My contacts have highly-classified communications from the Italian Prime Minister. The same Italian Prime Minister who is known to have links to the Sicilian Mafia. We know this guy is extremely devious and all we have are these flipping codenames to go on. We don't hold any intelligence on any of them and all we know is they are all expected to be present at a rendezvous with him tomorrow night. Unless you have somehow developed your own reconnaissance network with links to Icy Mike, the Walrus, the Angry Pirate, Hot Karl, the Flying Camel and the Cowgirl then my suggestion is *no*, Jennifer, you're not really going to be much help at all."

Sam stood up from his footstool, and wandered a little closer towards the whiteboard, perusing the list.

"Hmm. Icy Mike…" he murmured, rubbing his stubbly chin with a faraway look in his eye.

"Probably KGB," replied Florence, turning back to her whiteboard. "I doubt you know him, Jennifer."

"The Angry Pirate…" mulled Sam.

"Likely Somalian. Listen, I really need to get on," snapped Florence.

"And The Walrus…"

"Origin unknown. Seriously Jennifer, please don't interfere. I just don't have the time."

"Hmm. Hot Karl…"

"Jennifer, please fuck off, you're annoying me now."

"The Flying Camel..."

"Okay that's it, I'm getting my cosh out the desk," she scowled threateningly.

"And The Cowgirl..."

Florence pulled open a draw and took an extraordinarily heavy-duty cosh out of her desk.

"You realise this is a list of extreme sexual practices, right?" asked Sam.

Florence held her cosh steady as she looked back at the whiteboard and slowly scanned down the list.

"What are you talking about?!" Her face started to glaze over. "... are you sure??"

"Sure I'm sure. I was a sales executive at a very exclusive sex shop before I worked here, you know. You never heard of the Cowgirl? In fairness some of the others are a little more on the *exotic* side."

Florence looked at him bewildered. "The Angry Pirate??"

"Yeah, I probably wouldn't Google that if I were you."

She put down her cosh, sat down at her computer and immediately did an internet search for Angry Pirate. "Jesus Christ, the Italians are dirty bastards."

Sam perched back on his footstool. Florence tapped a number into her mobile phone and held it back up to her ear.

"Nathan? Yes. Call it off. The Italian PM is a class A pervert but other than that, we can drop the surveillance. Yes, really." She turned the phone off, flopped back down at her desk and looked over at Sam.

"Go home, Jennifer. I'll see you here in the morning."

* * *

Sam woke up the next morning in Ruth's converted bathroom with his usual fresh optimism. Although he had become accustomed to sleeping in the tiny half-sized bed, he was nevertheless relieved each morning when it was time to get up. After getting dressed and paying his compliments to Wordsworth on the stairs, Sam headed off to get the bus to Old Kent Road.

Sam arrived early at the entrance of the Videodrome store. Agent Krueger was still sitting behind the counter diligently fulfilling his undercover role as disinterested, spotty shop assistant. Sam pulled forward the temporary ID badge he had pinned to his lapel to expose it to Agent Krueger and introduced himself, assuming he may not remember Sam from the brief meeting the day before.

"Good morning!" he said cheerily. "My name's Samuel Juniper, I'm new here." He leaned in slightly and added in a hushed voice, "I work in the Department of Conspiracy," tapping the side of his nose.

Krueger did not look back at Sam. Instead he seemed to be pre-occupied with the feat of balancing a single HB pencil across the bridge of his nose as he leant back in his chair with his arms outstretched.

"I know who you are," he replied, without a flicker of interest.

"Right-o!" said Sam, hesitating briefly before deciding to just continue on through to the Betamax section. Once inside, he located the 1979 boxset of *Tinker, Tailor, Soldier, Spy* and slotted the tape into the video player in the same way he'd seen Milquetoast do the day before. He waited a few moments and then, once it had arrived, stepped inside the noisiest lift-car in the world. The lift slowly but obediently delivered Sam to the small lobby outside Florence's studio.

As he entered the office, Florence was already at DEFCON 2 which, to her mind, meant three laptops powered up, Sky News broadcasting on a wall mounted TV screen and several mobile phones being used to simultaneously text or call different people. This was fairly average for Florence at 8am on a Wednesday morning.

"Good morning!" smiled Sam optimistically. Florence didn't ignore Sam with quite the same degree of animosity with which she had done so the day before, but she did seem to acknowledge him with only the minimal number of facial gestures necessary. He was sure he saw a fraction of one eyebrow raise up ever so slightly. *Excellent progress,* he thought.

Sam settled himself onto his footstool workstation by the door, arranged his paperwork neatly over his knees and prepared his array of biros for a further morning of form filling.

It was about half-past nine when Sam finally accepted that none of his biros were working. They definitely *had* been working previously, but oddly they now appeared to object to aiding him with any further HR paperwork. He had some sympathy for them mind you, as he too felt he had overdosed heavily on paperwork in the last hour.

Pen-less and fatigued, Sam decided this might be a good time to try out the coffee machine in the corner. He walked over and stared at the intimidating appliance. There were a lot of buttons, two levers, a digital display and a teeny tiny chimney on the top.

Sam placed a cup under the spout and adopted a *lucky dip* strategy by pressing buttons randomly, hoping this would somehow result in a latte. At first it appeared that his luck was in. The lights on the machine twinkled, the teeny tiny chimney went *pssshht* and the cup filled with the blackest liquid known to humanity. It had the look of a swirling, deathly abyss and the aroma of a thousand tortured coffee beans being torn from their loved ones and thrown into a decaffeinated concentration camp. If dark matter came in a liquid form, Sam was fairly sure this coffee machine had just produced it.

He put the cup of dark matter to one side and tried once more to use an alternative combination of button pressing. Again the lights came to life and the teeny tiny chimney let out an obedient *psssshht* before the funnel ejaculated its caffeiney load into the cup below. This time the result was significantly more pleasing with the beverage looking and smelling distinctly more latte-like.

Sam picked up both cups and turned around looking for a suitable flowerpot to pour away the cup that contained Satan's bile. As he stood holding both cups, he noticed Florence was looking straight at him. Not wishing to appear thoughtless, he bounced comfortably into bullshit-mode.

"I made you a coffee!" he said smiling. Sam was kind of expecting Florence to ignore him, as that seemed to have been the steady nature of their relationship up until that point. As it happened, in spite of the mental list of tasks she had ticking through her mind and in addition to the migraine she could feel coming on at that precise moment, the one thing Florence did actually need right now was a cup of coffee.

"Oh. Okay."

Sam looked down at the two full cups in his hands trying to decide which one to give to her. "Do you like it black or white?"

"Black."

Oh balls, thought Sam. She's going to take one sip of this and then I'm going to get boiling hot, putrid smelling coffee plasma thrown all over me. He carried the cup of tar over to Florence and placed it on the desk in front of her.

She looked down at it, picked up the cup and took a sniff. Sam retreated to the safety of his footstool, cradling his own entirely normal-looking latte.

Florence took a sip.

Jesus Christ that was good, she thought. She was all coiled up and ready to lambast this moron's coffee making skills, but my god the boy had nailed it. It was the first time she could remember anyone managing to make her a coffee exactly the way she liked it, at least since Cornelius worked at the adjacent desk.

Sam looked on nervously. She was actually drinking it. She actually looked like it was… passable?

"Thanks," she said. "Good job, fuckwit."

* * *

Florence was relaxing back in her chair, slowly sipping at her tarry cup of joy. In amongst all her frenetic phone calls and urgent emails it was nice to decompress for a few minutes. She looked at Sam perched on his stool like some kind of unwieldly, office gargoyle.

"I wasn't just being mean, you know."

"I'm sorry?" Sam looked a little startled at the impromptu declaration.

"When I said to you yesterday, 'everything you think you know is wrong', I wasn't *just* saying it to be mean. To be clear, I *was* being mean, but I was also actually trying to help you."

Sam let this little marble of wisdom roll around his brain for a few moments. Was this another thinly veiled insult? Or was it in fact just a straightforward insult? He wasn't entirely sure.

"The examples I gave you; the Great Wall of China, bats, lemmings — it's true that they are all wrong, yet everyone believes them. But most of everything else they teach you at school is also wrong."

"Like what. What's wrong with school?"

"All of it. Religious studies. Geography. History. Maths. Science. All of it is just a load of half-truths at best because it's too complex to explain the real truth to kids."

"How can science be full of half-truths? It's science. It's in the name!" Sam felt he was on stable ground arguing the case for science. *Fair do's, Religious studies might have a fable or two, but science is science.*

Florence took a sip of her coffee. "Well, it depends where you want to start really. For biology, it's not true that we only use ten per cent of our brains, we don't lose half our body heat through our heads and your tongue isn't divided into handy taste bud zones. In physics, remember how you were taught the atom consists of a few electrons whizzing in circles around a nucleus of protons and neutrons. They called it the *Bohr* model, right? But it's not true. Atoms are actually made up in the atomic orbital model, which is way more complicated. Even Niels Bohr disowned his own original version, yet today that's what they still teach, because it's easier."

"Well that doesn't make it *wrong*. It just makes it simpler." Sam knew he wasn't that well equipped to get into a conversation about physics so changed topics. "So what's wrong with history?"

"Oh where to start?! Well, firstly history is only ever written by the victors. What was it Napoleon said? History is but a fable that everyone has agreed upon. For example, Columbus wasn't the first guy to discover America and Edison didn't invent the light bulb. Even when we get it right, we completely misjudge when things actually happened. The Roman Empire was around until the fifteenth century, but most people think it finished a thousand years earlier."

"Er, geography?"

"Just look at a map!" groaned Florence. "They all lie. For instance, despite how it looks on most maps, Africa is like fourteen times bigger than Greenland. Null Island doesn't even exist, yet you'll find it right there on a load of maps plonked in the middle of the Atlantic Ocean. Great Britain isn't the same as the United Kingdom. Iceland isn't covered with ice and Sudan has more ancient pyramids than Egypt. What we teach is often nonsense, yet we believe it because otherwise the world is so much more complicated."

Sam tried to take all these facts in at once and realised he couldn't actually remember any of them sufficiently in order to coherently argue with Florence.

"English? You can't tell me all the rules for reading and writing were lies?"

"Sure they are," laughed Florence. "All those rules; two spaces after a full stop, you can't start a sentence with a conjunction, and you can't finish one with a preposition. None of those are rules in the real world. You remember the 'i' before 'e' except after 'c' rule? Total baloney. You want me to prove it? Science uses weird words albeit English is fancier. There you go, pick that sentence apart and you'll find four examples disproving the rule."

"Maths?"

"Maths isn't filled with lies so much, but some of the numbers are illegal and they don't ever teach you *that* at school."

"What do you mean? What numbers are illegal?"

"Well there's a particular number with 1,401 digits in it that can be used to decrypt encoded movies on DVD players. A judge actually ruled in 2001 it was illegal just to own or transmit that number. More recently in 2012, our friends in China banned people from typing the numbers 89, 6 and 4 into search engines. Dangerous things, numbers." Florence swigged the last mouthful of her coffee and put the cup down on her desk, satisfied that she'd helped enlighten Sam.

Sam looked at her silently and decided that this woman was fucking mental.

The red phone on Florence's desk started ringing.

Eight Legged Freaks

Josie Griffiths was putting the finishing touches to her placard.

'SAY NO TO ANIMAL EXPERIMENTS!'

She'd used the post from an old 'For Sale' sign and nailed a larger sheet of fibre board to the front of it. She'd sprayed it all in yellow and painted the new lettering on in black. She'd decided to use blood red paint for the word 'EXPERIMENTS' as an artistic statement.

Josie stood back to admire her handiwork. Not bad she thought, stirring her paint brush in a jar of turps. She popped the jar back up on her shelf with all her other painting paraphernalia. The thing about being a social justice warrior was that you needed to have the ability to rustle up a placard for any occasion at very short notice.

"What do you think?" she asked Ralphy. He didn't reply but instead opted to lick his balls approvingly. Josie was fairly sure her placard would receive firm approval from her fellow activists at the meeting this afternoon. Her oversized woolly jumper had long floppy sleeves which had unfortunately draped in the paint at least four times during her painting session. Her unbrushed hair had red paint flecks in it and was equally floppy with a scruffy fringe hanging over her twinkly green eyes. Ralphy, for his part, had red paint on all four paws and was in the process of trampling it into the carpet of Josie's tiny flat.

Enough painting for now - the brush looked more or less clean and the paw prints would probably fade if she left them long enough. She figured there was just time to make something for lunch before heading off to meet the others at Leo's house.

"Beans on toast, I think!"

Josie's tiny, rented apartment had an even tinier kitchen. A Che Guevara poster took pride of place on the tiled wall above the sink and a cactus was slowly dying of dehydration on the windowsill. The compact worktop was filled with vegetarian recipe books and boxes containing vegan dog biscuits

Josie grabbed a tin of beans out of the cupboard and scraped some mould off a loaf of bread. She pressed the button on the front of the microwave to release the Perspex door, but instead of flicking open, the door just dropped off altogether. They clearly didn't make microwaves like they used to. Although, in fairness, this particular microwave was around thirty years old, so they apparently didn't use to make them that well in the old days either.

Josie wasn't entirely sure if it was safe to use a microwave if the glass door was missing off the front. Would it mean all the gamma rays would shoot out of the microwave and ping around the kitchen? She didn't want to risk it in case that meant that her and Ralphy would get laser beam cancer. But then again wasn't that what happened to Bruce Banner to make him into the *Hulk*? Unsure whether there was more likelihood she would end up with laser beam cancer or as the new *She-Hulk*, Josie opted for the safer option of a slice of bread dipped into a can of cold beans. Ralphy quickly snaffled any rogue beans from the floor, which had fallen from her soggy bread shovel.

Although she'd had better meals, she'd also had worse. And being one of the founding members of the Croydon Revolutionary Front, she had bigger problems. But nobody ever said saving the planet would be easy.

* * *

"Shank you, shank you, everybody shettle down." Leo Angelopoulos was standing in front of his mantlepiece with a clipboard. The rest of the team were gathered around sitting on his sofas or cross-legged on the carpet. Leo had pushed his TV into the corner of the room to make more space and he'd moved his radio and games console up onto the shelf out of the way. "Welcome to the thixth official monthly meeting of the *C.R.F.*"

The other four members of the Croydon Revolutionary Front offered a supportive round of applause. Leo's clipboard held a printed agenda for that day's meeting;

<u>Agenda for Croydon Revolutionary Front Team Meeting</u>

Register of Attendees
Update of Government Crimes
Meeting arrangements for the Protest
Any other business

"First thingth first, let us check who is here today." Leo clicked his pen ready to act as his own secretary and mark down the names of everyone who had turned up.

Leo's English was remarkably impressive for someone who only learnt it as a second language nine months ago. But as the person responsible for reading out the register, his pronunciation was less than ideal.

"Mrs Bimble?"

"I'm here, dear!" said Mrs Bimble. "I'm afraid Norman couldn't make it. He said he was too busy watching paint dry, cheeky bloody bugger he is sometimes." Mrs Bimble was sitting in the armchair by the window, busying herself knitting a scarf.

"Nithe to thee you Mrs Bimble. I hope Mr Bimble's paint ith dry very thoon. What about Red Kendall?"

"I am with you, comrade!" Red Kendall gave an animated *black panther* salute with his fist. His fiery red beard and strong Scottish brogue gave an intimidating intonation to his salutary greeting.

It was generally agreed that Red Kendall was by far the most committed member of the Croydon Revolutionary Front. It took very little to motivate Red Kendall to take up arms and rage against authority of any kind. He was constantly at readiness to take up all lost causes on behalf of just about any left-wing, anti-government, anarchist crusade.

"Miss Jothie Grithiffith?"

"It's *Griffiths*!" corrected Josie, cheerfully.

"Griffiffifth?" offered Leo hopefully.

Josie broke it down slowly to be helpful. *"Grif...fith...sss."*

"Griff...fish?"

"Sure, Griffish, that'll do," she smiled.

"Very good Miss Griffish. And I thee we have little Ralphy with us today also?"

Ralphy had been busy inspecting his own tail on the rug and so looked a little startled at hearing his own name called out unexpectedly.

"And finally do we have Mr Black?"

Elijah Black was sat at the back of the room wearing a black hat and black sunglasses. He nodded when his name was called but didn't speak. If ever there was a sinister-looking man, with a sinister-sounding name, who was nodding very sinisterly, it was Elijah Black.

"Thplendid! Everyone is here!" Leo skipped down to the second item on the agenda. "Aha! Miss Griffish is going to give us the update on the illegal government experimentation. Miss Griffish?

"Thank you Leo!" Josie cleared her throat. "Ok comrades. As we know from the news last night, a government leak has reported that the Home Office has sanctioned research into unethical experiments on animals. If *4Chan* is to be believed, scientists are reportedly working on transplanting a mouse's head onto a squirrel's body."

Josie paused for dramatic effect, although most people in the room appeared relatively indifferent to the idea of a squirrel with a mouse's head. Except Red Kendall of course. He was outraged.

"Bloody outrage!"

"It is indeed *very* outrageous Red, thank you" agreed Josie. "As we know this is a terrifying and inhumane development and we at the *C.R.F.* are going to expose their plans to the wider public and force them to admit their horrible experiments."

The *Croydon Revolutionary Front* had been assembled by Leo when he first came to the country last year. Initially he had been the only member for about three months as few people in Croydon seemed open to revolution. But after putting an advertisement in the Croydon Gazette, his membership had soared to five, including himself. Red and Elijah were the first to reply to the advert and then soon after Josie turned up at a meeting after running into Leo in a local library. Mrs

Bimble lived just up the road and liked to come for biscuits and a chat.

"I just don't understand why they chose squirrels?" said Mrs Bimble, carefully casting on a new needle. "I mean honestly, a squirrel's head looks just like a mouse's head anyway, doesn't it?"

"They're only using mice and squirrels now, Mrs Bimble," replied Josie earnestly, "but who knows what's next? Cats with crocodile heads? Dogs with flippers?"

"Ooh that would be clever," smiled Mrs Bimble. "They could use them as lifeguards at the beach!"

"But this is terrible, Mrs Bimble!" Josie was getting noticeably distraught. "We already know that Egypt accused the Israelis of possessing a fleet of spy dolphins armed with GPS and killer arrows. Our Government could be doing the same, trying to weaponize wildlife. What would David Attenborough say?"

"The British wouldn't do that, what a lot of nonsense," scoffed Mrs Bimble. "The King would never allow that to happen, surely."

"I wouldn't be so sure!" Red banged his fist on the sofa arm angrily. "We are just pawns in this despicable government's wargames. They would think nothing of training kamikaze pandas if they could!"

"Quite right Red, and we've got to stop this from happening," affirmed Josie. "And that's why we're joining the demo in Trafalgar Square tomorrow. The Home Office Minister Jeffrey Braithwaite is making a speech there, so we'll be right in the thick of it with thousands of other protesters to stand up to the government on behalf of the people."

Josie held up the placard she had made earlier that day, and everybody nodded approvingly.

"Exthellent poster Jothie," clapped Leo. "Okay, so the protest starts at Twafalgar Thquare at thwee o' clock."

"We're going to meet under the statue," confirmed Josie. "I'm getting the number 11 bus with Ralphy so if anyone wants to join us we'll see you at the bus stop at lunchtime."

"Shall we all have a nice piece of Battenburg cake now?" chirped Mrs Bimble.

* * *

Somewhere, a long way away, deep in the recesses of a scary looking building, a small brown monkey was secured to a table. The tiny animal was shivering with fear as two surgeons in white lab coats prepared their medical instruments around him. His head was braced into a fixed position and a leather strap was stretched across his open mouth, holding a ball gag in place and stopping him from biting.

The operating theatre was dark and foreboding and it certainly didn't match the clinical atmosphere of a normal veterinary hospital. The surgeons were muttering to each other and were feverishly pointing at the primate's skull and drawing on his shaved head in marker pen. They seemed to be sizing him up for a new hat, however the monkey was fairly sure that wasn't what he was actually getting. A third man was busy adjusting a video camera on a tripod and making sure it was focused nicely on the table with the monkey.

Standing next to the surgeons there was another person, but this was a smart man in a tie and a grey flannel suit. He looked well-groomed, with tidy hair but was looking relaxed while a young woman touched up his make-up a little more. The monkey was becoming more agitated, wriggling his limbs and nervously chattering.

His small muscles twitched and flexed as he tried to fight the restraints.

The man behind the camera clapped his hands and everybody took their positions. A tiny red LED light on the camera illuminated as it went into *record* mode. One of the surgeons took the cover off his scalpel and started to make an incision into the monkey's scalp.

* * *

Back at the Department of Conspiracy office, when the red phone rang it meant the Chief of Operations had a lead that needed swift investigation.

"Lawrence," answered Florence.

"The Home Office animal experiment rumours are escalating," said the voice on the other end. "Smart phone monitoring stations have picked up intel that sensitive information is being shared amongst a number of low-level subversive groups. The original source of the leak has not yet been identified."

"I'm listening. What's the official modus operandi?"

"Reconnaissance only at this stage, Agent Lawrence. We need you to infiltrate one or more of the subversive groups. Establish contact. Locate the source generating the information. Clarify motive and report back to the Rabbit Hole."

"Understood. Who are the activist groups being monitored?"

"Primary targets are the usual suspects so look out for the Anarchy Collective, Combat 18 and the Revolutionary Communist Tendency. There's also a bunch called the Clandestine Insurgent Rebel Clown Army and a few lesser known groups we don't have much information on yet, like the Zero Collective and the Croydon Revolutionary Front."

"Jesus, it sounds like the whole circus is coming to town?"

"Indeed. We'll fax you details of a demonstration being arranged for this afternoon. See what you can find out about them."

"All received. I'll report back in 24-hours."

Florence put the red receiver back in its cradle and thought for a few moments. A machine on her spare desk buzzed and promptly churned out a printed sheet of paper.

"Is that a fax? You people actually still use fax machines?!" asked Sam.

"Only for restricted information. Encrypted data gets transmitted from a Bluetooth vault via electro-magnetic beams. The hard copies disintegrate within hours so we can't be hacked."

Sam poked at the machine, looking for cables.

"We don't have time for this, Jennifer," said Florence, impatiently scanning the details of the fax. "We've got to get to Trafalgar Square."

* * *

Florence opened her desk drawer and perused the contents, trying to decide what she might need to take with her for a low-level surveillance mission like this. She opted for a small metal microphone device about the size of a jelly-bean, a set of universal skeleton keys and a burner phone. Florence kept around a dozen spare burner phones in her drawer.

She placed the items in her purple ruck sack, zipped it shut and then went over to a cabinet by the wall. She opened up the metal doors and quickly leafed through the variety of outfits hanging inside. She picked out a t-shirt with *Just Do It* written across the front, screwed up her nose and put it straight back in. Then she picked out another one with the slogan 'Yoga will save the world'. *That's better*, she thought. Next she picked out some grey jogging bottoms and a pair of trainers and placed them on her desk.

Paying no mind to Sam who was standing by his footstool watching her aimlessly, she whipped her blouse off over her head, kicked off her heels and pulled down her smartly-pressed trousers.

Sam, realising he was staring, quickly looked at the floor. The sight of Florence's toned physique in skimpy white underwear suddenly being exposed in the office was both unexpected and uncomfortable for him. She was at least ten years older than him, but somehow had a washboard stomach. He felt flustered, he felt awkward, he felt a little aroused, he felt — oh, he noticed she'd already replaced her clothing with a tracksuit and jogging bottoms. *Jesus, that was a quick change. Where does someone learn to change so quickly?*

Florence flung a t-shirt, some jeans and a baseball cap at Sam. "Put these on."

Sam looked around wondering if she was about to reveal a discreet changing area for him. She wasn't.

He awkwardly tried to turn side on as he unbuttoned his shirt and sloped it off his shoulders. He suddenly felt awfully exposed standing under the fluorescent tube lights. He tried to flex his skinny biceps and conceal his hairless, boney chest in case Florence was watching him. *God, what if she saw his nipples? His massive, over-sized areolas?! Hopefully she wasn't looking.*

Trying to pull his suit trousers off while continuing to flex his arms was tricky. *Oh crap*, Sam had forgotten he was wearing his Teenage Mutant Ninja Turtle Y-fronts today. *Why did he pick them to wear today? Why didn't he wear the M&S ones his mum had bought him before she went to Spain?* He really, really hoped she wasn't looking in his direction.

As it happened, Florence was not looking at Sam. She was keeping her head turned firmly towards the opposite corner of the room, biting her lip hard trying not to laugh out loud.

Sam got the t-shirt on as quickly as possible and pulled the new jeans up. Not a perfect fit but they'd do. He looked down at the t-shirt which had a white CND logo printed on the front.

"I kind of thought we'd be wearing black suits. Maybe dark glasses? You know, like secret agents?"

"Right, listen Jennifer. We're going to a mass demonstration in the middle of Trafalgar Square. There'll be a lot of people there but we're just looking to fit in and suss out what's going on. We don't go anywhere dressed up like secret agents. Remember what Milquetoast said to you; *Security through obscurity*."

"How did you know he said that to me?"

"He says that to everyone, dumbass. Now you're *not* operational, okay? I just want you to stay near me, watch what I do and follow my lead, right? Nothing silly. Remember, you don't know anything. You're just the twat that makes the coffee, yes? Say it after me; *I'm just the twat that makes the coffee*."

"I'm just the twat who makes the coffee!" confirmed Sam, happy to have a defined role at last.

He watched Florence tuck a small handgun into the waistband of her jogging bottoms. "Are we going to kill anyone?" he asked.

"What? No, of course not, why on earth would we kill anyone?"

"I just thought maybe that's what our mission was. Find someone bad and take them out."

"Christ no, just follow me. And don't try and kill *anyone*."

"Right, got it. I wasn't going to kill anyone, I was just checking."

Florence flicked off all of her computers and locked up her drawers. She grabbed the rucksack and made towards the door.

"Florence," said Sam.

"Yes?"

"Have you ever killed anyone?"

Florence looked at Sam and pondered if she really wanted to answer this question truthfully or to divert him onto another subject.

"Our primary role isn't to kill people, E-Squadron deal with those jobs. They conduct most terminations, eliminations and disintegrations. E-Squadron call themselves *The Increment* — that's how seriously they take themselves."

"Ooh. Where do they work then?"

"Classified. They have a compound full of all kinds of kit hidden somewhere; guns, helicopters, batmobiles, all that kind of shit."

"Wow, they sound awesome." Sam was imagining a platoon of Power Rangers. "Will we get to meet them?"

Florence looked at Sam darkly. "You really don't want to meet E-Squadron, Jennifer. If you do, it's usually because something has gone seriously tits-up. Something really bad. They turn up, kill the fuck out of everyone and then disappear."

"Oh. How will I know if I see one?"

"Well, they almost always come out in force, rather than one at a time. They dress all in black, head to toe, except for the parts of their bodies that have mechanical enhancements. Some of them have bionic arms, metallic legs, that sort of thing. Bunch of total psychos if you ask me. Stay well clear."

Sam tucked his T-shirt in. He felt glad he wasn't going to have to kill anyone today.

* * *

They left Florence's office in their disguises and got into the lift.

"So how do we get to Trafalgar Square? Do we get a cab? Do we have a cool car?" asked Sam.

"No, we don't have a cool car."

As the lift clunked and clanged its way back up to the video store, Florence looked down at her watch and seemed to make some adjustments. Sam wondered if they were going to get a taxi or a bus instead.

Once the lift arrived at the Betamax storeroom, the pair stepped out onto the threadbare carpet and Florence started scanning through the shelves of videos, much like Milquetoast had done before. The empty lift clattered away, its noise disappearing into the distance, much to Sam's relief.

"What are you looking for in here? Should I call a cab?"

"No cab..." murmured Florence, scanning along the racks. "Hmmm... *Captain Scarlett*... *Captain Morelli's Mandolin*... aah, here we are, *Captain Horatio Hornblower*!" Florence picked out the 1951 movie starring Gregory Peck, took the cassette out of the case and slotted it into the video player.

After a few moments, a new lift-car dutifully arrived and clanked into place within the shaft. Florence pulled open the iron shutter on the lift-car and concertinaed it sideways, waited for Sam to step in and then shunted it closed again.

The lift-car seemed to be a different one to the one they had travelled in coming up from Florence's office, but it was equally dark and noisy with an overpowering stench of engine oil. The mechanical grinding echoed through the lift shaft in the same way but had a slightly different interior, although this lift-car seemed to be equally keen to shudder itself to the point of collapse like the other one.

If Sam could have heard himself think over the racket of metallic wails, he would definitely be wondering why MI-51 had failed to invest in a modern, state-of-the-art lift system, or at the very least one that hadn't clearly been constructed during the early Victorian era.

After a few minutes, the lift-car came to a jarring halt. Florence grasped the grated shutter and dragged it back open so they could both step out into a small, empty hallway with a single, innocent looking door. Florence closed the iron lift-shutter behind them and opened the door in the corridor, stepping out into refreshing daylight.

Sam looked around outside, trying quickly to familiarise himself. He could hear cars, buses and the hustle and bustle of a busy city street. They were in an alleyway. A fairly dirty alleyway, with overflowing waste bins on one side and old tires stacked up against a wall on the other.

"Where are we?"

"Well, this little alleyway doesn't have a name, but that over there…" she said, pointing towards the open end of the alley, "…is *Trafalgar Square*." As they walked towards the opening, two of the lion statues came into view followed by the towering column with Nelson standing triumphantly at the top.

"I don't understand. How did we get here? We were in the video store weren't we? That's miles away in the Old Kent Road, isn't it?"

"The Betamax network. It covers pretty much most of London."

"What network? What are you talking about?"

"The Betamax network. The video store is just the access point for our department, but we have entry and exit points all over the city. Quickest way to get around if you know how to use it."

"So we can go anywhere we like? Like a magic lift?"

"No, don't be ridiculous Jennifer. It's a spectacular piece of engineering, but there's nothing magic about it. It breaks down quite a lot."

Sam followed Florence as she crossed Duncannon Street and started to try and anonymously mix into the amassing crowds.

"How long has it been there? How come nobody knows about it?"

Florence rolled her eyes. "The network was built around the same time as the first London Tube stations in the 1800s. The shafts mostly go horizontally, some go vertically, but they're way too narrow for the trains - they were mainly dug out for transporting tools. A few decades later when they weren't needed anymore, Disraeli converted them by installing pulleys and motors, like any standard lift of that time, only he utilised the horizontal shafts as well as the vertical ones."

Florence was carefully scanning the crowd as she spoke, trying to pick out any familiar faces from the rogues gallery stored in her brain.

"It was pretty much forgotten about until the 2nd World War, when Churchill used it during the Blitz. All of the entry points are in fairly obscure locations dotted all over the place. A back alley here, behind a launderette there, sometimes surfacing in a hidden part of a car park, that sort of thing."

"So that's why it's so old and crappy then, I guess?"

"Pretty much. MI-51 couldn't properly upgrade it these days without digging up half of London. They can just about keep it running as it is."

"But I don't understand. How can one lift be used for so many people?"

"Because it's not one lift. There are dozens of lifts running through a hundred different shafts."

"Oh, I guess that makes sense. What's with the videos? How do you ever know where the lift is going to take you?"

"Ah, that's what we call *The Knowledge*. Kind of like how cabbies have to learn the names of all the roads in the *A to Z*. The videos are just linked to servos and gears that send the lift to the correct destination. So you need to make sure you know which video cassette to pick and insert into the system - make sure you know your movies!"

The crowd seemed to be mustering around one of the lions, and more people seemed to be drifting towards that direction. In the middle, a man with a fiery red beard and a strong Scottish accent was shouting into a megaphone, trying to whip up some anger in the crowd.

A police helicopter circled overhead, and two riot vans pulled up along the edge of the pavement. As the square steadily filled up with more and more bodies a few chants began, and policemen started to look edgy.

"Let's head over there," said Florence, pointing towards a few placards bobbing along just above head height in the centre of the crowd.

Sam tried to make out what the placards said but could only read one that was emblazoned with distinctive black and red lettering; 'SAY NO TO ANIMAL EXPERIMENTS!'

* * *

Florence and Sam jostled their way towards the nucleus of the crowd. Looking around, Sam estimated there must be at least a hundred people milling around Trafalgar Square. Florence more accurately estimated around a thousand.

The man with the megaphone continued his rousing *Braveheart* speech. It seemed to be working as the rest of the crowd joined in with chants of "No dead mice! No dead mice!"

"Aah, a doggy!" exclaimed Sam, looking down at a scruffy-looking terrier. "What's his name?"

"This is Ralphy. He's a socialist," smiled a girl with scruffy hair holding a large placard.

"Can I stroke him?"

"Sure, knock yourself out," replied Josie.

Sam could best be described as a dog-lover. This was clear when instead of just stroking Ralph, he got down on his knees in the middle of the crowd, clasped the dogs furry face in his hands and nuzzled up to his forehead enthusiastically.

"Ohh boy, I love head-rubs! Grrrr. Yeah, head ruuuubs Ralphy."

Ralphy was less enthusiastic about head-rubs with Sam but was used to tolerating humans with apparent emotional difficulties.

Florence looked down at Sam, equally unimpressed.

"What the fuck are you doing?"

Sam cocked his head to look back up at her. "Head-rubs! This is Ralphy!"

Florence looked at the girl with the placard. "Sorry. He doesn't get out much."

Josie smiled sympathetically. "No problem. Hi, I'm Josie."

"Hello. I'm Florence. This clown on the floor is Jennifer."

Sam stood up quickly. "My name's *not* Jennifer, it's..."

"SAY NO TO GOVERNMENT EXPERIMENTS ON ANIMALS!" yelled the man on the megaphone. "SAY NO TO CUTTING UP MICE!"

The crowd was growing restless, and some noisy skinheads were goading police officers by the fountain. Mrs Bimble had a can of spray paint and was busy daubing the words 'Fuck da Po Po' on the bottom of Nelson's Column. Josie shouted across at her to pack it in.

On the east side of the square, a black Bentley with a small flag on the bonnet pulled up, flanked by two police motorcycles. Out stepped the Home Office Minister Jeffrey Braithwaite along with a team of burly security officers in suits.

The crowd immediately broke into a chorus of jeers and boos as they recognised him - even Mrs Bimble threw an empty bottle in his general direction. He was escorted by the security officers towards the front of the square behind some barriers, and then up some steps leading to a makeshift scaffold podium.

Leo Angelopoulos was standing behind Josie. He leant towards her ear and whispered, "Thith should be interesting."

The crowd had turned their chant to "Braithwaite Out! Braithwaite Out!" and other protesters had joined Mrs Bimble by throwing bottles, rubbish and even a rubber chicken at the lone figure of Braithwaite up on the stand.

Braithwaite tapped the microphone and said "Testing, Testing, 1, 2, 3," whilst looking across at a sound engineer crouched down by the barrier. This only seemed to motivate the crowd to boo even louder. A thumbs-up from the sound engineer further confirmed that the crowd could hear him clearly enough.

"Please," he implored to the crowd. "Please, good people of London! People! Friends! Please just hear me out!"

The crowd continued to jeer although some started to shush their friends, keen to hear what they could justifiably be outraged about next. The volume in Trafalgar Square dropped and slowly the number of incoming projectiles directed at the podium subsided. Sensing his opportunity to be heard, Braithwaite attempted to start his speech again.

"Thank you. Thank you to the people of the United Kingdom for listening."

He looked down at his handwritten notes, pausing to put on his glasses.

"I'm here to tell you today, you fine people, that this has all been a terrible, horrible mistake."

Braithwaite looked out across the crowd, taking in the placards and faces staring back at him.

"Yesterday, there was a leak from unknown sources, purporting a horrific and chilling story that this government is undertaking grotesque medical experiments on animals. Libellous stories reported that this government is implicit in barbaric trials on mice, squirrels and other defenceless mammals. Slanderous rumours accused us of trying to weaponize innocent creatures..."

The crowd quietened down further, carefully listening to what he was about to say next.

"… None of it is true. *None* of it. Not one tiny morsel of information that you fine people have been told is true."

Josie looked across at Leo and Elijah. She felt uncomfortable. *Had they made a mistake believing this story? Had they somehow been incredibly foolish?*

Braithwaite continued, "Please just think about it. None of it makes any sense. The very idea that we, the British Government, would seriously undertake such callous and crazy experiments is just outrageous. And the idea that my department, the Home Office, would sign up to such deplorable activities is an afront to British democracy."

He put down his notes and took off his glasses in order to emphasize his honesty. "Please understand, that my own daughter is studying to be a botanist. My son volunteers at the local animal shelter - my own flesh and blood, whom I love dearly. We are all resolute animal lovers and I have a proven record of supporting environmental causes. The very idea that my family and I would support any kind of illicit animal experimentation is personally, deeply troubling."

The crowd had fallen almost entirely silent at this point. There was a sense of integrity and truth in what the minister was saying and even the most ardent of protesters were starting to feel their protest may have been a wild goose chase, the result of malicious trolls on the internet.

"I can categorically tell everybody here today, that the British Government has not, does not and will not ever conduct this kind of experimentation. There is no evidence for it whatsoever because it is a total fabrication, it is misinformation of the highest order and you my friends have been lied to."

An uncomfortable feeling swept across the crowd as remorse sank in. The minister's speech had been unusually categoric in its denial and he was absolutely correct that there had been no evidence to corroborate the rumours.

People on the edges of the crowd started to drift away. Police officers suddenly looked more comfortable, and a malaise of normality settled across Trafalgar Square.

MP Jeffrey Braithwaite remained on the podium, looking out across the crowd. He felt proud he had delivered the speech of his career today. He knew he would be rewarded with numerous positive front pages the following morning. He looked forward to fish fingers and chips with his wife Sarah tonight.

9½ Weeks

Somewhere, a long way away, deep in the recesses of a scary looking building, a group of men in suits sat around a table overlooked by an oversized television. The TV screen was showing live footage of the events in Trafalgar Square on the BBC World Service.

At the head of the table sat an elderly man with a creased, Mediterranean complexion. He stroked his chin thoughtfully, then looked up at a clock on the wall.

"Ok it is time," he said in broken English. "Proceed - release the footage now."

* * *

Back at Trafalgar Square, Josie was no longer holding up her placard. Feeling deflated and despondent, she looked at Elijah, Red Kendall and Mrs Bimble.

"I'm sorry guys. I guess we were wrong about this one. Anybody fancy a coffee?"

"Oooh maybe an Irish one," smiled Mrs Bimble.

Florence looked at Sam and whispered, "Well, that was all a little storm in a tiny tea-cup, wasn't it?"

Leo, meanwhile, looked troubled.

"There's thumthing strange going on here," he said to Josie. He was looking down at his mobile phone, scrolling and clicking. He used his hand to shield the screen from the sunlight and pressed play on a video file.

Josie got out her own phone, although having decided several years ago to avoid a modern smartphone she was stuck with her ancient, turn-of-the-century handset, which was incapable of accessing social media. She looked over Leo's shoulder to see what it was that had grabbed his attention.

The video showed a clip of a struggling monkey, strapped to a table. His eyes were wide and bloodshot, with lines drawn across his shaved head in marker pen. Doctors in lab coats were leaning over him but their voices were inaudible.

The camera panned in as they cut into the monkey's scalp and droplets of blood trickled down its face. They inserted steel probes into the pitiful creature's exposed brain causing it to screech in terror. As one of the doctors fiddled with the probes, the monkey's left arm raised into the air, revealing a prosthetic metallic claw.

Josie put her hand over her own mouth, retching at the gory spectacle. "Leo, this is gross! Why are you looking at this?"

"Hang on a thec. Keep watching!"

The shaky footage panned out to show a little more of the grim-looking surgery. A countdown timer on the video was coming to a close with around ten seconds left when they saw the most shocking image of all. As the doctor continued to make incisions, behind him there was another figure in a smart, flannel suit. His identity was clear to see.

Josie gasped.

The man in the flannel suit was watching the operation intently with a demented sense of satisfaction on his face. Throughout all of the horrific footage, the most disconcerting thing of all was that this man in the flannel suit was clearly none other than the man on the podium, the Home Office Minister Jeffrey Braithwaite.

* * *

Leo immediately tagged the video with Braithwaite's name and pressed the 'share' button, instantaneously uploading the video to his Twitter feed. And also to Instagram. And TikTok. And Reddit. And YouTube. And WhatsApp. And Pinterest. And even Facebook, which nobody used anymore.

Within moments, people in the crowd started to take their mobile phones out of their pockets. Less than a minute later, a whole chorus of electronic alerts could be heard pinging from people's phones. An eery hush swept across Trafalgar Square as the whole crowd collectively scrutinised their own mobile phone screens simultaneously as if they were all in some impromptu mass worship.

Sam looked at Florence, "What the hell's going on?"

"I'm not sure. But this doesn't seem good."

Up on the podium, Jeffrey Braithwaite was equally perplexed at the sight before him. He leant backwards towards an aide standing behind him, covering his hand over the microphone.

"What are they all looking at? What the fuck is going on?"

The aide was busily looking at her own phone. "Something bad, sir. We need to get you out of here. Now!"

Just as she said these words far up on the podium, the simmering crowd down below in the square suddenly erupted into a crazed mayhem. Angry shouts roared out as a flurry of bottles, coins and stones rained down on the podium. The number of people instantly seemed to swell as they surged forward, tearing down barriers and flinging cones at police officers diving for cover. Screams of 'murderer' and 'psycho' were aimed up at Jeffrey Braithwaite. The minister's security officers huddled around him, manhandling him back down towards his car, as red-faced protesters spat and hurled obscenities at him on the way down.

Sam looked around as paving slabs were being ripped up and hurled into the fountains, and protesters clambered over the lion statues, daubing them with paint. A shocked and confused Braithwaite was bundled into his Bentley as men and women pounded on the windows and bonnet with outrage. Police officers tried to fight them back with their batons to create a gap through the crowd so the car could make a getaway.

Red Kendall ripped his shirt off Hulk Hogan-style and ran into a cluster of flak-jacketed policemen while Mrs Bimble berated a WPC with her umbrella. Josie instinctively reached down to grab Ralphy to prevent him being trampled.

Elijah had climbed up onto the side railings and was throwing pebbles at Braithwaite's car as he ducked down inside. As the Bentley pulled away through the crowd, a trio of police riot vans screamed down the Charing Cross Road into the fray. On the south side of the square, police with riot shields formed up in a line as a large truck with a water cannon parked behind them.

"We have to get out of here," said Sam. "This has gone bananas."

"Grab those mopeds, we need to follow that car," said Florence, pointing at two mopeds parked up along the pavement edge.

"How do we start them? We haven't got the keys!"

Florence reached into her rucksack and pulled out her bunch of skeleton keys. She used one to start up her moped and then unhooked another key and tossed it at Sam. "Here, use this. It'll start any vehicle." Sam shoved the key into the ignition slot, pressed the start button causing the moped to bubble to life first time.

"We haven't got helmets!" he shouted over the revving engines.

"Don't crash then!" Florence shouted back, accelerating away in the direction of Braithwaite's car.

One problem, thought Sam. He'd never ridden a moped before. He'd only ever ridden that little pink bicycle when he was being chased onto that tube train, and even that had stabilisers fitted. *Oh well, how hard could it be?* He twisted the throttle grip on the right handlebar resulting in the two-wheeled beast roaring away doing a wheelie - unfortunately in the complete opposite direction to Florence.

Sam did his best to wrangle the handlebars in the direction he wanted to go but the stubborn little moped was more determined to forge its own path, directly into the middle of the angry crowd.

* * *

As the violence spilt out of the pedestrianised part of the Square, surrounding traffic had ground to a halt. Taxis honked their horns and stranded buses became a further target for the unruly mob to take their anger out on.

Police squads reinforced themselves and tried to get into a defensive formation with their riot shields. Other Police on horseback arrived from Marble Arch, breaking through into the meleé, as tear gas was launched into the areas of most hardcore aggression in an effort to disperse people.

In response, wild-eyed youths broke off fragments of concrete and hurled them through the air, trying their best to provoke the police to break ranks and engage in a street brawl. Red Kendall was beating his chest and screaming in the face of a police Alsatian, goading it to fight him.

The Alsatian was more than willing to accept the challenge.

Mrs Bimble was being coaxed to safety by Josie, who in turn was trying to protect Ralphy by cradling him under her jacket. They headed eastwards towards The Strand, hoping to find a way out of the sudden chaos. As they weaved between the mob, a water cannon sitting on top of an armoured police truck opened up its payload on the crowd, firing a ragged torrent of freezing water in their direction.

Josie threw her arms around Mrs Bimble, shielding her from being knocked off her feet but Ralphy fell from her arms and instinctively darted across the road seeking shelter.

"Ralphy!" she screamed, chasing after him. "Ralphy, fucking stop!" She sprinted through the parked traffic trying to catch up with him but was grabbed by a towering, surly policeman in full riot gear.

"Get back over there, pikey!" he snarled, throwing her to the floor in one savage movement.

"Fuck you prick, I'm trying to get my dog!" she spat back at him, grabbing a traffic cone and swinging it square into his ballsack. The riot cop crumpled to the ground but as she looked up, four of his angry riot cop friends were bowling rapidly towards her, unfurling their batons and readying their CS gas. Josie reached up to shield her face, anticipating the blows about to come raining down on her, but as she did so, a guy on a moped appeared screaming out of nowhere and smashed head on into the riot squad, sending all four of them tumbling away like skittles.

As the moped lay on its side with its wheels still frantically spinning, the man stood up and started dusting himself down. Josie instantly recognised him as the guy called Jennifer who was enthusiastically nuzzling her dog earlier.

"That was amazing!" gasped Josie.

"It was?" replied Sam. A little dazed, he wasn't entirely sure what he just did, but the carnage of four fully armoured police officers looking concussed on the floor was definitely a bad sign.

"Quick, we've got to find Ralphy and get out of here." She grabbed Sam's hand, urging him to start running with her. Sam was limping a little at first but managed to break into a lopsided run alongside her, as Ralphy suddenly bounded out from a nearby side street to join them.

They sprinted down The Strand, Josie flicking her head around to check they weren't being chased by the cops. As the crowd grew more distant behind them, they eventually slowed back down to a brisk walk as the noise from Trafalgar Square disappeared. Josie was laughing hard as she tried to catch her breath.

"That was *so* funny! I can't believe you rescued me like that! It was like something out of *The Dukes of Hazzard*."

"I didn't mean to—"

"I know you didn't mean to hurt them, but it was still funny! I don't think I've been rescued by a guy on a moped before." Josie picked up Ralphy again and gave him a kiss on his furry head. "Come on, let's get away from here - we can walk up towards Covent Garden. I'll get you a coffee and a cake for that."

* * *

Florence pulled over to the side of the road on her moped, realising Sam wasn't following her. She took her mobile phone out of her rucksack and called him.

"Where the fuck are you? You're supposed to be following me!" Sam seemed to be coughing up a lung or two at the other end of the line as he relayed his location. "What do you mean you're going for coffee? *Who with?"*

She turned the engine of her moped off so she could hear him a little better. She was out of range of the rioters now and Braithwaite's Bentley had disappeared towards Westminster. Sam seemed to be saying he had hooked up with some protesters from the Croydon Revolutionary Front and was off to Covent Garden for a cosy post-riot chat. Florence thought for a moment. "Ok I'll meet you there in fifteen minutes."

Hmm good work Jennifer, this could be just the break we need, she thought.

* * *

Sixteen minutes later, Florence was sitting in Mama Mary's Colombian Café drinking a Black Caribou.

Sam was having a Raspberry Piccolo Cappuccino and Josie was drinking a vegan oat milk latté. Ralph was tied to a lamppost outside the café, sniffing curiously around the carcass of a decaying sparrow.

After another five minutes, Red Kendall and Elijah bounded excitedly into the café to join them.

"That. Was. Bloody immense!" roared Red, holding his arms in the air triumphantly. He had a swollen eye and a chipped tooth but was beaming like a huge, savage Cheshire cat. Josie jumped up to welcome them both with a hug. There were jubilant fist bumps all round, followed by enthusiastic pats on the back. Braithwaite was vanquished, the government had been shown to be liars and they'd had some jolly fun fisticuffs with the Feds to boot.

"What happened to Leo and Mrs Bimble?" Josie asked.

Red plonked himself down at the table. "Mrs Bimble demanded one of the police officers take her home in a squad car - crazy old lady. Didn't see what happened to Leo, but I hope he didn't get arrested. We escaped in an ambulance and crashed it through the roadblock on Northumberland Avenue."

"Well, you're not going to believe what happened to me..." enthused Josie with an excited grin on her face. She went onto regale her fellow justice warriors with her own adventure and introduced Jennifer as her new moped-riding hero for saving her from 'at least ten brutal rozzers trying to beat her ass senseless'.

Sam was about to interject and correct her about his name when Josie wrongfooted him with an unexpected question, gesturing towards Sam and Florence. "So how long have you guys been together?"

"Together? Us? Oh! She's not my girlfriend! We work togeth—"

"He's my little brother!" Florence interrupted sharply.

"Oh. Righto." Josie pondered how they could look so starkly different but decided it was best not to offend anyone by questioning it.

"How come you look like chalk and cheese then?" waded in Red Kendall, fearlessly happy to offend when necessary.

"Different dads," answered Florence confidently.

Sam initially felt confused but quickly cottoned on to the subterfuge Florence was deploying and decided he should try his best to help with the deception.

"Yeah. Our mum was kind of a slag. You know, she put it about a bit," he smiled cheerfully.

The table fell uncomfortably silent. Even Red Kendall looked disappointed in him. Florence stared at him blankly, wondering if it was somehow possible to physically zip his mouth shut.

Sam quickly tried to redeem himself. "Well, what I mean is, she wasn't a total slag. At home she was lovely. It wasn't like she was wearing a basque and suspenders while doing the hoovering. It was just at work. She sometimes got a bit. You know… a bit slaggy… because… she was… umm…"

Sam wracked his brains to think of a word to say. *Any word. What should the next word be? A nurse? An air hostess? A trumpet player?? Jesus Christ brain, just think of a job!*

"A prostitute! Our mum was a prostitute!" he finally blurted out.

Florence's shoulders slumped as she held her head in her hands. "I'm going for a cigarette." She stood up and headed out towards the front of the café.

Sam supped on his raspberry coffee medley, hoping someone would change the subject away from his make-believe, promiscuous mother.

"So who are you with?" asked Red Kendall pointedly.

"Huh? Who am I *with*?" repeated Sam, slightly bewildered. "My sister. She was just sitting right here next to me."

"He means, what group were you with at the demo?" clarified Josie. "We're the Croydon Revolutionary Front. The famous C.R.F! You must've heard of us?"

"Oh sure. Yeah, everyone's heard of you guys. The good ol' C.R.F! I've heard lots of good things about the C.R.F. Yep, great reputation you guys have."

"So? Who are *you* with?" pushed Red, belligerently.

Sam looked around in mild panic trying to think of a suitable acronym, desperately hoping Florence was going to be back very quickly. He hated improvising.

"Oh, well we're with the…" he found himself staring at the various condiments laid out on the café counter looking for inspiration, "… with the S-U-G-A-R."

"The *SUGAR*?" queried Josie, looking puzzled. "I'm not sure I've heard of them. What does it stand for?

"Um. Well. Yes, we're fairly new actually. We're the… Society… for Underground… erm… Galactic… Armed… erm… Resistance!"

Josie's eyes widened. "The Society for Underground Galactic Armed Resistance? Wow they sound mental, I need to find out more about them. Where do they meet up?"

Jesus, stop asking me questions, thought Sam. "Oh we kinda just hang around at the video store on the Old Kent Road. A lot of them are… er… movie nerds."

Red enthusiastically joined in. "Is that right? I'm a bit of a film buff myself, y'know. I think I might look them up too!"

Suddenly, there was a loud, shrill, yelp coming from outside. Everybody froze and looked round towards the window. Moments later, Florence swept back through the front door of the café having finished her cigarette.

"What on earth was that noise?!" asked Josie. "It sounded like Ralph, is he okay?"

Florence wiped her finger on a napkin as she sat down. "Oh you mean that little dog out there? Yeah he's fine, he was just barking at a car I think."

"It didn't sound like he was barking at a car…?" Josie stood up and leant forward in order to see out of the front window. Ralph was still safely attached to the lamppost, but he was now looking back at her with a cross look on his furry face.

Florence tapped her watch and nudged Sam with her shoulder. "We'd better go, bruv. We've got that *thing* that we've got to do tonight."

“Right, yes the *thing*, sure.” Sam swigged back his cappuccino and smiled sweetly at Josie as he stood up. “Thanks for the raspberry coffee!”

“No problem,” winked Josie. “Listen I’m sure you’re really busy with the whole ‘armed galactic resistance’ thing right now, but on Saturday night we’re having a planning meeting for the C.R.F. team at Leo’s place. You could come along if you fancied it? Maybe meet some of the others?”

“Sure, I could do that. I don’t think I’m doing anything important Saturday. I don’t think we have any *things* we’ve got to do.”

“Great!” Josie scribbled Leo’s address on a napkin, folded it and handed it to Sam. “Kicks off at 7pm, I’ll save you a seat.”

Sam and Florence said their goodbyes to their new friends and headed for the door. As they left the café, Ralphy’s tail dropped between his legs, as he growled nervously at Florence.

“What on earth did you do to that dog?” asked Sam, looking back over his shoulder at the angry pooch.

“Ask me later,” said Florence. “I need to get home and wash my hands.”

Ten Things I Hate About You

Somewhere, a long way away, on one of the upper levels of a scary looking building, an elderly man with a creased complexion removed the stopper out of a crystal decanter and poured an aging Scotch into three glasses. He passed one to each of his companions and then gazed out of the window across a dusky plain.

"Gentlemen, today's operation was a resounding success. The seeds of uncertainty have been sown and the path to discrediting the British has begun."

He raised his glass and chinked it with the other suited gentlemen. "To our brilliant and as yet undetected neophyte. When the dogs of the British Government are finally on their knees, they will be begging to return what is rightfully ours. Hail Crypteia"

"Hail Crypteia," echoed his smiling companions.

* * *

The following morning, Florence received a pink memo on the fax machine, summoning her and Sam to an emergency *the-shit-has-hit-the-fan* meeting.

The-shit-has-hit-the-fan meetings were called whenever there was a potential international incident evolving, and the Home Office Minister starring in a video helping to mutilate a monkey was certainly considered a potential international incident.

These meetings always made Florence nervous. Knowing that each of the department heads would all be sitting there swinging their dicks around the unnecessarily large boardroom table would be bad enough, but on this occasion she knew the White Rabbit would be twitching his metaphorical whiskers in her direction, after yesterday's events at the demonstration.

Sam followed Florence up to the Betamax room and waited whilst she checked through the video racks, looking for the right movie.

"So where are we going for this meeting?" he asked.

"The Boardroom. It's in the White Rabbit's warren. That's why I'm looking for the 1951 copy of *Alice in Wonderland*."

"Ah, that figures." Sam's mind wandered back to the first time he walked into the video store with Milquetoast, at the start of the week.

"Florence. When I spoke with Mr Milquetoast, he said that our job is to specialise in *black propaganda*. Do you know what he was talking about?"

"He's correct. That's exactly what we specialise in." Florence picked up a copy of the animated classic. She leant against the desk with the video player and looked at Sam.

"Listen. If you want to persuade a certain demographic to support you, you might try love bombing them with misleading information. That's what they call *white propaganda*. It's all bullshit, but ultimately it's obvious where the fake information is coming from."

"Right. So I'm guessing *black propaganda* is the opposite of that?"

"Kind of. If you decide to disguise what you're doing, so the target demographic doesn't even know where all this bullshit is coming from, that's what they call *black propaganda*. It's when information isn't only false, but it also pretends to originate from a different source, adding a further layer of subterfuge."

"And that's what we do, is it?"

"Not really, that's what we're trying to stop. But the problem is black propaganda is everywhere. Even when it fails, it actually succeeds. Once you get suspicious of it, you see it all over the place. Even if nobody believes it, the intention is to spread suspicion and confusion so that no one knows what's actually true anymore."

"Like when the Russians were fucking about with the American elections?"

"Exactly. At this point it doesn't really matter if they were interfering or not, the fact is there was so much shit being flung around that now half of the American population don't trust the results of their own elections regardless of the original reason. In short, democracy ends up eating itself."

"Did the Russians really fuck with the American elections?"

"Probably. They've been dicking around with American presidents for years. They used to fund the American Communist Party back in the Fifties just to annoy McCarthy. Thing is, it worked. And the Yanks spent decades accusing each other of being Commies."

Florence tucked her blouse into her trousers and smoothed the imaginary creases out of her immaculate blouse, then slotted *Alice in Wonderland* into the video player.

"The problem we've got after yesterday," she said, "is now someone is dicking around with us, and we don't even know who they are, let alone what they want." Sam and Florence got into the lift, which then headed off in an ambiguous direction towards the White Rabbit's warren, somewhere in London.

The journey was relatively brief, and they were soon stepping out of the lift-car. Florence was familiar with the route and led Sam through the labyrinthian corridors, while Sam did his best to keep up with her brisk pace until they finally reached the boardroom door.

Florence double-checked she had no creases, braced herself, knocked on the door and walked in.

* * *

The MI-51 Boardroom wasn't really a boardroom. It carried the air of a Grand Masonic Hall combined with the seductive ambience of a 1920s ballroom. The high walls were clad in dark wood and decorated with gilded oil paintings depicting venerable-looking Victorian gentlemen. Distant chandeliers twinkled in the overhead offering a sultry glow across the chamber. It was a room of paradoxes which instilled a sense of intimidation into anyone entering it for the first time. It was very large yet managed to maintain a sense of eery intimacy. It looked ancient, without being dusty, worn or old-fashioned. It was a place of miniscule details and world-changing decisions.

The Grand Reform Club aesthetic was interrupted by an excessively large, ornate, dark oak table occupying the centre of the burgundy carpet. The circumference of the table would comfortably contain the entire footprint of an average-sized London apartment and was surrounded by twenty five evenly spaced leather bound chairs, enough to cater for two people from each department - plus the White Rabbit, holding court on a slightly larger gold-trimmed throne.

Sam followed Florence to their allocated chairs which were accompanied on the table by a brass plaque identifying them as the Department of Conspiracy. He looked across the table and considered the other people sitting around it.

Directly next to them were the two Heads of the Department of Interrogation. Sam felt confident he could identify that the friendly faced, blonde guy was probably Mr Nice, while the grizzled thug with a scar on his cheek was undoubtedly Mr Nasty.

Further around the table, the Department of Propaganda consisted of a professional-looking woman who'd possibly just stepped out of a salon and a man who looked like he'd always prefer it shaken not stirred. Both looked like they would be extremely comfortable promoting the privileges of a members-only tennis club.

The two spectacularly prim-looking weasels representing the Department of Bureaucracy appeared to have built a temporary fort with books and paperwork stacked up on the table around them. They looked to be undertaking some kind of pre-meeting *book-a-thon* as they flicked through multiple tomes readying themselves for the impending verbal intercourse.

Out of everybody at the table, Sam decided he would be most likely to go for a drink with the two guys sitting behind the brass plaque for the Department of Subversive Toys. They looked to be the most out of place characters and appeared to be very casually dressed. One of them was unusually tall, possibly seven foot in height. His uncomfortably skinny frame, large head and googly-eyes gave him the presence of a child's make-believe alien friend. He covered his mouth with his palm as he whispered excitedly to his Subversive Toys colleague. Conversely, his colleague was shorter, fatter and sported a poorly-managed beard. He seemed to be stifling giggles at whatever googly eyes was whispering to him. The idea of the two of them being employed to invent and devise new toys seemed entirely plausible, thought Sam.

Then he caught sight of a teenage girl on the far side of the table, sitting directly adjacent to the White Rabbit. The shaven head and nose gave her a distinctly androgenous look, which Sam instantly recognised as the girl who'd crashed into him when he was wearing the sandwich board from Super Mario's sex shop. *So she was the one who'd stuffed the map into his hand and then disappeared into the nearby toilets!* Sam thought back to the incident over a month earlier and realised that toilet must have been one of those locations linked to the Betamax lift system, and that was how she disappeared.

He strained to read the brass plaque on the table in front of her; *Agent Socrates*. That sounded like a pretty cool name to him, definitely better than *Jennifer*. As he continued to stare, Agent Socrates suddenly winked at him. Sam was immediately startled and wasn't sure whether it was polite to wink back or not – what was the wink etiquette with strangers? Rather than risk a full wink, Sam opted to blink in response, hoping that would be appropriately civil.

"Ahem." The White Rabbit cleared his throat, causing the room to immediately fall silent.

"We, my friends," he began slowly and gruffly, "are under siege."

The White Rabbit hunched his elbows on the table and spoke with gravelly tones. His square jaw carried heavy jowls and shadowy bags were set low under his eyes. He was a bulky, heavy-set man, with the manner of a cranky bison, weary of the tiresome jackals around him.

His neck had all but disappeared into his shoulders as if the weight of his hefty skull had forced it downwards over the preceding decades. Tufts of white hair and a walrus moustache helped give the White Rabbit the appearance of a particularly cantankerous bunny.

"Yesterday's disappointing revelations about our Home Office Minister have," he briefly paused in order to moderate his choice of words carefully, "*dismayed* His Majesty."

The White Rabbit was always careful to be selective in describing who his organisation was actually serving. He knew politicians were fleeting and prime ministers were short-lived. His loyalty, and therefore the loyalty of his organisation, was very much betrothed to King and Country before all else.

"Communications. What have *you* got?"

The White Rabbit didn't use names, only departments. He reasoned that this was to satisfy security protocols, although in truth he had long since stopped trying to remember the names of everybody who had worked for him after so many years.

The Department of Communications consisted of two studious-looking females who prided themselves on being consistently on the pulse of all activity, occurring everywhere, at any time. Their information came from a deluge of sources including emails, internet searches, smart phones, games consoles, CCTV, traffic cameras, court transcripts, intercepted radio transmissions, satellites and of course their infamous fleet of pigeon-cams, which happily mixed with real pigeons in city centres up and down the country. They also had a trusted network of informants, moles, grasses, narks, snouts, snitches and snakes who would happily sell their grandmas for the right price.

"We've been investigating Braithwaite. We know that he reads *The Times*, has marmalade on his toast, is environmentally conscious and has paid off his mortgage. His family all check out - his daughter is working on a botany PhD, his son is at 6th form college and his wife likes going to the gym. She's also having an affair with her yoga instructor. In summary, we *don't* believe Braithwaite has the capacity or inclination to go rogue or actually undertake this experimentation of his own accord."

The White Rabbit seemed to acknowledge this with a grumble of agreement, although it might equally have been indigestion. "Propaganda. What do you have?"

"Initial investigations indicate a classic *disinformation* attack," confirmed the professional-looking woman. "At first we weren't sure if the video footage had been edited using software, but analysis confirms that whilst it's not CGI, it is probably staged. Somebody has gone to a great deal of effort to make it appear real. Clever use of the Kuleshov effect gives it away. We remain confident this is something similar to the KGB's Operation Infektion in the eighties."

Around the table, other people scribbled notes. The relevance of this being a *dis*-information attack helped frame the issue for the other departments. Whereas mere *mis*-information related to unintentional mistakes such as incorrect statistics or translations, *dis*-information was rather more serious as it indicated deliberately fabricated evidence intentionally created for the purpose of a planned conspiracy. The third category was of course *mal*-information, which related to the deliberate disclosure of an individual's private or personal information. When that ex-boy/girlfriend circulates pictures of you with a cucumber stuck between your butt-cheeks, that's definitely *mal*-information.

"Do we think this is KGB?"

"Negative sir," joined in Propaganda No.2. "This footage doesn't fit with anything we've seen from the Russians before, and in recent years they've been more occupied with the Ukraine."

"Hostilities. Who do we think *is* involved?"

The Department of Hostilities looked like they'd just returned from a *GI Joe* mission. Their pseudo-military outfits trimmed with shoulder slung pistols and utility belts gave Sam the distinct impression that they had probably abseiled into the meeting via ceiling vents after kayaking up the Thames.

"We concur the footage is *not* of Russian origin, sir. Not slick enough to be the Chinese or Saudis. We've deployed the *Black Knight* satellite to investigate various South American cartels, nothing showing so far. We've also got eyes on the Grey Wolves, Hamas, Hezbollah, the Islamic Revolutionaries, Muslim Brotherhood and the Vanguards of Conquest and nothing showing. Our intel suggests this is someone close to us or more likely a new, unknown adversary."

Everyone sitting around the table looked across to the White Rabbit to see who was next. He appeared to be deep in contemplation or possibly fallen asleep, no one was quite sure. Then he turned to look at Florence and Sam.

"Conspiracies?"

"Yes sir," acknowledged Florence.

"Who is this… person?" The White Rabbit flicked his hand in Sam's direction.

"This is Jennifer, sir. He's a trainee, started this week."

"Actually, my name's Sa—"

"Shhh!!" rebuked Florence sharply at Sam.

Sam silenced himself. Why did she insist on calling him Jennifer he wondered? Perhaps she actually thought his name really *was* Jennifer.

"Sir, yesterday we started to infiltrate a group known as the Croydon Revolutionary Front. We don't know if they're *directly* responsible, but we think they might lead us to further information. Jennifer here will be embedded further within two days."

"I see," grumbled the White Rabbit. "And you think it's safe to embed this 'trainee' into a potential terrorist organisation?"

"He's our best option at the moment. He seems to have generated a rapport of sorts. I've implanted a microphone into an asset belonging to one of the suspects. I'll be able to monitor activity remotely"

"Asset?"

"It was a dog, sir."

Googly eyes from the Department of Subversive Toys looked confused. "How did you manage to implant one of our microphones into a *dog*? You can't just attach it to a collar, they were designed to be surgically implanted?"

"I had to improvise. I inserted it via an exposed cavity."

The White Rabbit raised an eyebrow suspiciously. "You deployed the microphone… *orally*?"

Florence looked uncomfortable. "The animal was uncooperative, sir. I decided it would be more effective to insert the microphone as a suppository."

The White Rabbit looked unusually startled. "I see…"

Sam looked horrified. He whispered at Florence "*You stuck a microphone up his butt?!*"

"*Shh. We can talk about this later*," she whispered back.

"We're taking quite a risk here, Conspiracy. I hope you know what you're doing," cautioned the White Rabbit.

"I understand that sir. We do," replied Florence.

Sam put his hand up.

"Why is your hand up?" The White Rabbit looked around the room confused. "Why is his hand up?"

Everybody looked at Sam with his hand up.

Florence shout-whispered at Sam, "Put your hand down moron!"

Sam slowly moved his arm halfway down. "Sir. I might need some help with something sir," squeaked Sam nervously. His voice box had seemingly rebelled, independently deciding that speaking several octaves higher would clearly be an ingenious new way to make him look like a twat.

"What sort of... *something?*" frowned the White Rabbit.

"Well, it all happened kind of quick sir, and I had to create a persona, so they'd trust me. I kind of let slip that I'm part of a different activist group. That's why they liked me I think."

"What sort of... *activist group?*"

Florence stepped in. "I'm afraid he said he was part of the Society for Underground Galactic Armed Resistance. I apologise sir, I wasn't in the vicinity when he created this cover story."

"The Society for Underground Galactic what?! I've never heard of them."

"No, sir. They don't exist sir."

"SUGAR for short, sir," clarified Sam, helpfully.

The White Rabbit shook his head, bemused. "I see."

"We're going to need help substantiating this cover story, sir," said Florence. "We might need a blog, some leaflets and posters, that kind of thing."

The White Rabbit fiddled with his wristwatch, and after a few short moments, a familiar face hurried through the door and strode confidently across the boardroom. Sam watched as Milquetoast walked directly up to the White Rabbit and leant in closely to confer with him.

The White Rabbit whispered some brief instructions, Milquetoast nodded obediently and then swiftly spun around on his toes and disappeared back out of the door again.

"Right, trainee. Listen to me." He pointed towards Sam. "Your job is to monitor this group. Follow them. Find out what they know. I want you being involved in everything they do. But don't take any affirmative action. If we see a threat, we'll send in support to intervene. You just watch and listen, got it? And put your hand down."

Sam put his hand all the way back down. Support sounded assuring, but Sam wondered what he meant by 'intervene'.

"Communications. Deploy a squadron of pigeon-cams - I want them following this boy everywhere he goes. Subversive Toys, provide the trainee with a Mk IV surveillance kit before he goes undercover. Also, set up this Galactic Resistance nonsense as a cover story for him. Make sure its airtight."

The studious-looking females and Googly Eyes all nodded in acknowledgement of the White Rabbit's instructions and rapidly made notes.

He then turned to Agent Socrates. "Notify E-Squadron that we may be requiring their back up - Right, off to work people."

* * *

Somewhere, a long way away, in the security room of a menacing-looking building, a silhouetted old man sat at a large computer screen. He was undertaking a video call with the neophyte, many miles away.

"Our queen has reported your progress to me. You have served The Crypteia well," said the old man. "You are drawing nearer to your goal of becoming a crimson guard with each successful mission."

It was a great honour to even be considered. An essential part of the agoge was to undergo an exile and successfully complete the trials.

The old man continued, "The next target will be the British Chancellor. You may proceed with stage two of your mission in London. And good luck."

* * *

Josie was eating a strawberry Pop-Tart dipped in mayonnaise for breakfast, but there was something troubling her. It wasn't the dubious clash of sweet and savoury in her mouth and it wasn't the red paw prints on her carpet that had disappointingly failed to evaporate overnight.

Every now and then, she thought she heard an irritatingly faint sound emanating from somewhere within her flat. It was almost imperceptible to the human ear, but she was becoming increasingly aware of a distant whistling tone. As soon as she turned her head to try and identify the source, it promptly ceased.

The television was turned off, the microwave was still broken, and the fridge produced an entirely different electronic hum. She sat down next to Ralphy and tickled him on the belly, wondering if he could hear it too.

Ralphy looked back at Josie. He was still quite cross about what he considered to be 'the café incident'. He also still had a sore bottom.

Ocean's *Eleven*

Editorial meetings at the West Dulwich Gazette generally consisted of all reporters showcasing their best story of the week, in the hope of getting a front page. Bobby Noggins had managed two front pages this year and was looking for a third in order to be included in the annual lucky draw bonus pot.

His current workload included a number of ongoing investigations that had limited potential. A drunk man from Streatham had allegedly been beaten up by the real invisible man, firefighters in Norbury had rescued a duck from a lake and an old woman from Thornton Heath was very cross because she'd just realised that she had been posting her letters into a dog poop bin for the last two years. Whilst all of these stories would make solid page four or five stories in the Gazette, Bobby didn't see them as Pulitzer Prize material.

One of the main challenges when working for such a small-time publication was sorting out the wheat from the chaff. And where he found the jaded chaff, he saw it as his job to put a dramatic spin on it and turn it into golden wheat. It was his job to figure out the *alternative facts*.

Alternative facts was a term introduced across the Atlantic in the United States some years earlier, which Bobby rather liked. After Republican politicians made inflated claims regarding the size of the crowd that was present at the new president's inauguration ceremony, journalists had challenged them.

Journalists argued with simple logic that *alternative facts* are not actually *facts* at all, they're simply *lies* however Republicans countered this and doubled down on their claims. Their justification argued "Two plus two is four, but also three plus one is four. Partly cloudy is the same as partly sunny. A glass half full is also a glass half empty." Bobby agreed with the politicians that these could reasonably be considered *alternative facts* and he found it easy to subscribe to this logic, which in essence he had translated as 'you have your version, I have mine'.

Bobby stared despondently at the wire framed in-tray on his desk. Amongst the pile of junk mail and unopened letters, he noticed a large, brown padded envelope.

It wasn't addressed to him personally, but it had the office address on the front. It was not handwritten, but rather consisted of individual letters cut out from a magazine which had in turn been sellotaped on to the envelope. There was no stamp and no postmark which, Bobby knew, meant the padded envelope had been hand-delivered personally.

"Did anybody see who dropped *this* off?" he asked, waving the envelope in the air. Mr Peterson looked up from his desk and shrugged, Janice shook her head and everyone else just continued with their work, ignoring him.

He peeled off the seal and tore the top of the envelope open. He gently tipped it upside down allowing the contents to slip out onto the desk. Bobby stared down at the scattered contents in front of him. He slowly refocused and, one by one, rearranged the photographs that had emerged, so that they were all facing him in an orderly fashion.

He felt a lump in his throat as a wave of uncomfortable nausea swept across him. There were a dozen photographs, all depicting the government's Chancellor of the Exchequer enthusiastically gorging himself on a sumptuous meal. What was immediately disconcerting was that the chancellor was fully naked in all of the pictures. His large, hairy man-boobs and flabby beer belly were fully exposed, and his eyes looked glazed in a euphoric stupor.

In several pictures, the chancellor was accompanied by his lovely wife, who was equally naked and looked to be joyously participating in her husband's antics. The photographs had a grainy quality, of the type that had been snapped spontaneously during a night out with friends in a club or restaurant.

Bobby did a quick search on the internet which confirmed the faces he was looking at were definitely the British chancellor and his renowned socialite wife, Gloria. The images of some grotesque naked feast was not what Bobby found disturbing though. The concept of receiving illicit, nude or private photos of public figures was hardly novel in this day and age. What Bobby found shocking, what he found truly horrific, was the distinct images that confirmed what the cocaine-addled couple appeared to be feasting on.

He rearranged the photos and realised they could be ordered in a clear sequence. The sequence indicated the beginning, middle and end of some kind of opulent Caligula-inspired banquet. Bobby realised the diabolical pair were happily using a large carving knife to slice tender, pink cuts of flesh from what could only be described as a young, pert, motionless, female body.

He placed his hand over his mouth as the sickening enormity of what had landed on his desk seeped into his brain.

Not all stories required *alternative facts*. Some stories just wrote themselves.

The Chancellor of the Exchequer was a cannibal. And so was his lovely wife.

* * *

Florence was preparing Sam to go undercover.

"Remember what the White Rabbit said: Your job is to monitor the C.R.F. at Saturday's meeting and follow them around, nothing else. We'll be listening to everything that's being said, and the pigeon-cams will also be following you."

"How do they put the cameras in the pigeons? Do they shove them up their bottoms too?"

"Don't be ridiculous, Jennifer. They're not real pigeons, they're drones. Like robots. They just look real. Here…" She flicked on one of the big screens on her desk, pressed a few buttons and then grainy footage appeared on the monitor.

"See? This is pigeon No.1079. He's in Birmingham at the moment."

"What's he doing in Birmingham?"

Florence scrutinised the screen. "Staking out a mosque by the looks of it." She then picked up a small, mobile speaker on her desk.

"Listen!" she said, beckoning Sam towards the speaker.

"What am I listening to?"

"This is the dog-microphone. The one inside Ralphy."

Sam listened but could only hear snoring. "Why can I hear snoring?"

"I guess Ralphy snores. Either that or your little social justice warrior snores."

Florence picked up what looked like a stapler and walked round her desk, closer to Sam.

"Close your eyes."

Sam closed his eyes. Florence stapled something into the back of his head.

"MOTHERFUCKER!! WHAT DID YOU JUST DO TO ME?!"

"It's a skull receiver. Means I can talk to you and give you instructions. Nobody else will be able to hear me but to you it'll be clear as day. Hopefully."

Sam rubbed the back of his head and scowled at Florence. "Couldn't you just have told me you were going to staple a speaker into my head?!"

"Don't be such a baby. Right, empty your pockets."

Sam stood up and pulled out his wallet and a few coins then placed them on her desk. Then from his other pocket he produced a piece of tissue and his prized three-leafed clover encased in laminated plastic.

"What the fuck is that?"

"It's my three-leafed clover. It's lucky."

"How is that lucky? It's supposed to have four leaves to be lucky?"

"It used to have four leaves, but one dropped off. That's why I had it laminated."

"You're an idiot."

"I'm keeping it," replied Sam indignantly, putting the clover back in his pocket.

"Whatever. Right, when you're undercover keep your pockets empty. Prevents you leaving anything behind that might give your real identity away."

Sam picked his belongings back up off the desk and tucked them away.

Florence sat back down at her desk. "Now you've got to go and report to the Department of Subversive Toys to get your authorised surveillance kit before you go home for the day. See if you can use the Betamax lift system without getting lost."

"What video do I need?"

"Look for *Mary Poppins*. The original one with Julie Andrews."

Sam wondered if maybe they were going to give him a magic flying umbrella but decided it was best just to wait and see.

"Florence," he said.

"Yes, Jennifer."

"Do you really think they're dangerous? The Croydon Revolutionary Front, I mean. They don't seem very dangerous to me?"

"Probably not," replied Florence. "But hopefully they'll lead us to whoever *is* behind all this."

"I see." Sam hoped not. Josie seemed nice when he'd met her, and he didn't really want her to get in trouble.

"Florence?" said Sam.

"Yes, Jennifer."

"You do know my name's not Jennifer, don't you?"

Florence stared intently at her mobile phone and pretended not to hear him.

* * *

Sam stepped out of the lift into the Department of Subversive Toys. As he did so, a brown shoe came spiralling towards his face. Sam instinctively ducked as the airborne footwear shot over his head and plummeted into the lift shaft behind him.

"Sorry!" yelled a voice from the far side of the workshop. "Prototype rocket shoe! We're having problems with the hover mode."

Sam cautiously looked around him, readying himself for any other incoming projectiles. The floor of the workshop was filled with a hotch-potch of bundled cabling, paint splodges and the charred remnants of failed experiments.

A workbench on the left side spilled over with bubbling test tubes and flickering electrical apparatus. Precariously balanced piles of manuals and crates of paraphernalia obstructed access around the workshop whilst unsettling blue smoke was emanating from a generator in the corner.

"Hello! I'm Eugene!" said the tall googly-eyed man from the Boardroom meeting, shaking Sam's hand enthusiastically. "You must be Jennifer?"

Eugene then promptly called out over his shoulder to his short, fat colleague sitting at the back of the workshop, "37.2 degrees, O negative, blood pressure 115 over 65, low iron count, minor wheat allergy, sleeps on his left side, needs one ear syringed and he's masturbated fourteen times this month."

"Forty times?!" yelled out the short, fat man from the back.

"No, fourteen! He's masturbated fourteen times this month!"

"Oh good. I was going to say forty seems a bit high."

"Sorry, what was that?" enquired Sam, as politely as he could muster.

"What was what?" asked Eugene.

"That. The 'he's masturbated fourteen times' thing?"

"Oh that! Look at this!" Eugene excitedly pulled a white glove off his hand and held it up towards Sam. "We call it the Michael Jackson Glove. It can read all your vital signs with just a handshake. Still in beta-testing at the moment. Not much good for moonwalking though!"

Sam raised his eyebrows, pondering whether to refute any of the glove's intimate findings. Eugene meanwhile had already bounded off across the workshop and was fiddling with a hamster. Sam followed him, cautiously observing the array of half-finished projects on display. The hamster didn't seem to be moving much.

"Is that a real hamster?"

Eugene giggled. "Here Roscoe! He just asked if it's a *real* hamster?"

Roscoe also giggled at the back of the workshop. "Tell him its real!"

"Yeah its real," said Eugene, still giggling. "Here, give it a stroke!"

"I don't think so."

"Yeah go on, stroke him."

"I don't want to. He'll explode in my face or electrocute me or something."

Eugene looked disappointed. "Fair one. It's only a little shock though. So, you're here for your Mk IV surveillance kit, I suppose?"

"I guess so. Agent Lawrence sent me down."

"Right you are!" Eugene reached up to a top shelf and pulled down a cardboard box. "Here we go." Eugene pulled out a small fabric pouch with a nylon strap attached to it.

"It's a bum bag," said Sam, matter-of-factly.

"It's *not* a bum bag. It's a Mk IV surveillance kit." Eugene unzipped the pouch and tipped out the contents. Sam watched as a small torch, a pen and a lip balm tumbled onto the desk next to the inanimate hamster.

Eugene carefully picked up one of the items. "This is not just a lip balm. It's an emergency flare. Twist clockwise if you've got chapped lips but twist *anti*-clockwise to launch a red flare to a height of four hundred metres."

Sam examined the tiny tube and tried to commit to memory which way did what.

Eugene then picked up the pen. "This is not just a pen. Click the little button on the end once if you want to write with it, *twice* if you want to use it as a flamethrower."

Sam picked up the pen and eyed it with concerned suspicion.

"Don't point it at your eyebrows, Jennifer," warned Eugene, considerately. Sam immediately pulled the pen away from his face.

"And *this*…" he said, picking up the final item, "… isn't just a torch. Press this *green* button if you want it to light something up. Press this *red* button if you want to engage the x-ray facility." Eugene demonstrated by pointing the torch at a wall and pressing the red button.

Sam stared at the area on the wall where the torch beam was pointing, realising that he could see straight through into the room next door which was full of computers.

"Woah! *That* is incredible."

"Like I said, it's not a bum bag." Eugene packed the items back into the pouch and handed it to Sam. "Now this is only the Mk IV version. We can't give you the latest Mk VII until you're out of probation."

Sam wondered what outlandish curiosities would be found in the Mk VII bum bag but then found himself distracted by the room next door with so many computers.

"So what's that room for?" He pointed towards the door which was emblazoned with red prohibitory signage denying entry on pain of death and warning of toxic hazards within.

"Oh, that's the Infinite Monkey Room. It's part of an experiment we're working on."

Sam felt alarmed at the thought of a monkey experimentation room. "You don't mean like the experiments the Home Office Minister was doing, do you?"

Eugene giggled again. "Here Roscoe, he wants to know if we're doing experiments on real monkeys?"

"Yeah tell him they're real!" laughed Roscoe from the back. "Tell him we hate monkeys, and we hate hamsters."

"I'm literally right here," said Sam, looking directly at Roscoe.

Eugene stopped giggling. "You're right, they're not real monkeys. It's just a theoretical experiment. You know how they say if you had a monkey hitting random keys on a typewriter for an infinite amount of time, eventually the monkey would type out the entire works of Shakespeare?"

Sam nodded, still looking suspiciously at the door.

"… Well, we're testing it. Only, we're doing it with computers. We've got two thousand servers in there mimicking the actions of over ten million monkeys, constantly typing randomly, twenty-four hours a day. They've been tapping away for twelve years now."

"And have they come up with anything yet?"

Eugene rubbed his chin. "Not really, no. We got a new Harry Potter book, but it wasn't very good. Harry died on the third page. Just seems a shame to turn them off now after they've worked so hard."

"So do I need any other bits of kit?"

Eugene checked his list. "Nope, that's it I think. Roscoe is writing a blog for your Society for Underground Galactic Armed Resistance cover story so if you get asked any awkward questions you can point them to that."

Sam picked up the bum bag and walked back over towards the lift. He'd had quite enough electro-hamsters and infinite monkeys for one day.

"Nice meeting you, Jennifer. Remember, anti-clockwise! And don't point it at your eyebrows!"

Sam stepped into the lift and bid Eugene farewell with a mock salute. He really needed to go back to Ruth's and get some proper sleep. Undercover tomorrow. With a bum bag.

* * *

The next morning, the Chancellor of the Exchequer woke up in a good mood, ready to enjoy a well-earned day off. As it was a Saturday, he was looking forward to a cooked brunch followed by a round of golf at Wentworth. His wife Gloria was still asleep, so he decided to get up a little early, make some coffee and maybe have a breakfast cigar in the back garden. He popped his dressing gown over his loose-fitting pyjamas, tucked his podgy feet into his furry slippers, grabbed his mobile phone off the dresser and headed down the stairs of his Victorian house.

His joints always creaked first thing in the morning and his eyes were always a little blurry until after 8am. As he clomped slowly down the stairs he checked his phone. That couldn't be right? At first glance it looked like he had 94 missed calls and 319 text messages. At second glance, it had jumped up to 323 text messages. As the Chancellor slowly got to the bottom of his stairs, he could see some commotion through the obscured glazing of his front porch. This was unusual as it was rare for there to be any sort of kerfuffle in this particularly leafy and pleasant part of Kensington.

He took the chain off the door and unlatched the two security bolts in order to investigate what was going on outside. As he swung open the door, the chancellor was met by an assault of camera bulbs flashing in his face and jostling journalists thrusting microphones towards him.

"Chancellor, is it true you and your wife ate a young girl?"

"Chancellor, what does human flesh taste like?"

"Chancellor, how long have you been a cannibal?"

The chancellor looked down at his pyjamas to check he was all tucked in. Unfortunately he wasn't, and a picture of his flaccid penis would appear later that day on the internet. Although in the circumstances, this was currently the least of his problems.

"What are you all talking about? What the hell is this?!"

"Chancellor, how many people can you eat in one sitting?"

"Chancellor, are you a breast or leg man?"

"Chancellor, what did you have for pudding?"

"No bloody comment!!" bawled the chancellor angrily, slamming the door shut in their petulant faces. What the hell was this? He picked up the newspapers that were scattered on his hallway floor. His flabby face was on every single front page, accompanied by damning headlines in bold lettering.

'Government Minister Implicated In Tawdry Spectacle' announced The Times. 'Cannibal Of The Exchequer' read The Express. 'Filthy Tory Pervert Munches On Virgins' screamed The Sun.

He took the newspapers into the kitchen and lined them up on the breakfast bar. He quickly scanned through the first few paragraphs of each front page, trying desperately hard to decipher the scandalous details that had been printed about him.

Up in the bedroom, Gloria awoke from her slumber and could hear unfamiliar noises coming from downstairs. She heard the shouting outside, followed by the front door slamming. Then a short pause followed by a loud, dull thud.

She jumped out of bed, ran quickly out of the bedroom and skipped down the stairs to see what the hell was happening. As she entered the kitchen, the first thing she saw was a bright crimson puddle on her polished marble tiles, shortly followed by the sight of her husband's body lying motionless on the floor. Blood was oozing from a deep cut on his forehead and one of his hands was clutching his chest.

* * *

Josie was incandescent with rage and was bellowing down the phone at Leo.

"Honestly, what on earth is going on with these clowns in the government? First the Home Office Minister is doing crazy animal experiments, next thing the bloody chancellor is some kind of perverted cannibal?! I mean, who the hell is next Leo?"

Leo sounded equally disgusted. "It is absolutely dithgusting!" Everybody is going crazy about it on thocial media."

Josie and Leo had been having one of their pre-meeting phone calls to set the agenda for that evening's gathering of the C.R.F. With the latest news about the Chancellor of the Exchequer, which was splashed all over the newspapers that morning, everyone was abuzz with a groundswell of anti-government fervour that had gripped the nation. Notably, the additional information that the chancellor had subsequently collapsed and died of a heart attack on his kitchen floor had not yet been released into the public domain, however even this was unlikely to curb the hostility currently being directed at His Majesty's government.

"This could be our chance to make our mark tonight, really get the C.R.F. on the map," said Josie. "We need to do something big, and we need to do it sharpish. Get the public on our side and really stick it to the government!"

"Don't worry about that," agreed Leo. "I have something thpecial in mind for tonight already, and its going to put us thmack banger on the map!"

"Thmack banger?" asked Josie.

"Yeth, thmack banger."

"Oh, you mean smack bang?"

"That's exactly what I thed, thmack banger."

Josie and Leo continued gossiping excitedly about all the newspaper revelations and eventually both agreed they were far too busy to keep chatting. They had lots to do and would catch up more later at the meeting.

"Oh, and bwing some torcheth," Leo chipped in as they said their goodbyes.

Josie put the phone down, figured she'd give it half an hour and then she'd start getting ready for the meeting. She would have to look in the messy drawer to find some torches and she also wanted to wash her hair before she went out. She didn't want their potential new member, Jennifer, to see the red paint flecks from her previous placard-painting session. On second thoughts, she might just wear her knitted bobble hat.

* * *

Meanwhile, after he'd put the phone down to Josie, Leo went straight off to start rearranging the furniture in his lounge ready for the meeting. He brought in an extra chair from the garage for their new member from S.U.G.A.R, hoovered the carpet and then excitedly tidied up the pile of magazine cuttings on his table. With the lounge all ship-shape, he grabbed some of his favourite bowls from the kitchen and poured some crisps and nibbles into them, then made some of his special home-made baklava which was Mrs Bimble's favourite.

* * *

Elsewhere, a few doors down, Mrs Bimble was busily knitting a scarf. Knit one, pearl one. It was nearly finished, and she was very satisfied that she had included all of the colours of the rainbow. She often found plenty of time to knit, mainly because Norman was always busy in the loft adding touches of acrylic green paint to the tiny trees bordering his model railway.

Previously Mrs Bimble had knitted a bobble hat for Josie, a pair of mittens for Leo and a Christmas jumper for Red Kendall. Now she was knitting something colourful for Elijah. He definitely needed brightening up and she felt sure the green, red, turquoise, orange, yellow and blue neck warmer would be just the ticket to cheer up his day.

* * *

As it happened, Elijah Black had the lights off in his house. He preferred the dark. A creature of the shadows, a teacher once called him. After yesterday's escapade in Trafalgar Square, he and Red Kendall had wandered down to Shoreditch for dinner and had fun until the early hours.

Elijah was looking forward to seeing him again tonight. Red had told him he had a surprise for him. Elijah looked in the mirror, sizing up his black outfit. He was wearing his favourite black Stetson hat, dark sunglasses, black jeans and a black polo-necked shirt. He looked at his feet, trying to decide which shoes would suit his outfit. He had a choice of the black brogues, the black loafers or his black Chelsea boots. He chose the black loafers. Red seemed to like him in the loafers.

* * *

Whilst Elijah was pondering that evening's footwear choices, Red was in the process of snapping a pool cue in half at the Rose & Crown pub in the High Street. After disputing the result of a game of pool, he had taken exception to being called a 'cheating, ginger, fuckpig' and as such, was about to retaliate with a more physical gesture of his own.

Within a few moments, the saloon bar at the Rose & Crown had broken out into a full on bar brawl with chairs flying across the room and glasses smashing on the slate floor. As punches were thrown and lips were split, the landlord attempted to restore order by dramatically pulling a concealed shotgun out from behind his bar.

The brawling subdued momentarily, and Red gently placed his splintered pool cue down onto the green baize. An alarm bleeped on his watch, reminding him of the meeting at Leo's house in an hour.

"Och, well that'll be me for today, gentlemen. I've got places to be! Fare thee well!" And with that, Red Kendall downed his Snowball in one, slung his jacket back on and cheerfully strolled off out of the pub. He was also very much looking forward to seeing Elijah tonight. The ring he had secretly bought for Elijah as a token of his love was safely tucked away in his pocket.

Twelve Monkeys

Just after 7pm, Sam was on his way to the C.R.F. meeting. He was walking down Cranfield Street being followed shortly after by six conspicuous-looking pigeons. He had concealed his bum bag as best he could under his sweater and was hoping he wouldn't be mistaken for a time-travelling tourist from the 1990s.

"*Stop looking so uncomfortable*," said a voice in Sam's head.

"I *am* uncomfortable," answered Sam. "It's this stupid bum bag."

"*Just for the record*," said Florence's voice, "*If you're speaking to me, I can't hear you. You can hear me through the skull speaker, but remember the only microphone is inside Ralph. Unless you're anywhere near the dog, you might as well be talking to yourself!*"

Sam checked the map on his phone, but he wasn't picking up much of a signal. Josie had written down Leo's address on the napkin as 25 Windermere Avenue, which was somewhere near Elephant & Castle. Now it should have been just a short walk to Leo's house where the meeting was taking place, but Sam had managed to get himself a bit lost when he decided to cut across the park.

He looked around at the street signs, trying to figure out his precise location and identify the simplest route.

Although tempted, he correctly guessed that firing off the lip balm flare would be premature at this stage.

"*Next left,*" said Florence from somewhere deep inside Sam's head, "*then 200 yards on your right.*"

Sam and his entourage of pigeons headed off down Windermere Avenue. The suburban post-war houses looked tired but friendly. As he got to number 25, he could see through the curtains that there were already people inside the front room. He rang the bell and within moments Leo appeared at the front door welcoming him in.

"Greetingth comrade, welcome to my humble house!" Leo performed a dramatic but convivial bow as he held the door open. Sam recognised him from being amongst the crowd at Trafalgar Square, even though Leo hadn't gone on for coffee afterwards. Sam said hello, smiled politely and walked in, as the six pigeons perched themselves on Leo's front garden wall and cooed innocently.

Leo guided Sam through the hallway and into the front room where the others were already sitting and nibbling on Wotsits, Pringles and Cheeto's.

"Jennifer! Here, come and sit next to me!" beckoned Josie, excitedly padding the cushion next to her on the sofa.

Mrs Bimble was sitting on the other side of Josie eating a baclava, Elijah was squished cosily next to Red Kendall on the two-seater and Ralphy was curled up on the rug having a snooze.

"Right! Everybody here," smiled Leo as he came back in, clapping his hands together.

"And with our new VIP member!" beamed Josie, tipping her head repeatedly in Sam's direction, trying her absolute best not to seem overly excited.

"*Somebody's pleased to see you,*" sneered Florence inside Sam's head.

"Shush, I'm concentrating!" rebuked Sam out loud.

"Huh?" asked Josie confused, "What are you concentrating on?"

"No one else can hear me dummy. You sound like you're insane!" said Florence.

"Oh umm, sorry Josie... I just meant I was concentrating on what Leo was saying... like, cos I'm uh super keen to stick it to the... aah... government?"

"Huzzah!" roared Red triumphantly. "Power to the proletariat!"

"Quite right," joined in Mrs Bimble. "Power to the prostitutes!"

"He said power to the *proletariat*, Mrs Bimble," whispered Josie. "It means the common people, not the prostitutes."

"What's wrong with the prostitutes?" asked Mrs Bimble.

"Well, nothing really. It just sounds a bit wrong to say *power to the prostitutes*. It's kind of not what we're all about, is it?"

"Well I think they're lovely," said Mrs Bimble, indignantly.

"So does Jennifer," said Leo. "His mum is a prothtitoot!"

"Well I think that's lovely, dear." Mrs Bimble reached across and patted Sam's knee reassuringly. "I'm sure your mother's a very sweet prostitute."

Sam tried to smile politely.

"Can we start the meeting now?" asked Leo.

"Hang on sweetheart. I've got a little present in my bag." Mrs Bimble fumbled around in her large shopping bag and pulled out the long, knitted scarf she'd been working on and passed it across to Elijah.

"I made you this, dear. To keep you snuggly when Red's not around."

Elijah took the multi-coloured monstrosity and scrutinised it, somewhat horrified.

"I thought it would brighten you up a bit. All this black is a little bit, you know, morbid?"

"But… I'm a *Goth*? Mrs Bimble, I wear black because I'm a *Goth*. You do know what a Goth looks like, don't you?"

"Well you can still be a Goth dear, now you'll just look like a happy little Goth?"

Red Kendall was chuckling to himself. Since he and Elijah had been together, he'd never seen him sport a single thread of colour in that time. "Put it on ya big dandy, the old lady worked hard on that!"

Elijah reluctantly draped Mrs Bimble's scarf around his neck but still felt despondent. "I look like Doctor fucking Who going to a funeral."

"You look like Joseph the techni-colour dream twat!" laughed Red.

Josie giggled. Seeing Elijah the Goth resplendent in the flamboyantly coloured scarf did make a refreshing change from his normal Dark Lord of the Sith / cowboy outfits. It had taken Elijah so long to come out in the first place, and it was only Red's belligerent affection that had given Elijah the confidence to even admit his feelings were reciprocated. Josie knew the thought of displaying full Pride colours on a scarf would have been excruciating for him just a few short months ago.

"Well I think you look lovely poppet," smiled Mrs Bimble.

"So do I," grinned Red, ruffling Elijah's hair. "You look proper distinguished." Red didn't want Elijah sulking tonight, especially given the special gift he had hidden in his jacket pocket for him later.

Elijah stroked the scarf with his hand and smiled bashfully at Red. "Okaaay… I guess I'll give it a go. Thank you Mrs Bimble."

"Super!" smiled Leo. "Ok, onto bithnith."

* * *

The control room at MI-51 had evidently been designed by somebody who admired the aesthetics of NASA's Mission Control Centre. It was slightly smaller but remained a bristling hive of activity. A wall of overhead LCD screens looked down on several banks of workstations equipped with computer modules, telephones and notepads.

Florence was sitting at one of the front desks in her role as the mission supervisor. Around her were the department Heads from Confrontation, Hostilities and Communications. A transcriber was ready to write down everything that was heard over the radio transmissions and IT technicians were fiddling with electrical equipment and trying to tune in the pigeon-cams. The White Rabbit was prowling up and down the centre aisle maintaining a watchful eye over the operation.

"Update?" demanded the White Rabbit.

"Our agent is embedded, sir. Comm's are up and running. Pigeon-cam feed is on screens one to six above. But the dog-mic is a little intermittent. It should have been implanted at surface level. We're not sure if it will broadcast clearly from deep inside the dog."

"I see. What have we picked up so far?"

"Random chatter only, sir. Mainly about the chancellor being a cannibal. And then the Home Office Minister's monkey experiments. And something about a scarf."

"A *scarf*? What sort of *scarf*?"

"We think it might be code. Maybe a disguise of some sort," chipped in the Hostilities department.

Florence was busy focusing on the incoming feed. The sound was distorted and even when it was working it was still being muffled by the snoring of the dog, so they weren't picking up every word clearly.

"Communications? What have you got?"

"Sir, the suspect's games console has been disconnected but we're undertaking a building survey with the Black Knight."

The Black Knight was a satellite currently in near polar-orbit, though it could be diverted on specific trajectories as needed. The unique equipment on board the Black Knight was capable of undertaking a full geo-spatial scan of pretty much any building or structure in the world, thereby producing a three dimensional layout both inside and out. In order to disguise this capability, the Department of Propaganda had previously gone to considerable lengths to inject bizarre conspiracies about the Black Knight into the public consciousness, including the rumour it was either space debris or, alternatively, of extra-terrestrial origin. This had proved a most effective smokescreen and was often cited on social media.

"What is the Black Knight showing us?"

"Standard small, terraced house built circa 1950s. Five people at ground level in the front room, plus our agent and the canine. Two accommodation rooms downstairs, two bedrooms upstairs and a bathroom. There is something odd though, sir."

"Go on?"

"One of the bedrooms will not scan. We can't see inside it, sir."

"Why not? Is the Black Knight glitching?"

"No sir, we believe the room may have defensive measures in place. We think it might be lead-lined preventing our internal scan."

"I see," said the White Rabbit. "We need to arrange to get a forensic team inside that house when it's vacated and find out what's hidden in that room."

* * *

Leo had a big banner he had been working on that he was looking forward to showing everyone. It was folded up ready in the corner of his lounge but made a handy seat to perch on. He had laid out a street map showing a small part of London and was busily drawing on it with a red felt pen.

"We go along thith alleyway, then we thneak up the stairwell at the back of the building and up onto the roof. When we're up there we can drop our big C.R.F. banner down over the front of the building!"

"Oh my god this is sooo naughty Leo," gasped Josie. "What if we get caught?"

"Och, we won't get caught," joined in Red. "It's not like we're breaking into Downing Street. It's just a boring Home Office building. We'll be off the roof and gone before they even know what's happened."

"Correct, and I've made *theeth*!" Leo lifted up a brown suitcase and opened the lid to show his friends what was inside. To everyone's amazement it contained at least two dozen bloated water balloons, each one a different colour.

"*Water bombth*! And each one is filled with different colour paint! When we've dropped the banner we'll be able to thplash the balloons on all the policemen and watch them exthplode on their heads! Then we'll escape out the way we came in."

"Well that'll make an awful mess of their uniforms, won't it?" asked Mrs Bimble disapprovingly.

"Yeth! That's the point, thilly!"

Just then Sam heard Florence's voice in his head again. "*Sam, we're struggling with the comms because of the dog snoring. We need you to wank the dog.*"

Did she just tell him to *wank* the dog? Why the hell did Florence want him to do that?

"I'm *not* wanking the dog!" Sam blurted out.

Leo promptly ceased explaining his plan and stared at Sam blankly. Josie, Red and Elijah also stared at Sam with considerable concern. Mrs Bimble didn't stare at Sam but did help herself to another piece of baklava.

"Jesus Christ Jennifer, WAKE THE DOG!!! Why the fuck would I be asking you to wank the dog?!"

Oh yeah. That makes more sense thought Sam. *Dammit.* Sam stroked Ralphy on his back and tried to smile inoffensively at the other faces in the room. The ones that were looking back at him very suspiciously.

"See, I'm just stroking Ralphy. I didn't want any of you to think I was wanking him, y'know? Just in case that's what it looked like I was doing?"

"I don't think any of us thought you were trying to wank Ralphy," said Josie, bewildered.

"Sure. I know. Sometimes it can just look like you're wanking a dog though. Even if you're just giving it a friendly stroke. I just wanted to be absolutely clear with you all. I don't do that. At least not to other people's dogs. Or my own dog! I mean, I haven't got a dog. But if I did have one, I wouldn't wank it off. I'd just stroke it. Like this."

Everyone was still staring at him uncomfortably.

Ralphy woke up as Sam stroked him and yawned, blissfully unaware of the nature of the conversation. If he had been aware, Ralphy would have been rightfully offended.

"For God's sake stop talking about wanking bloody dogs. Change the subject you cockwomble. Talk about anything else!" Florence sounded furious.

"I think I need to go to the loo!" Sam stood up looking for an escape route out of the conversation.

"It's upstairs," said Leo. "Thecond door on your left."

Sam stepped over Ralphy and hurriedly walked out of the lounge and up the carpeted stairs. As he reached the top he heard Mrs Bimble say, "I think that boy is a bit strange, you know."

As Sam reached the upstairs landing, he realised he hadn't been paying attention to Leo's directions. He picked the door that he figured was most likely to be the bathroom and tried the handle although it was firmly locked. He tried the second door which opened but turned out to be Leo's bedroom.

Third time lucky and the final door revealed a rather unseemly avocado-coloured, 1970s style bathroom suite. Sam didn't actually need a wee, so decided he would just wait for a minute or two, flush the loo, wash his hands and head back downstairs, desperately hoping the conversation had moved on.

* * *

The control room at MI-51 had gone into *high alert* state. The muffled communications from the dog-mic were still intermittent, but there was enough dialogue being heard to cause jitters. The transcriber had picked out some concerning key words which were worrying the White

Rabbit, specifically the words 'Downing Street', 'bombth' and 'exthplode'.

"Sir, this is starting to sound like a terrorist cell!" declared the head of the Hostilities Department. "Request permission to deploy armed support?"

"Sir we're reading this wrong - they don't fit a terrorist profile at all!" responded Florence.

"Standby," said the White Rabbit, noting Florence's protest. "Get armed response ready but don't deploy. We need to find out when they're planning their attack."

"Sir, we've contacted the onsite security at Downing Street," said the Confrontation Department. "They're putting the building on lockdown now just in case."

"Good work. Get the PM out the way. Send him to Chequers or something."

"I'm not sure we've got this right, sir?" said Florence. "We're only hearing snippets of conversation."

"Keep listening then. Your man could be about to crack a dangerous splinter cell. This lot sound like professionals to me."

* * *

When Sam got back downstairs he was relieved to find the subject had changed. Josie was handing out torches to everyone and Leo was passing around ski-masks. He gave one to Sam as he walked in.

"Ooh what are these for?" smiled Sam, trying his one on.

"So we don't get theen of course."

"Here take one of these too," said Josie, passing him a big black torch.

"Oh I've got my own torch already!" Sam reached under his jumper and into his bum bag to pull out the x-ray torch that Eugene from the Department of Subversive Toys had supplied him with the day before.

"Ooh that's a little one you got there," teased Josie.

Sam smiled as it occurred to him Josie was flirting a little bit. "It's not the size, it's where you point it!" Sam immediately tried to demonstrate the power of his little torch by pressing the red button and pointing it directly at Josie.

Sometimes in life, there are moments when time seems to stand completely still. Like when one talks derogatively behind a friend's back at the exact same moment in time they realise they're talking to precisely the person they happen to be denigrating. For Sam, this was one of those moments. As he pointed the torch, he found himself staring, slack-jawed at Josie's naked body. Like, very naked. At what point she had decided to get completely naked in a room full of people Sam couldn't quite recall, yet there she was, most definitely naked and female and lovely.

Sam's brain was working in slow-motion. The left side had already joined the dots and was trying to communicate to the right side that Josie wasn't naked, and that he had accidentally pressed the red *x-ray* button on the torch instead of the green *illuminate* button. Sam was the proverbial rabbit caught in the headlights, frozen in time. His eyes darted around the room at everyone else to see their reactions.

In a peculiar twist of happenstance, Leo appeared to have put his ski mask on wrongly and was still struggling to align the eye holes, Elijah and Red seemed to be engrossed in forensically examining Elijah's new scarf and Mrs Bimble had nodded off. Ralphy looked confused though. Josie, meanwhile, was staring directly at Sam wondering why there was no dazzling light beam coming out of his torch, oblivious that her bare body appeared exposed to the entire room.

Sam's thumb flicked the red button off and Josie's clothes magically reappeared. Sam felt his heart start to beat again.

"Here, I think you better take this one after all," grinned Josie, handing Sam her big black torch. "Your one's rubbish!"

Leo finally managed to get the eyeholes of his ski-mask aligned. "Right then! Everybody ready to do thith?"

Josie, Red and Elijah all stood up off the sofas, but Mrs Bimble was still snoozing on the sofa, covered in crumbs.

"I think we should leave Mrs Bimble here with Ralphy," said Josie. "She looks so comfortable."

"Wait, what?" Sam was confused. "Where are we going?"

"The big plan," confirmed Josie. "What do you think we've been talking about all evening?"

"WE'RE GOING NOW?!"

"Of course we're going now. Tonight's the big night, when did you think we were going?"

"I thought we were going to do it in a few weeks or something. Or Christmas maybe. Or next year?"

Josie laughed. "Of course not, silly. We've got to strike while the iron's hot, we'll be all over the front pages by the morning; *Heroic Justice Warriors Embarrass the Evil Government!* Unless you don't think you're up to it?"

"No... of course I'm up to it... I just didn't realise it would be so soon..."

"Right then, thaddle up and let's go thmash the oppressors," instructed Leo.

Everybody was feeling suitably riled up and enthusiastically followed him out of the house.

* * *

"They're deploying now, sir! They're going to attack tonight!" shouted the Head of the Hostilities Department.

"Action stations!" declared the White Rabbit. He slammed the emergency Red Alert button on the main control console. Although this meant a full on Red Alert was officially underway, in reality it just resulted in the red beacon on the wall illuminating and revolving rapidly. But it certainly made the control room seem a lot more serious.

Florence was holding the portable speaker to her head in order to drown out all the control room kerfuffle and focus on what was going on at Sam's location. She was still hearing less and less via the dog-mic, and all the shouting in the control room wasn't helping. She wasn't sure if Sam was still in range of Ralphy or not.

"Sir, I'm not sure it's an attack at all — it sounds like a protest of some kind?" queried Florence.

"It's definitely an attack, sir!" insisted the Hostilities Department. "Pigeon-cam 4 has identified that they're carrying a suitcase out of the flat. The Black Knight satellite has scanned it and we think it contains bombs of some kind."

"Deploy the entire pigeon-cam fleet!" commanded the White Rabbit. "I don't want to lose them anywhere on the streets of London."

"Sir they're getting on a No. 148 bus towards Westminster. Do you want us to secure the bus?"

There were a variety of methods that MI-51 liked to use to *secure* a bus. Invariably this could include deploying a stinger to burst the tires, remote-tazer of the driver, electrifying the chassis (and thereby electrifying all the passengers onboard) or tractor-beaming the bus into a layby.

"Not yet..." replied the White Rabbit, stroking his whiskers and gazing at the overhead monitors. "Let's see where they're going!"

Florence breathed a sigh of relief that Sam wasn't going to get electrified. *"Jennifer, listen to me, you've got to get them to stop as soon as possible! Get them to stop!"* she said over the radio link.

The Control Room staff continued to press buttons and watch the overhead screens intently, following the bus's route. After a few minutes it crossed Westminster Bridge and came to a stop on the north side of the river.

"Sir, they're disembarking the bus in Westminster! We have them surrounded by pigeon-cams," reported the Hostilities Department.

"Of course, they must be targeting the Houses of Parliament. This could be catastrophic!" said the White Rabbit. "We need to put an end to this little insurrection. Send in E-Squadron, now!"

* * *

As Josie got off the bus with the others, she noticed that there seemed to be an unusually high number of pigeons around. There were pigeons perched along the steel fences, pigeons waddling up and down the pavement, a flock of pigeons circling overhead and pigeons sitting on every bus, car and taxi in Parliament Square.

"Have you ever seen so many pigeons? They're everywhere."

"Maybe it's an attempted *coo*," laughed Red.

Leo checked his map and started heading towards the far side of Parliament Square, with the others following behind him. He looked up at a big white building with ornate sculptured architecture and flags protruding out across the frontage. "Thith is the one," he said, leading them down a narrow alleyway at the side of the building.

Red had the bulky banner folded up under one arm and was holding Elijah's hand with the other. He had the ring in his pocket, ready for the right moment.

Josie was trying to stand close to Sam, wondering if he might decide to hold hands with her too. Sam, meanwhile, had decided not to try and hold Josie's hand as he didn't want to seem too keen and scare her off.

"So all we've got to do now is thcramble up there." Leo pointed up at a black-painted, fire escape structure that was bolted to the rear of the eight-storey building. It wasn't entirely obvious whether the metal stairs were held in position by the rust or purely by gravity.

Sam could hear Florence in his head again but was struggling to catch what she was saying. *"Jennifer listen to me, you've got to get them to the top as soon as possible! Get them to the top!"*

What was the rush? wondered Sam, but not wishing to screw up again after dogwank-gate, he decided to hurry the gang along.

"Come on guys, let's do this." He grabbed Josie's hand instinctively and tugged her to follow him up the steel steps. Josie blushed and realised she rather liked Sam taking charge. Leo, Elijah and Red followed on closely behind, shining their torches up as they ascended the rickety structure.

Several pigeons appeared to be nesting in the steelwork as they reached half-way up. The wind was picking up the higher they got, and the stairs were starting to creak.

"I'm not sure this was a great idea after all," said Josie looking down.

"Sure it is," replied Sam, hurrying her along to keep Florence happy. "Come on, we're nearly there."

As they finally reached the roof, everyone was starting to puff and wheeze. Sam was first onto the flat roof still clutching Josie's hand followed by Red, Elijah and then Leo. The roof had a gravel surface and was pretty empty with the exception of several air-conditioning units whirring in the darkness.

Sam looked out across the edge of the building and realised he was still grasping Josie's hand in spite of his decision not to look too keen. They had a view right the way across Parliament Square. To the far side of the square were the ancient Houses of Parliament, with an illuminated Big Ben at one end and Westminster Bridge twinkling in the distance.

"It looks kind of romantic, don't you think?" smiled Josie.

"I guess it kind of does," replied Sam. He could feel his heart beating hard again, and he was sure it wasn't just because he'd hurried up eight flights of stairs.

Red dropped the folded up banner onto the gravel with a loud thud. "Right! Let's get this fucking thing rolled out then."

Red and Elijah unfurled the banner and started laying it out flat across the roof. Leo held a torch for them as they pulled out the corners to straighten it up. Fully stretched out it was nearly the length of a tennis court.

"Great job on this, Leo. They'll see this for bloody miles," said Elijah excitedly.

"Right, everybody take a corner and we'll drag it to the edge." Red often took the lead when it came to practical things. It was one of the things Elijah liked about him - always loud, always enthusiastic and always taking charge unnecessarily.

Sam heard Florence's voice in his head. *"Sam what are you doing?? I said get them to STOP! How did you get up there so quick??"*

Oh bugger thought Sam. *Get them to stop*, not *Get to the top.*

Sam was glad the signal was coming through much clearer now that they were on the rooftop, but something was wrong - Florence was sounding uncharacteristically panicky.

"You've got to get out of there!! E-Squadron are coming, do you hear me? I repeat, E-Squadron are coming!! Get yourself away from the rooftop!!"

E-Squadron? thought Sam. *The ones that carry out all the 'terminations and disintegrations?' Why the hell were they being sent in for a bunch of clowns with water balloons and a banner?*

Sam looked around, trying to figure out where they could be hiding. He couldn't see anyone behind the air-conditioning units, and he was certain no one had followed them up the stairs.

Through the blustery wind, Sam became aware of a sound breaking through from the distance, a rhythmic beating sound.

"Get out of there now!!" pleaded Florence in his head.

Josie saw Sam suddenly looked distracted. "What is it? What are you looking for?"

"Josie, there's something I need to tell you…" Sam sensed the rhythmic beating sound was getting steadily louder and was coming from across the Thames.

"Get off the rooftop! Get off there NOW!!" screamed Florence.

Within seconds, the rooftop was suddenly vibrating and bathed in neon-white brightness as searchlights blazed down from above. Three huge black military troop-carrier helicopters loomed overhead, their massive blades beating through the air and forcing turbulent gusts across the rooftop. The deafening noise of the engines roared down, causing Josie and Sam to cover their ears. Leo was already running for cover by the stairwell while Elijah and Red were trying desperately to cling onto the banner, as the wind took hold of it and flapped it around wildly.

The three helicopters steadied and hovered overhead. A rear door opened on one of them and an armoured figure started to lob tin cans down onto the roof, initially bouncing harmlessly on the gravel surface. Moments later, they ignited into thunderflashes across the rooftop with disorientating loud cracks and blinding flashes of light. A tannoy sounded from one of the other helicopters.

"THIS IS E-SQUADRON. YOU ARE UNDER ARREST. DROP YOUR WEAPONS AND PUT YOUR HANDS BEHIND YOUR HEAD. DO NOT ATTEMPT TO RETALIATE. ANY RETALIATION WILL RESULT IN YOUR TERMINATION, ELIMINATION OR DISINTEGRATION."

The helicopters steadily lowered themselves closer to the building. Two ropes were thrown out from the cargo doors of each aircraft, followed by the synchronised deployment of a dozen armed soldiers abseiling in rapid formation down onto the rooftop. Infra-red targeting beams cut through the air as the soldiers shouted angry instructions that *must* be complied with.

Josie and Sam immediately knelt down on the floor with their hands in the air, cowering as the soldiers pointed their weapons at them threateningly. Red also capitulated, releasing his grasp on the banner and putting his hands behind his head to demonstrate he was not resisting, as a soldier appeared behind him and swiftly snapped steel cuffs over his wrists.

On the other side of the roof, Elijah was still gripping onto the other end of the flapping banner, which whipped up into the air and dragged him flailing across the rooftop like a rag doll. The soldiers instinctively swung their rifles around at him as he floundered helplessly in the darkness while the wind pulled him and the banner towards the edge of the roof.

From all across the roof, soldiers screamed out commands towards Elijah; *Desist! Stop running! Stand still! Halt! Don't move!* The roar of the engines drowned out their words as Elijah was still unable to stop himself being dragged around helplessly. A soldier with night-vision goggles yelled "Final Warning!" before opening up a hail of automatic gunfire which rattled across the roof towards Elijah, shredding through his skinny body and collapsing him to the floor.

As his body lay bleeding onto the gravel, Elijah's eyes glazed over and his hand released its grip on the banner which spiralled away in the wind.

"ELIJAH!! NOOOO!!" Red screamed out in anguish as he looked across at Elijah slumped in the darkness, swathed in his multi-coloured scarf. Red turned and glared at the masked soldier behind him. "YOU FUCKING BASTARDS! WHAT HAVE YOU DONE?!" He tried to clamber back onto his feet, but the soldier immediately slammed a rifle butt into the side of Red's neck, sending him crumpling back to the floor.

Sam and Josie looked on in shock as they watched Red writhing and groaning in the gravel, and Elijah's body laying lifeless on the other side of the roof.

A muscular soldier with a mechanical arm marched up to Sam. "Trainee Agent Juniper, I'm Captain Flex. The White Rabbit sends his regards, he says you've done a good job. Come with us, sir."

Josie stayed on her knees as Sam was helped back up onto his feet.

"*Trainee Agent Juniper*?" asked Josie, stunned. "What the fuck!?"

"It's not what you think Josie. This has all gone wrong."

"Gone wrong?! What do you mean? Why the fuck is he calling you that?"

"Josie, I'm not who you think I am… I didn't get the chance to tell you."

Are you kidding me? Have you set us up?!"

"I… I didn't set you up… I didn't realise this was all happening!"

"You fucking set us up! And you just got Elijah killed? What the fuck is wrong with you? Is your name even Jennifer, or is that a lie too?!"

"Don't worry, sir," interrupted Captain Flex. "We'll take it from here. We need to get you into the chopper."

One of the helicopters touched down gently on the rooftop and Sam was forcibly ushered into the rear cargo door by two of the soldiers.

"You two-faced piece of shit," yelled Josie. "You fucking horrible, lying—"

"Shut up bitch." Captain Flex rammed the butt of his rifle into her neck, knocking her into unconsciousness.

The soldiers secured the rooftop and transported Red and Josie's unconscious bodies into one of the cargo bays. Elijah was zipped up into a body bag.

Leo meanwhile, had managed to escape with his water balloons.

* * *

Back in the Control Room, the White Rabbit turned off the *Red Alert* button.

"Sir, we've got Captain Flex on the comm-link with an update."

"Patch him through," said the White Rabbit.

One of the overhead screens momentarily scrambled itself and then cut into a video transmission coming live from one of the helicopters.

"Sir, this is Captain Flex. Operation complete. Trainee Agent Juniper has been successfully recovered. We have two terrorists in custody, one male and one female. One termination. One terrorist escaped from the rooftop with the explosives before we deployed. We have drones out looking for him now but no sign as yet. All choppers en route back to base."

"Good work Captain Flex. Stand your men down. And tell Trainee Juniper he's done an outstanding job. Get him checked out by the medics tonight and tell him to report to me in the morning."

The White Rabbit walked over to Florence's console and patted her lightly on the shoulder.

"Well done Agent Lawrence. Your team has just saved the Houses of Parliament, Guy Fawkes would be turning in his grave. How does it feel?"

"Sir, I'm not sure we *did* save anything. I think we might've called this one wrong."

"Nonsense. You heard Flex, they had bombs with them. Two terrorists in custody and one terminated. I'd call that a good night's work. Get yourself some sleep and we'll debrief in the boardroom tomorrow morning."

The White Rabbit marched up the aisle and out of the control room.

Florence slumped back in her chair. She held her head in her hands and wondered how everything had become so fucked up so quickly.

Apollo *13*

Somewhere, a long way away, an elderly man with a creased complexion was trimming his bonsai tree with a tiny pair of pruning scissors. He held a monocle in his left eye socket and was leaning forward to focus on the tiny leaves.

"Stage two appears to have been an unmitigated success, but clearly not quite in the way we anticipated?" He directed his words towards an adjutant standing by the door.

"Indeed, Your Excellency. It would appear the British Chancellor's heart was rather weaker than we thought."

"Good," replied the old man snipping a fragile stem. "It would appear our little undercover neophyte continues to exceed expectations also?"

"He will be an excellent addition to the elite Crimson Guardsmen if he completes his final mission. He has been instrumental in creating a diversion in Westminster this evening. The British security forces are busy chasing the amateur renegades whilst their government collapses around them."

"Aah, of course they are. The British are always most excitable when they're busy chasing shadows. And the neophyte is safe?"

"We believe so, Your Excellency. We lost direct contact, the communications equipment linking him to us was destroyed as planned. But we expect him to re-establish contact in the morning."

"Good. Pass on my congratulations to him. And I wish to speak to our queen."

"Certainly, Your Excellency. May I ask, with the Home Office Minister disgraced, and the chancellor now dead, is it time to instigate Phase Three?"

The elderly man lifted the bonsai tree up from his desk and carefully carried it across his office to place it by the window, so it could bake in the hot sun the following morning.

"It is time. Commence *Operation Medusa*. Their arrogant prime minister will be the next pig roasted on our fiery spit."

"Understood Your Excellency," said the adjutant. "Hail Crypteia."

* * *

The next morning, Sam arrived at the video store early. For the first time in a long time, he had not woken up in a good mood.

When he entered the building, he did not attempt to make any small talk with the video shop assistant. When he picked out the 1951 copy of *Alice in Wonderland* he did not stop to browse the other movies with gentle amusement. As he got into the lift he kicked the black and yellow cone to the side slightly, instead of carefully stepping over it. When he got out of the lift, he didn't even say thank you to the lift in his head.

As he got to the boardroom door, Sam couldn't decide whether to knock on the door politely or just throw it open and storm straight in.

Sam was cross. And when Sam was cross, everybody had better watch out. Sometimes if he was cross, he would blatantly ignore people instead of giving them a cheery hello. Other times, he would walk through doors without even bothering to knock on them first. If he was *really* cross, he would sigh very, very loudly so that everyone would know just how cross he really was.

Sam knew he was smart-mouthed enough to put people in their place. He would respond to acts of rudeness with a swift and damning riposte, verbally stunning any adversary with his wit, incisiveness and boldness. Oh yes, when Sam Juniper was cross, any surly or objectionable characters would soon shrink in fear as they were cut down to size with one of his withering, Churchillian quips.

At least, this was how Sam imagined it could be. Unfortunately, the truth was he usually had a habit of stumbling upon a Churchillian quip whilst he was lying in bed, dwelling on the incident some several hours later. Often at this point, he would re-enact the entire incident in his head, embellishing the narrative with the precise comeback he wished he'd thought of at the time.

This tended to be Sam's actual reality; suffer a daily indignity, get cross about it, stifle the anger for twelve hours or so, release the anger in an unhealthy inner monologue with a questionable version of the incident, fail to get much sleep, repeat once more the following day.

Sam decided to knock on the boardroom door on this occasion (although later tonight, he would no doubt recall to himself how he angrily kicked the door open causing it to fly off its hinges).

"Enter!" called out the White Rabbit.

The boardroom was much quieter than when he'd last been in there. It was just the White Rabbit standing with Milquetoast, and they were both talking to Florence.

"Come in, come in my boy!" Milquetoast had a big smile on his face with his arms open welcomingly.

Florence saw the sullen look on Sam's face. "Morning Jennifer. Quite a night last night, eh?"

"Last night was a triumph!" beamed Milquetoast warmly. "You have smashed a dangerous splinter group, we have two terrorists in jail, and you prevented a bomb attack on the Houses of Parliament. Quite the young prodigy, our new trainee is."

Sam felt very uncomfortable. *How could they think that the Croydon Revolutionary Front were a dangerous splinter group? Josie and Red weren't terrorists, they were just over-enthusiastic activists.*

"They weren't *bombs*, they were water balloons filled with paint!" replied Sam.

"Nonsense, the Black Knight scanned the suitcase and identified bombs," declared the White Rabbit loudly. "And our Hostilities Department confirmed it using our Pigeon Cams, and they're hardly ever wrong! Unfortunately the terrorist that escaped still has the case of bombs with him, so we don't yet have that evidence in our hands."

"Not yet, sir," clarified Milquetoast, "but it shouldn't be long until we have him in custody too."

"Jennifer, the situation escalated very quickly. We thought you were in danger," consoled Florence, hoping to settle Sam.

"They had a *banner*, for goodness' sake!" implored Sam. "They were just trying to carry out a *protest* against the government. They were just going to drop it over the side of the building!"

"Captain Flex didn't report finding any banner?" mused Milquetoast.

"That's because it blew off the side of the building! The backwash from your stupid helicopters was blowing everything all over the place!" said Sam indignantly.

"Now, now," countered Milquetoast, calmingly. "If there even *was* a banner, it doesn't change the fact that they had clearly taken up a position with line of sight of Parliament. And our communications picked up all of their conspiratorial planning. We have evidence of them talking about exploding bombs around Downing Street. You've foiled a potential terror attack in the heart of London, young man. You should be proud!"

"I just don't understand why you think they were so dangerous?" Sam knew Josie wasn't a terrorist. He felt he knew her a little better, and he was sure that most terrorists wouldn't look as nice as she did if they had an x-ray torch pointed at them.

"We don't believe they were a harmless activist group," insisted Milquetoast. "They were armed conspirators caught in the act of an insurrection against His Majesty's government. The two we have arrested will be tried by a jury but for now they're off the streets."

"Quite so," smiled the White Rabbit. "And as a result, I have something of a surprise for you, young Jennifer."

The White Rabbit opened a wooden box on the table, and lifted out a small, silver medal on a ribbon.

"This is for you." He pinned the medal onto Sam's lapel. "This little pendant is a Conspicuous Gallantry Medal for services to your country. And with this, I'm pleased to confirm that you are no longer considered to be a mere trainee. I hereby confer the rank of full Agent on you, congratulations *Agent Jennifer*."

Sam looked down at the medal and lightly touched the blue ribbon. He was a little stunned, but not because of the medal, and not because he was now being recognised as a full agent. He was stunned at the thought that Josie might be sent to prison.

"Wow, a medal," smiled Florence. "Get you, *Agent* Jennifer!"

Milquetoast silently nodded at Sam approvingly. "An excellent start to your career, young man."

"Thanks," said Sam, quietly.

"Right," said the White Rabbit. "Much to do today! You've neutralised one threat to our national security, but there are plenty more still out there! I suggest you head back to your office and start planning your future investigations, Agent Jennifer."

Sam looked at Florence briefly, and then turned around and walked towards the door. He didn't really know what else to say, nobody seemed to be listening anyway. Maybe the right words would come to him later, probably when he was lying alone in his bed that night. But for now all he could do was what he always did; stifle his frustration and dwell on what he should have said later.

Sam paused as he got to the door. Not this time.

He turned and looked back at Florence, Milquetoast and the White Rabbit who were still standing on the opposite side of the big, round table.

"You're wrong, sir."

The White Rabbit turned his head to look back at Sam. "I beg your pardon, young man?"

"I said, you're wrong sir."

Milquetoast and Florence looked a little uncertain. They were acutely aware that nobody ever told the White Rabbit he was wrong.

"And how is that so?"

"I haven't neutralised a threat to our national security. You have created one."

The Boardroom carried the eery silence of a graveyard at 4am. The White Rabbit's eyes darkened, his eyebrows lowered and he glared at Sam.

"I suggest you choose your next words very carefully, young Jennifer."

"I didn't ask to be sent to spy on those activists yesterday, but you told me to. I didn't ask for a flock of demented pigeons to follow me around London, but you sent them to follow me. I didn't ask for three Black Ops helicopters to attack us, but they did anyway. I didn't ask for a bunch of GI Joes on steroids to start firing their fucking rifles at us, but you let them. I didn't ask for two innocent activists to be put in handcuffs and sent to jail, but you let it happen."

The White Rabbit's fists were clenching, and his face reddened. Milquetoast looked aghast and Florence's jaw slowly dropped open, but Sam knew he couldn't stop.

"I didn't ask for a young man to be shot dead in cold blood, but you let it happen. You made all of these things happen, sir, not me. And all you've achieved is to stigmatise some activists and alienate them further. How do you think real terrorists are created?"

Sam took the silver medal off his lapel and tossed it on the table. "And I didn't ask for this either."

Sam turned around and walked away towards the door. Before he left there was one thing left he had on his mind.

"And stop calling me Jennifer. My name is *Sam*."

* * *

Mrs Bimble was at home reading the Daily Mail. Ralphy was asleep at her feet and Norman was up in the loft assembling a track intersection.

The first six pages of the Daily Mail were dedicated to a story about a foiled terrorist plot in Westminster the previous night. Candid photographs of Josie and Red accompanied the story proclaiming them to be seasoned terrorists intent on destroying democracy through means most foul.

How funny, thought Mrs Bimble. *As if sweet little Josie and that oik Red Kendall could ever do such a thing. They were cheeky little scamps, but they certainly weren't terrorists.*

She looked down at Ralphy. "Well it looks like I'll be dog-sitting you for a little longer than expected, young Ralphy."

Ralphy looked up at Mrs Bimble, and then gave her slipper a lick. He had decided he quite liked Mrs Bimble, she fed him pieces of baclava and let him sleep next to her fireplace. What was not to like?

Admittedly, Ralphy had been a little confused about Mrs Bimble the night before. When they were at Leo's flat yesterday evening, Josie and the others had all abruptly got up and departed, leaving him and Mrs Bimble behind to carry on snoozing. The confusing thing though, was when Mrs Bimble woke up, promptly set fire to Leo's house and then departed with Ralphy.

Josie never used to set fire to houses before she left. Josie used to run around her flat looking for her keys, pat him on the head and then leave. He was sure he couldn't remember her setting fire to stuff on the way out.

Still, he felt sure Mrs Bimble probably had a good reason to set fire to Leo's house. Maybe it was just one of those things that humans did sometimes.

Ralphy went back to sleep. Josie would probably be back soon.

* * *

Josie and Red were being held in one of the government's undisclosed secure detention centres somewhere in Berkshire. Two armed police officers were positioned outside the interview room and CCTV cameras were mounted in each corner.

Josie and Red's arms were both manacled with wrist braces. They were sitting at a table before Senior Commissioner Reinhard of the Crown Prosecution Service, under the special measures of the Terrorist Act 2000. This permitted the government to hold people in detention prior to their trial if they suspected them of acts of terrorism. It allowed time for a thorough investigation to take place prior to the court date which, in the case of Josie and Red, probably wouldn't take place until a year or two later.

In addition to Commissioner Reinhard, there was another man in the room - Rodney Cumberland QC was a state appointed lawyer provided to Josie and Red, in order to ensure due process and advise them accordingly.

The evidence of their wrongdoing was not in dispute - as far as the government was concerned, they had already been caught red-handed. Commissioner Reinhard's role was merely to inform them of their rights and explain the ensuing process. Unfortunately, Commissioner Reinhard had clearly also read the Daily Mail that morning. His mind was decisively made up that the two people before him deserved minimal consideration of their so-called rights.

"People like you... *people...*" Commissioner Reinhard spat the word like he had a filthy taste in his mouth. "You come over here and you prance around, taking our jobs and smoking your weed in your stupid hats, driving your fancy sports cars, without jobs, leeching off decent hard working British people, not paying tax and talking in your own language! You make me want to vomit!"

The two armed police officers outside the room could hear Reinhard's offbeat tirade through the door. They looked at each other and rolled their eyes - fucking Reinhard was off on one of his rants again.

"I'm fucking Scottish, ya wee prick," said Red. "And she's from Bromley!"

"I don't care if you're both from *Buckingham fucking Palace*!" screamed Reinhard. "When I'm done with you, you'll be strung up by your balls wishing you'd never stepped foot past Hadrian's fucking wall!"

"Objection, Your Honour," proclaimed Rodney Cumberland. The commissioner stopped and looked at Rodney with disdain.

"I'm not a fucking judge, you imbecile. Don't call me *Your Honour*!" cussed Reinhard.

"Oh," said Rodney, "sorry, what should I call you?"

"Commissioner. You call me Commissioner, moron."

"Certainly. Objection, Commissioner Moron."

"*Why* are you objecting?"

"Umm, well this defendant doesn't have any balls. You wouldn't be able to string her up by them I'm afraid," Rodney gestured towards Josie's genitalia.

"He's right," confirmed Josie, spreading her thighs. "No balls down there!"

"You don't *need* to object! We're not in a fucking courtroom!" growled Reinhard.

"Oh right. Yes, I see. Ha. Hmm. I just wasn't sure how best to interject if I needed to raise any points in their defence? You seemed kind of huffy?"

It was becoming clear to Josie and Red that their 'government appointed lawyer' may have been appointed to them primarily because of his inexperience and general ineptitude.

"Defence? What do you mean *defence*? They will be found guilty of high treason, sedition, lese majesty *and* plotting to bomb the Houses of Parliament. What in-the-shit kind of *defence* can there be for these two wretches?!"

Rodney thought hard. In fairness to him, he hadn't been given much time to consider the case and formulate a coherent defence, so instead he found his memory straining back to remember any historical defence strategies he had studied while doing his law degree a year or so ago.

"Well, umm maybe the… Urban Survival Defence?" offered Rodney.

"The *what*?!" asked Reinhard.

"The Urban Survival Defence! Bernie Goetz used it when he shot four people on a New York subway. He said he was being attacked by them."

"Nonsense! No one was attacking them."

"Ok, well how about the Twinkie Defence?"

"There's no such thing you buffoon!"

"Sure there is. Dan White used it when he murdered Harvey Milk. He said junk food made him do it."

Josie and Red were looking at Rodney with increasing concern.

"Or the Matrix Defence? Lee Boyd Malvo said he carried out the Beltway sniper attacks because he thought he was trapped in the Matrix."

"What you're saying is utter hogwash. Stop talking rubbish, man."

"It's not hogwash. What about the Taxi Driver Defence?"

"Am I talking to myself? I don't fucking care about the Taxi Driver Defence!!"

"John Hinkley Jr used it when he tried to assassinate Ronald Reagan," Rodney continued. "He said Jodie Foster made him do it."

"Right. That's enough!" Reinhard banged his fist on the table and pointed at Rodney. "You shut the fuck up. And you two are going to be taken to Belmarsh until you're ready for trial."

Rodney continued undaunted. "Then there's the Sleepwalking Defence or the Evil Twin Defence…" He wasn't just making these up – Rodney's knowledge of historical defence strategies apparently extended far beyond that of anybody else in the room.

"I SAID, *SHUT THE FUCK UP!*" Reinhard grabbed hold of the table and flung it towards the wall. "GUARDS! GET YOUR BACKSIDES IN HERE!!"

The two armed police officers obediently came into the interrogation room.

"TAKE THESE TWO PIECES OF SHIT TO BELMARSH. MAXIMUM SECURITY, ARMED RESPONSE VEHICLES TO FOLLOW! AND GET THIS BLITHERING ARSE OUT OF MY BUILDING. I DON'T WANT TO SEE HIM HERE AGAIN."

Rodney stood up and smiled politely at Josie and Red. He felt satisfied he had handled the interview extremely well and was sure his new clients knew they were in safe hands.

Josie and Red looked at each other. They knew they were fucked.

* * *

Outside 25 Windermere Avenue, the street had been cordoned off by the Police. Yellow and black barrier tape was stretched across the road at either end and police officers ambled around, shooing away nosey onlookers. MI-51 forensic agents had been dispatched to the address simultaneously as the helicopters were being deployed last night in order to investigate the lead-lined bedroom, but by the time of their arrival the house was already a fiery inferno. Teams from the local fire brigade had battled the flames valiantly but by the time they had finished their operations there was little left other than a pile of blackened and sodden embers.

Forensics had sifted through the remains under orders from the White Rabbit, however it was clear that whatever was being hidden in Leo's mysterious second bedroom, was now destroyed beyond all recognition. The best they could conclude was that the room contained some serious electrical equipment - possibly long range communications devices.

An old lady with a small scruffy dog approached one of the police officers at the barrier tape to see what was going on.

"Ello luv, what on earth is all that mess?"

"House fire," said the police officer. "What does it look like?"

"Oooh, I say. A house fire! Anybody dead?"

"I'm not allowed to say. But I don't think so."

"Well how long till I can get up the road? I wanna go to the off-licence."

"No idea. Road will be open when it's open," replied the policeman.

"Can I ask you a question, luv?"

"If you must."

"What's it like being a fascist puppet?

"Look, I'm busy here. Sod off you daft old goat."

"Come on Ralphy, we'll go the long way round. Better get out of here before Officer Ballbag calls for back up."

* * *

An hour later, Florence was back at her desk tapping on her keyboard and Sam was sitting at his footstool workstation making notes.

He was refusing to talk to Florence and she wasn't talking to him either, although admittedly she wasn't entirely clear what the stand-off was specifically relating to at this stage. But there was no way she was giving in.

Sam's eyes flicked up from his notebook just as Florence's eyes looked back down at her screen. Moments later, Florence glanced back up and Sam immediately made it look like he was engrossed in his notes.

This went on for some time. Neither of them were really doing any particular work, but they were going to make damn sure it looked like they were the busiest. Sam was actually doodling a dinosaur on stilts and Florence was browsing cat memes.

Florence looked up over her monitor again, momentarily catching Sam's gaze but then he pretended to be staring at the ceiling, thinking.

"Ok, this is ridiculous. Sam, *I'm sorry.* Is that what you want to hear?"

This had caught Sam off guard. He definitely wanted her to apologise but felt it was a bit unfair of her to just surprise him with it like that. He wanted to maintain the high ground so tried to come up with an eloquent and dignified response.

"Well I'm not sure I accept your apology. And on top of everything else, that poor dog still has a microphone up his arsehole."

"Look, the comms weren't working well, the dog-mic clearly wasn't powerful enough to transmit from deep inside his butthole. It was my mistake, but the dog will be fine. Eventually it'll pop back out and probably start working again so we'll just have to go and retrieve it then.

But I do agree with you, the White Rabbit might have over-reacted on this one."

"You *knew* that Josie and the others weren't terrorists. Why did you send the bloody Starship Troopers in?"

"I *didn't* know that Sam, and I *didn't* send anyone in. Look at the evidence that the White Rabbit was responding to…"

Florence started counting the examples on the fingers of her left hand, "They were kicking off at that rally with all the other nutcases; they mentioned Downing Street; they were talking about attacking policemen; Leo was going on about exploding things; they had ski masks with them when they were arrested; they were carrying a suitcase full of suspected bombs." She had run out of fingers on her left hand. "They were even standing on a rooftop next to the Houses of Parliament in the middle of the night. Sam, come on, it sounds really bad when you look at it like that - cognitive dissonance is a weird thing. Do we really know for definite they are all innocent or have you just convinced yourself of it?"

Sam looked glum. He knew everything Florence was saying was right, but he felt sure Josie wasn't a terrorist.

"I guess. But Florence, we killed a man. We shot Elijah dead and put Josie and Red in handcuffs. You heard the White Rabbit, those two will be locked up for years and Elijah is never coming back."

"Sam, have you ever heard of something called the Backfire Effect? It's when we have strongly held beliefs, and yet when we are provided with strong evidence that contradicts those beliefs, instead of changing our minds we just double down on our original beliefs in spite of any better information."

Sam knew Florence was suggesting that this was what he was doing. In spite of obvious evidence to the contrary, he still believed Josie and the gang were innocent in this tangled mess.

"Think of it like this," she continued. "Take the shape of planet Earth. Most right-thinking people these days accept that it's a globe. Okay, maybe an oblate spheroid but never mind that — it's a big round ball, right? But imagine if someone showed you incontrovertible evidence that it was flat. How long do you think it would take for you to change your mind? There's been all kinds of studies to show people still wouldn't change their mind and would continue to stick to what they've believed for years before."

The door unexpectedly opened and as if by magic Milquetoast appeared.

"Actually Agent Lawrence, I'm not sure you're telling young Samuel the full story! The studies you're referring to were indeed conducted by a certain scientist by the name of Mr Brendan Nyhan at Dartmouth Research Establishment, and the findings of the Backfire Effect experiments have been published in numerous essays ever since," announced Milquetoast.

"Hello Mr Milquetoast," said Sam.

"And greetings to you Agent Juniper. However, the irony of the Backfire Effect research is that a series of follow up studies undertaken in the years since the original experiment entirely failed to corroborate those original findings. Indeed, it appears that quite the opposite is true, as there were countless examples in later experiments that in general people are *more than willing* to moderate their beliefs, so long as the new evidence is emphatically empirical."

Florence stared at Milquetoast loathingly. She was irritated by his interruptions at the best of times and certainly didn't like being corrected by him.

Milquetoast smiled warmly at Sam. "Even the good Professor Nyhan himself later accepted the new findings discredited his own. He agreed entirely that it would be awfully ironic if later evidence contradicting his *Backfire* theory, simply provoked him into doubling down on his own theory. However, regardless of this, many people still ardently elect to only quote the original hypothesis. It's just much easier that way, I suppose. Is that not so, Ms Lawrence?"

"Why are you here Milquetoast?" asked Florence, abjectly rolling her eyes.

"I was wondering if I may have a little tête-à-tête with our new young agent here? Perhaps with a little privacy?"

Florence sighed. "Fine. I need some fresh air anyway. Don't sit in my chair, Milktits."

As Florence left the room, Milquetoast gently closed the door behind her. He glanced around the room trying to decide where he could sit, in order to make their conversation a little less formal - a little cosier perchance. He noted Sam perched awkwardly on his footstool workstation but opted not to question why he wasn't sitting at the vacant desk.

Aiming to demonstrate solidarity with sulking Sam, Milquetoast elected not to sit at Florence's desk or to sit at the other vacant desk. Instead, Milquetoast took off his hat, laid his cane gently against the wall and lifted out a second footstool from behind the wall cabinet. He unfolded it adjacent to Sam and awkwardly sat down onto the top step, lifting both his feet up onto the lower step like some ungainly leprechaun.

"Well you certainly gave our illustrious leader *what-for* this morning, young Samuel!" he said breezily.

"I guess I did. Is the White Rabbit annoyed with me?"

Milquetoast chuckled. "Oh yes. Bloody seething he is. But he knows you might be right."

"Really?"

"Of course. He might be a surly, cantankerous old walrus but he didn't get where he is today by not knowing when he might have made a mistake."

"So, will Josie and Red be released?"

"Good God, no man. They've already been locked up and are probably being packed off to Belmarsh as we speak. The government needs to be seen to have acted swiftly in the face of terrorism, especially at the moment."

"Oh," replied Sam despondently.

"You must understand Samuel. They are really just pawns. Tiny pawns in a game of global chess. Collateral damage if you like. And as you know in any game of chess, pawns are always the first to be removed from the board."

"So they really are going to stay locked up?"

Milquetoast didn't answer. His old bones suffered a little from arthritis and he was wondering if he would ever be able to elevate himself back out of this footstool.

"There are greater games afoot, young Samuel. You played your part to perfection yesterday, and although the White Rabbit is on the warpath at the moment, he knows you show great potential and now he also knows you'll stand up for what you think is right. So we need *you* to look into something else. Something rather urgent."

Milquetoast handed Sam a charred memory stick, retrieved from the remains of the previous night's housefire in Windermere Road.

"This was retrieved by our forensics team last night, Samuel. There's an audio file on here - I need you to get it unscrambled and listen to it. The prime minister is at Chequers at the moment, but he could still be in significant personal danger, even there. Speak to Florence and between you work out what resources you'll need to set up a stakeout before the PM ends up going missing."

Milquetoast slowly levered himself out of the footstool, with all the grace of a giraffe climbing out of a tree.

"Mr Milquetoast," said Sam, "You didn't answer my question. Are they really going to stay locked up?"

"I couldn't possibly say, young Samuel. Perhaps a guardian angel will step in and place those little pawns back on the board. Who knows?"

Milquetoast put on his hat, picked up his cane, winked at Sam and then swiftly departed from the office.

* * *

Leo Angelopoulos was peeking around the side of a wheelie bin, making sure the coast was clear. No cars, no CCTV, no people - time to make a run for it. He sprinted as quickly as he could across the road and darted into a muddy back alley.

The alley was narrow and ran along the back of a row of suburban back gardens. Leo walked tentatively down the alley, counting the gardens as he passed by them.

He was cold and he smelt a bit but after twenty-four hours of avoiding the police, he was pleased to be surviving. As he got six gardens down, he stopped, looked behind him to make sure he wasn't being followed, and then peered over the top of the fence.

He could see a small, manicured lawn, a tiny pond and some colourful flower beds. He placed a foot on the frame of the fence panel, grasped the top edge and hauled himself over. As he landed he bent his knees and rolled onto the floor like a commando. He got up and carefully checked his surroundings to make sure no one had spotted him, then tip-toed up to the back of the house and tapped on the back door.

At first he heard a dog yap, and then the door opened.

"Hello Leo, I wondered where you'd got to!" smiled Mrs Bimble.

"The Poleethe are crawling everywhere," breathed Leo, "I've been avoiding them all night."

"Of course you have dear, you must be wet through! Come in and have a nice cup of tea."

Ralph was looking up at Leo. Ralph thought he smelt alright actually.

Mrs Bimble fetched some of Norman's clothes from upstairs so Leo could change into something dry, and then put the kettle on. Leo quickly got changed in her lounge, flopped down in her armchair, and slowly started to thaw out. Mrs Bimble brought in a tray with a teapot and two cups along with a small tin of baclava.

"Well it sounds like you all had quite the adventure last night?"

"I'm so tired," replied Leo. "I couldn't go back to my houthe, it was all cordoned off by the cops."

"Just as well dear, I burnt it down after you left."

"Oh." Leo mulled this new information over for a moment. "All of it?"

"All of it."

"I thee. Any particular reason why you burnt my houthe down after we left?"

"It was for the best. Would you like some baclava, dear?"

Leo took two pieces and dipped one in his tea, despondently.

"You can stay with me for the time being young Leo. Until things, you know, calm down a bit."

"Where is your husband?"

"He's up in the loft of course, playing with his railway. Norman loves that railway. Spends hours up there he does. Bloody old fool."

"I have some things I have to thort out. I've got to go to Frinton-on-Thea."

"I know you have my little iced doughnut. No rest for the wicked."

Leo felt a little uneasy. Mrs Bimble seemed to be unnervingly calm for an old lady who had just burnt his house down the night before.

* * *

Josie stumbled as she stepped up into the back of the armoured security van. The wrist braces made it difficult for her to balance and the surly security neanderthal was not interested in helping her maintain any degree of dignity as she got in. Red was already manacled inside the van, ready to be transported to Belmarsh.

The van doors were slammed shut behind them and they heard an industrial security bolt clunk into place.

The van interior consisted of a bench on either side, no windows and a tiny roof light which was just enough to assure any occupants that they hadn't gone entirely blind. Josie could just make out Red's fiery orange beard in the gloomy light.

"I'm sorry, Red. I got us into this. I feel like Elijah's death was all my fault."

"Aww shut yer puss, fannybaws. None of this is your fault. That prick Jennifer is the one to blame in my book."

"I know. He's such a two-faced bastard, Red. Y'know, I'm embarrassed to say I think I fancied him a little bit, but I never even knew his real name. I can't believe I'm such a mug."

"Ye fancied him? Naw shite, ya daft bint. You had it written all over yer face."

"I know. I hate him, Red. I hate him so much for what he did to us. And to Elijah."

Red looked distant. "Did I tell you I was going to ask Elijah to marry me that night? I bought a ring and everything."

"I'm so sorry, Red. It's all so messed up. You must be devastated about that on top of everything else."

"Well that's one way of putting it, lass. I'll tell you one thing though, one day I'll find the bastard who pulled that trigger on Elijah. One day."

Josie and Red sat in silence waiting for the van to start.

"What do you think's going to happen to us?" asked Josie.

"Judging from that mad fucker Reinhard, we'll be slammed up in Belmarsh for a year or two just waiting for a trial. Eventually when we get to court, Reinhard is going to make damn sure they throw the book at us and then we'll be held at His Majesty's pleasure for another decade or so."

"You make it sound like it's inevitable, Red?"

"If Rodney Cumberland is our lawyer, then yes, I'd say it's pretty inevitable. The bloke's named after a fucking sausage. I thought Reinhard was going to go all *Chewbacca* on him at one point and rip his arms off."

Josie had never seen *Star Wars* but vaguely imagined a green alien with a cosmic arm-pulling machine. Red saw her despondency and wondered how he could cheer her up.

"Talking of Chewbacca, did you know the biggest trending search term on the web about him is 'Do Wookies have teeth in their buttholes?'"

"What? Why on earth would anyone search for that?"

"It started off as a joke in the TV show *Peacemaker*. But now so many people have googled it to see if it was true, that it was added into a comic. The rumour spread and now it's official canon."

She still looked despondent.

"Say Josie, what do you call Chewbacca when he's got chocolate stuck in his fur?"

"I've no idea, Red."

"A chocolate chip Wookie!"

Josie chuckled. She didn't understand his joke in the slightest but knew Red was just trying to distract her from their dire situation and she appreciated the effort.

They both felt the van rock slightly as the security neanderthals clambered into the cab seats in front of the opaque partition. The engine spluttered to life and a brief whoop of the sirens indicated that they were on their way to Belmarsh.

They sat in silence for the next ten minutes wondering how long the journey would be. They could feel the van stopping and starting in the traffic and could hear the two security guards in the driver cab chatting. Now and again one of the guards would slide open a small hatch to check on the prisoners and then quickly slide it closed again, saying nothing.

After a while they felt as if the van was pulling into a layby before coming to a stop. Josie and Red listened as they heard muffled voices outside and then one of the doors at the rear of the van suddenly swung open. An old man stepped into the van, closed the door behind him and sat on the side-bench next to Josie.

Red and Josie watched him curiously as he adjusted his collar slightly, and then the van pulled away again.

He had a boney face, neatly combed grey hair and delicate half-moon spectacles perched on his beaky nose. Josie noticed he was dressed quite immaculately and had his hands rested on the handle of a carved mahogany walking cane. An ornate gold wristwatch on his right arm glinted in the gloom as the van jostled over speedbumps.

"Josephine Louise Griffiths and Reginald 'Red' Kendall. How nice to make your acquaintances," smiled the man.

"And who the fuck might you be?" asked Red.

"Me? Oh, I'm nobody," smiled the man. "Nobody of importance anyway. I was just in need of a short lift and the kind gentlemen escorting you were generous enough to oblige me."

"You don't look like a nobody?" Josie probed, eyeing his gold watch suspiciously.

"Appearances can be quite deceptive, my dear. You really should pay them no mind."

"Well that much is true, ye old knacker," agreed Red. "The whole reason we're in this poxy van is because of a jobby-flavoured fart lozenge pretending to be Josie's pal."

"Quite so, Reginald. A most eloquent description of your current circumstance it would seem."

"So how do you know our names?" asked Josie.

The man ignored the question and adjusted his spectacles. "Are you familiar with the concept of Plato's Cave?" he asked, smiling pleasantly.

Josie and Red looked suitably blank.

"The great Socrates once regaled us with the story of a group of wretched, ignorant, troglodytes who were regrettably chained inside a dark cave. The pitiful creatures were manacled facing one of the walls of the cave, and that wall is all they could ever see for the entirety of their miserable lives. However, within the cave, there was a campfire burning behind them, casting shadows on the wall. Each time a rat crept by or a spider spun his web, the troglodytes would excitedly watch the shadow puppets created on the wall, which provided them with a narrow two-dimensional perception of reality."

"Are you saying we're going to be chained up in a cave?" asked Josie, wearily.

"Not in the least, my dear girl," he continued. "One day, one of the troglodytes broke free of his chains and escaped out of the cave and into the big wide world. He was overwhelmed by the colourful beauty and vivid splendour and his brain filled with new insight of the real, three-dimensional world."

"So what did he do?" asked Red curiously.

"Well he rushed back to the cave of course, to share his insights with his fellow troglodytes. Unfortunately, in spite of the magnificent stories he told them, all they could see were just the same old shadows and so they shunned him - they considered him to be a lunatic."

"And the point of this story is what?"

"The point, my fine hirsute friend, is that you and your young companion here have briefly escaped the cave. You are one of the few who have been able to see behind the security curtain. If you are able to shed the metaphorical shackles of perception then you have an opportunity to see the truth behind the pantomime. What you do with that knowledge, is entirely up to you."

"Well now, that's the problem isn't it," Red held up the literal shackles securing his wrists. "These are a little difficult to shed."

"They would certainly appear to be quite substantial wouldn't they, Reginald." The man looked down at his wristwatch and appeared to be winding it up. However, instead of winding the clockwork mechanism, his thumb and forefinger pulled out an inch long universal key, which was equipped with delicate spring-loaded teeth.

Gently taking hold of Josie's hand, he slotted his skeleton key into the wrist restraints and wiggled it around. After a brief moment, the restraints clicked and released from her wrists. The man then repeated the process with Red's handcuffs.

Josie and Red looked mildly stunned as both sets of manacles dropped to the floor.

The man then tapped his walking cane on the front bulkhead as if to signal the driver, and the van made a sudden and sharp turn to the left and came to a stop.

"I do believe this is my stop!" he announced.

"Wait!" said Josie. "Who *are* you?"

The man paused and looked thoughtful. Then he reached into his top pocket and pulled out an elegant business card which he placed on the seat as he stood up. He opened the rear door of the armoured van and stepped out.

After exiting, he turned to face them. "Remember, you have both seen behind the curtain — you have become aware of the existence of the secret security services operating in this country. The other troglodytes will not believe your stories, but you should use your new-found knowledge wisely. Good day to you both." He tipped his hat and then walked briskly away from the van.

Josie and Red stared at each other, and then at their manacles on the floor, and then at the wide-open van door, flapping in the wind. Then they looked back at each other.

"What does the card say?" asked Red.

"It's just a phone number, and one word?"

"What word?"

"Milquetoast?"

"What does that mean?"

"I've no idea. Do you think he's coming back?"

"I don't think so. Should we… just go?" asked Red.

Josie tentatively approached the open door towards the back of the van and peered out of it. There was nobody around, so she stepped out. Red followed, and they slowly walked around to the front of the vehicle. There were no longer any guards sitting in the cab. The van had come to a stop in a layby somewhere on the outskirts of West London, but the security guards, the car that was supposed to be escorting them and the mysterious old man all just seemed to have disappeared into thin air.

"Well what do we do now?" asked Josie. "Have we just escaped?"

"I'm not sure," replied Red. "But the keys are still in the ignition."

"Okay then. Get in. I guess we have just escaped."

1408

The Spring of 1969 was unseasonably chilly. A polar low had slipped over the British Isles, dragging bitterly cold winds across the country, resulting in flurries of snow in mid-March.

Milton Sears sat dejectedly on a park bench near Holborn, gazing sympathetically at a half-melted snowman. Milton's arm rested on a brown leather suitcase as he watched a Routemaster Bus carefully negotiate the treacherous roads as it meandered towards Piccadilly.

Today, Milton's illustrious career in Her Majesty's Secret Intelligence Service had come to a rather abrupt end. It had lasted less than two years and he'd just been informed his services would no longer be required. What the Director General had actually said was rather more damning;

"There is no longer a need for sneaks and spooks to be exchanging clandestine messages in the classified section of The Times newspaper. The incident with Maclean and Burgess has frankly cast doubt on all of you, so the PM would rather you were gone. Thank you very much. Now fuck off, there's a good chap."

Donald Maclean and Guy Burgess - a despicable pair of smug, two-faced Cambridge tomfools if ever there were. Their defection way back in 1951 was just the tip of the iceberg, but when Philby followed them in '63 the whole stinking house of cards started to tumble. There were even rumours that Blunt and Cairncross were being investigated but that seemed hard for Milton to believe, they had both seemed like stand-up fellows. But it was starting to look like all of the old guard was rotten to the core.

As a result, trust in all of the Secret Services had been eroded and the whole organisation was being discretely dismantled. The chaps working at MI-1 were the first to be dispatched at the end of last year. Who knows what careers they would find out in Civvy Street - maybe a code-breaker could go on to write crosswords or something? Their demise was shortly followed by MI-4, and then MI-17. Finally, it was the turn of Milton's branch, MI-9 Clandestine Operations.

When he had been recruited during his second year at Oxford, he'd felt privileged. He'd initially been approached by his sociology professor because of his tenacity and acumen. After a few initial cloak and dagger meetings, he'd found himself on a train to Bletchley and promptly signing the Official Secrets Act.

But where had that got him now? Sitting on a bench in Bloomsbury Square Gardens, without a job and eighteen months' experience which he wasn't allowed to tell anyone about.

"I've been looking for you!" called a gruff voice from somewhere behind him. He looked around to see the bulky figure of Charles Lapin trudging through the slush towards him, a heavy trench coat pulled tightly around his shoulders. "They let you keep the briefcase then?"

Milton patted the leather case. "Indeed they did, old chap. A memento of my time in the service."

Charles grimaced and sat down next to him. "You shouldn't be so sentimental, Milton. We all knew the circus would be leaving town soon. It'll be a different world with NATO running the show. Bloody Yanks."

Milton liked Charles. He was a hulk of a man with fists the size of pineapples and the face of a bulldog. He had a surly, belligerent manner and lacked the etiquette that came so naturally to Milton, but his directness was refreshing and he understood the world of spycraft well. Milton's first assignment had been in Paris where he had met Charles who was stationed out there supporting London's French counterparts. Whilst there, Charles had quickly built himself a reputation as an unbridled pragmatist and a courageous young agent. Rumours were abound that he had single-handedly defended France's new nuclear deterrent from the clutches of anti-De Gaulle renegades.

Milton pulled a handkerchief out of his pocket and polished a few flakes of snow off the lenses of his large square glasses. He looked at Charles huddling for warmth in his coat. Charles's pale blond hair and his distinctive matching moustache gave him the air of a man more advanced in his years, although in truth he was only a few years older than Milton.

"So the powers that be have elected to close down the Paris bureau as well, have they?"

"They have," replied Charles, pulling his lapels closer together.

"Do you know what you're going to do then, old bean?"

"I have a few ideas. Let's go somewhere and talk, Milton."

* * *

The Summer of 1979 was long and dry. The British government was enforcing drought restrictions and lush green lawns across the United Kingdom started to turn yellowy-brown.

Charles Lapin mopped his heavy brow with the cuff of his jacket as he stomped along Chancery Lane, panting heavily. As he turned the corner into Furnival Street, he could see Milton already up ahead, waiting by the fire exit door as agreed.

Milton's wiry body was leaning casually against a wall while he fiddled with a bunch of keys. Charles had originally considered that Milton's spindly frame and beaky nose rather gave him the appearance of a precocious bird and his twitchy mannerisms had done little to dispel this image over the years. Although he didn't rate Milton's physical strengths, Charles certainly valued his strategic prowess. Over the last decade he had proved invaluable in securing resources to support their little private enterprise, and now he had finally acquired a substantial new premises from which they could operate.

"Morning," mumbled Charles.

"Salutations, on this fine day!" declared Milton, selecting a particularly rusty key.

The building was an oddly industrial setting for one being located in the heart of London. There were no windows but instead a large mechanical hoist was bolted to the red brickwork overhead and a ventilation grille was fitted across the first floor level. Milton slotted a brass key into the fire exit door and pushed it open.

As both men went in, Milton tapped a switch and flickering bulkhead lights strained to illuminate a dingey passageway. At the end of the corridor, a rusty spiral staircase took them several storeys down, deep underground.

"So this is it?" asked Charles, blinking as he surveyed the vast concrete vault at the bottom.

"This is it," replied Milton, triumphantly.

"It's… a bit shit."

"Oh it'll brush up, old chap. A bit of spit and polish."

Charles stalked around the empty void, trying to visualise it being operational. "And tell me again how this fell into our hands?"

"It belonged to the Services Research Bureau in the 50s and 60s. When they were disbanded, their assets were reallocated to MI-9. Only MI-9 was then disbanded before they'd registered it as part of their official estate. A little creative accounting with enough people who possess somewhat flexible morals, and voila! Our new headquarters for discreet corporate espionage."

Charles grunted. He shunted open an old door in the vault, which creaked as he forced it through the matted strands of spiders' webs. "And you said there were tunnels linking it to other parts of London?"

"Indeed there are, old man." Milton enthusiastically skipped across the vault. "Lift-shafts and tunnels criss-crossing from Camden to Clapham and from Stratford to Southwark. There's even a pulley system left over from the war. We really would have unencumbered access, right across the city."

Charles grunted again, but tried his best to at least look a little impressed. He swept the cobwebs from his face as he stepped through the doorway and tried to feel for another light switch.

"And *this* will knock your socks off Charles…" Milton flicked the switch for him.

Far above their heads, an array of rickety chandeliers lit up another dusty chamber. The walls were clad with flaking timber panels and tired looking oil paintings were hung on the walls.

"What the hell was this? It looks like a bloody ballroom."

"That's exactly what it was my good man, back in the war. Created to cater for the aristocracy during the Blitz. It's rather jolly, don't you think?"

Charles shook his head. "This all has to come out Milton. We're trying to set up a professional operation. We don't need a bloody ballroom."

"Not a ballroom, you grumpy buffoon," Milton strode out into the centre of the room and flung his arms aloft. "Imagine this as our boardroom!"

Charles slowly raised an eyebrow, as he pondered the potential of the space. Maybe Milton had a point. "And where does *that* door go?"

"Who knows? There are doors everywhere, corridors running off into lobbies and stairwells leading to hidden areas all over the place. It's like a rabbit warren."

Charles nodded, thoughtfully. "Hmm, a rabbit warren. I like that."

* * *

The Autumn of 1989 saw the Berlin Wall finally being torn down, and Germany was at last re-unified. As the Eastern Bloc disintegrated, democracy slowly started to spread across Europe. The Cold War was finally over.

Milton sat at a tiny circular table in their massive boardroom. Opposite him sat Charles who was brooding over a memorandum he had received from the Prime Minister's Office. The other man sat with them was the rambunctious Major Phillip Longshanks, in his perfectly tailored Army uniform.

Milton had brewed a pot of tea and had made some hot toast with butter for them to share during their morning breakfast meeting.

"This is not the end of the war gentlemen," grumbled Charles. "I'm afraid this memo says it is only just the beginning."

"That's just government hogwash, Charles," boomed the Major. "Bloomin' scare tactics from the Admiralty trying to drum up finance for some more blasted aircraft carriers no doubt."

The major had joined their little outfit two years before, after leaving the Yorkshire Regiment. Having joined the Army straight from school at sixteen, he had now completed his twenty-two distinguished years' service and had been honourably discharged. Although his chest proudly displayed an array of medal ribbons, he would often be heard exclaiming how his proudest moment was meeting Elvis Presley back in 1974.

"I fear not, Pip," replied Charles. "The days of the Soviet Union may look numbered after perestroika, but this report says their threat will return. It may take twenty years, maybe thirty years but the elite within the Kremlin will rebuild and a new Cold War will be initiated when they try to reclaim parts of Eastern Europe. In the meantime, any temporary vacuum of power will undoubtedly be exploited by radical new threats from around the world."

Both Charles and Milton were around ten years older than Major Longshanks, but his bombastic, military demeanour had proved to be more than capable of having his voice heard. "Oh horseshit, Charles. The Soviets are nothing but a third rate junta with fourth rate tanks now. As for the rest of the world, everybody hates the British, they'll all just have to get in line."

"Tea, chaps?" Milton removed the woolly cosy from his teapot and poured Earl Grey into cups for himself, Charles and the Major. He then carefully apportioned milk from a small jug into each cup and gestured towards the plate of toast inviting his companions to help themselves. "Regardless of the presence of any possible horseshit, gentlemen, there are unfortunately more pressing concerns."

Charles sipped his tea, then screwed his face up. "How pressing?" he asked, swiftly adding several spoons of sugar to his cup.

Milton pushed his circular, wire-framed spectacles up the bridge of his nose. "Well old bean, you may not realise it, but we currently live in a world where information crawls into the public consciousness at a snail's pace. The BBC and the newspapers are often days or even weeks behind current events. But news of the future is going to be spread much quicker. Tomorrow's conspiracies will spread instantaneously, and they'll be in the palm of everyone's hands within the blink of an eye."

"Poppycock," snorted the major, his mouth full of toast, "how the blazes is that going to happen?"

"Technology, my fine fellow," retorted Milton. "They're already working on a network of computers that will connect the entire world at the touch of a button! It'll be utterly ubiquitous and totally anonymous. They're going to call it the *Interweb!*"

Charles stroked his platinum moustache. "And *this* is why we're being officially activated."

"Activated?" Milton held his cup and saucer still, the word piquing his interest.

"That's what this memo says, Milton. The PM wants our little private operation upscaled to meet these new threats. They know we can stay out of the spotlight, so now they want us back in-house. We are to be re-classified as MI-51."

Milton looked concerned. "Assisting local firms with corporate espionage is one thing, Charles. But we don't have the resources for upscaling, we've been running on a shoestring for the last decade."

"A budget has been allocated Milton - a significant budget."

"We'll need more people," replied Milton, rapidly calculating the cost of such an escalation of activity, "new specialists in Propaganda, Hostilities and Technologies."

"I agree," said Charles. "Pip, I want you to start taking charge of recruitment - interviews, entrance exams, that sort of thing."

The Major nodded his head, and helped himself to another piece of toast.

Milton tapped his fingers on the small round table. "We're going to need a bigger table."

"A much bigger table," agreed Charles. "Gentlemen, if we go down this path it won't be an easy one. Protocols of the past will need to be re-introduced. I will issue you codenames for your own safety. I suggest you use them."

"Maybe I could be called Thunderfist?" suggested Major Longshanks.

"I will choose the codenames Pip," replied Charles.

"Dragonclaws?"

"I don't think so."

"Wolfdagger?"

"Your codename will be *Longstocking*," concluded Charles with finality.

Milton tried not to laugh.

"And you, Milton, shall be known as *Milktoast*," declared Charles, nodding towards the jug and the plate Milton had kindly provided in his breakfast offering.

Milton placed his cup and saucer down onto the table and frowned. "Milktoast? How remarkably uninventive of you, Charles. And isn't that a little close to *Milton?*"

"Fine, pronounce it however you like, I really don't care. Unless you'd prefer to have the codename Teapot?"

Milton and the Major looked at each other, trying to decide who had been awarded the most disappointing codename.

Charles's whiskers twitched as he raised his cup in readiness for a toast. "Gentlemen - to Her Majesty's first new security section in over forty years..."

Milton and the Major responded by raising their teacups in a show of unification.

"... To MI-51 - the most secret of all the secret services."

* * *

The Winter of 1999 buzzed with anticipation. The end of the century beckoned and December was spent by people across the world making new millennium party plans. Whether or not the rumoured Millennium Bug would bring technology crashing around their ears was yet to be seen.

"I don't understand why we can't just have buttons?" asked Ben, staring at the video player.

"Because it's a bloody secret lift, isn't it!" snapped Charles. "It's got to be accessible to all our agents, but I don't want any Tom, Dick or Harry waltzing in here off the street and pressing the button that takes them all the way over to Furnival Street. I'll end up with a bunch of blasted tourists posing for photographs outside my office."

"But we're in the back of a video shop! No fucker is even going to come in here. You realise everyone uses DVDs now? And they're supposed to last forever so will never be replaced."

"Come, come, now Benjamin, we've been through this." Milton was used to the young man's irascible outbursts. "Do try not to vex the White Rabbit."

"Cocky little shit." Charles stomped off towards the front of the newly acquired video store, muttering under his breath. The strain was showing on Charles's face after so many years. Bags were starting to form under his eyes and his once lustrous platinum blond hair was starting to thin into chalky tufts. The powerful stocky build he had as a young man was slowly and steadily heading south.

"But it's going to take forever to know which flipping movie takes you to which part of bloody London. Who's even heard of half of these?" Ben grabbed a copy of 1981's *Chariots of Fire* and held it up as 'exhibit A'.

"Then I strongly suggest you spend a little time learning about the history of filmography from before your limited lifetime, young man." Milton snatched the video out of Ben's hand and placed it back in the rack. "Your generation didn't invent popular culture you know, Benjamin."

Ben Cornelius had left University the year before and Milton, having identified his formidable potential, had agreed to bring him into the fold as his young protégé, much as he had been himself so many years ago. A much needed injection of young blood, as MI-51 continued to expand, although for now he was being limited to odd-jobs and maintenance tasks.

Ben gazed down the lift shaft forlornly. "I don't know how you put up with that gnarly old butt-hurt," he mused.

"Appearances can be deceptive, Benjamin," sighed Milton. "You may just see a cantankerous old sod in his fifties but be assured, when he was your age, our illustrious leader was quite brilliant."

"You're not going to start banging on about your old days as a spy are you, Uncle? Save the world from World War Three, did he?!"

"Yes, Benjamin. I believe he did."

Ben scribbled a note on a piece of cardboard; 'THIS LIFT IS KNACKERED – DON'T FALL DOWN THE SHAFT!' and stuck it on the wall next to the chasm. Ben wasn't a fan of lifts at the best of times and sensed that one day they would be the death of him.

"There you go then Uncle M, that should stop anyone falling down there. Any more exciting jobs for me today?"

Milton sensed his nephew was still sulking. He walked closer and gently placed his hands on Ben's shoulders. "The White Rabbit really does think a lot of you, Benjamin, and so do I. I know you have potential far beyond the menial tasks we're asking you to accomplish at the moment. Putting up signs and drawing schematic maps of the lift system is clearly a waste of your talents but soon the White Rabbit might end up assigning you to your own department, perhaps even a new department. Something you can develop and grow in the years to come."

"But I don't know anything about your sneaky-beaky stuff," whined Ben. "The whole thing is run like a giant frigging *conspiracy!*"

Milton contemplated Ben's skillsets. He was certainly anfractuous, pernicious and capable of considerable artifice when needed.

"Well if you have an eye for such things young Benjamin, I think perhaps one day we might have to create the Department of Conspiracy and have you head it up for us."

15 Minutes

Back in the present day, Henry Morley looked out across the rolling landscape of Chequers. As Prime Minister of the United Kingdom it was his entitlement to enjoy his weekends at the official country residence that had served countless prime ministers since 1921. Located in Buckinghamshire just over an hour from Downing Street, the Grade 1 listed, stately manor was steeped in history and teemed with elegant paintings and ornate statues. The extensive grounds included sumptuous lawns and well-tendered orchards.

It had possibly been the worst week of his tenure as PM so far.

The bubbling civil unrest about ministerial back handers, cronyism and other illicit goings-on had been fuelled by ravenous media speculation and culminated with a mass demonstration at Trafalgar Square. This had led to the resignation of his long term Home Office Minister, Jeffrey Braithwaite who was now being investigated by Scotland Yard for alleged illegal animal experimentation.

As if this hadn't been bad enough, to add to this his long-time friend and confidante, who also happened to be the Chancellor of the Exchequer had succumbed to a heart attack shortly after it was revealed in the newspapers that, of all things, he was a cannibal.

On a personal level, an odd diversion had proved to be a telephone call from his elderly mother earlier that morning. Although of relatively good health for her age, she had reportedly suffered a break-in at her small bungalow in Frinton-on-sea. Oddly, very little had been stolen aside from a single dress, some underwear and a wig. His mother had chosen not to report the incident to the police as the items were worthless, but it was nevertheless somewhat disconcerting.

It was a small mercy that the recent terrorist attack on the Houses of Parliament had been foiled by security forces. That aside, he did wonder if things could get any worse. Surely, he was due a break soon?

"I'm off for a bit of fresh air," Henry announced to his security detail. "I'll just be in the gardens having a walk. Kindly hold my phone calls for a bit, would you?"

The security officer nodded and muttered into a microphone in his shirt cuff.

"The skipper says I need to accompany you, sir."

"Good god, I'll only be twenty minutes. Let a man have a little solace."

The security officer muttered into his shirt cuff again. "Understood, sir. Skipper says ten minutes."

"Shitting hell," growled Henry, grumpily. "I'm the bloody prime minister and I've still got a curfew?!"

Henry wandered off down the gravelled path and stepped onto the manicured lawns. It felt like a world away from the hustle of Central London and he'd started to forget how therapeutic nature really could be.

He decided to take his shoes and socks off, enjoying the cool soft grass between his toes. As he walked further from the trusty old mansion he looked up at the clear blue sky and the tumbling fluffy clouds, deciding that perhaps things weren't so bad after all. He had his health, he had a happy family and his reign as prime minister was well into its second term, a considerable feat for any head of state in this day and age.

On the far side of the sloping lawn, there was a small, wooded copse comprised of lofty fern trees and carpeted with wild flowers. He wandered in amongst the bluebells and smiled as he saw a few squirrels scurrying for cover. For the first time in months, he was able to enjoy the tranquillity of peacefulness, with just the sparrows chirping in the treetops for company and the gentle breeze causing leaves to rustle. Henry turned to gaze behind, back through the tree trunks where he had just walked from, which were now silhouetted against the backdrop of the open gardens and the historic old house.

Henry felt entirely relaxed at the exact moment a baseball bat struck him hard on the back of his head. He dropped his shoes and socks and flopped down into the bluebells.

* * *

Josie started driving the van in no particular direction, getting used to the sluggish steering.

"Stick to the speed limit, Josie. We dinna know if they're looking for us or not right now. I'm not sure if we should be trusting that old guy." Red opened up the glove box to see if there was anything useful left behind by the security drivers.

"Bingo! One of them has left their mobile phone here."

"Careful Red, they could have bugged it. They could be using it to track us."

"Josie, we're driving towards London in a marked police van. I'm pretty sure if they wanted to track us, we're making it as easy as possible for them."

"Yeah I know. I just don't trust anyone right now, Red."

"Aye, I make you right, lassie."

"So where should I be heading?"

"I'm not sure. We could do with some answers. We could do with getting hold of that two-faced rat too."

Josie guessed Red was referring to Agent Juniper or whatever his stupid name was. "Why don't you Google that group he said he was part of? *SUGAR*, wasn't it? Was that even real?"

Red checked he had a signal and then tried a few different search terms. "Ah, here we are. The Society for Underground Galactic Armed Resistance. They've got a blog, Josie. Maybe they are real after all?"

Red scanned through the amateurish website, looking for any names that might give them a clue.

Much of the blog was filled with ambiguous claims regarding sasquatches and Loch Ness monsters. Red got side-tracked and went quiet as he read an article about the Dalai Lama once being a paid CIA agent.

"Red! You're not supposed to be reading it all. You're supposed to be finding clues for us."

"Och, right. Okay, how about this then? There's a postal address on here to say correspondence should be sent to *Videodrome* in Old Kent Road." Red put the phone on his lap and looked at Josie. "Didn't that twat say something about hanging around in a video store? I'm sure he mentioned that when we were all in Mama Mary's Café?"

"You're right Red, good thinking. If we hang around outside long enough, we might see what sort of people are going in and out and be able to get some answers from the *SUGAR* clowns."

* * *

Florence and Sam were hunkered around her desk craning their heads towards her computer speakers. Florence had unscrambled the audio file from Milquetoast but the sound quality wasn't great.

So far it had just consisted of an elderly man with a Greek accent giving instructions to two or maybe three other people on the call, with the others seemingly agreeing with whatever he had to say.

"Operation Medusa is ready to commence my friends…"

Sam scribbled down 'Operation Medusa!!'.

"The target will be acquired this weekend. We have contacts inside the residence who will notify us when he is alone…" continued the recording.

Sam scribbled down 'this weekend!!'.

"He will be suitably incapacitated, restrained and the anaesthetised…"

Sam scribbled down '~~anneesthattize~~' '~~aneserthertised~~' '~~aneathasatize~~' 'knocked out!!'

"We will have one of our drivers ready to transport him to room 1012"

Florence paused the audio file. "Room 1012, hmmm. Thoughts?"

Sam tried his absolute hardest to look thoughtful. "I… think… maybe… it's a room number? Like in a hotel perhaps?"

Florence looked at Sam, very disappointed. "A hotel room. You think? Jesus Sam, I know it's a flipping hotel room number, but which hotel!?"

"Oh yeah. I see. Well I guess a really big one?"

Florence thought for a second, and then spun round in her chair to reach her other laptop. She tapped in *MI51.co.uk* and started to search the database on the encrypted intranet.

"Ok, so in London, there are only four hotels with more than a thousand rooms. The Regal, The Mayfair Plaza Hotel, The Park Royal Hotel and The Sutherland.

So it looks like The Sutherland closed last year and The Regal is undergoing restoration, which narrows it down to just two possible locations."

"But how does Milquetoast know it's the prime minister they're after?"

"He doesn't, he's guessing. But it's a good guess. And if you're right that Josie and her pals are innocent then the real antagonists could still be out there, and that's what we could be listening to right now. Following on from the Home Office Minister and the Chancellor of the Exchequer, the next logical choice would be the PM. Especially if they're calling it *Operation Medusa!*"

"You mean because he's like, really ugly?"

"No dummy because Perseus chopped her head off. They might be saying the prime minister is the *head* of the British Government."

Sam nodded, gravely. Then he grinned and started bouncing in his seat a bit. "This is great, isn't it?! It's like we're doing a *real* investigation with *real* detective work."

"Sure Sam, I'm having a blast."

"And I'm like Mel Gibson in *Lethal Weapon* and you're Danny Glover, and we're chewing the fat and bouncing ideas off each other, and having loads of banter like real partners, and figuring out what the bad guys are up to!"

"I don't have partners anymore, Sam."

Sam wasn't listening. "Or like *Bad Boys*. No, no, like in *21 Jump Street!* You'd be Channing Tatum and I'd be Jonah Hill and we'd bust into the hotel room and we'd be like *Blam! Blam! Blam!*" Sam mimed shooting an imaginary firearm at various things in Florence's office.

Florence looked at him, waiting for him to finish shooting things.

"Blam! Blam! Blam!" he continued, taking aim around the room.

Sam looked at Florence. His imaginary gun was still loaded but he'd run out of targets.

"Have you finished?" asked Florence patiently.

"Yeah, I've finished. Thanks."

Florence pressed play on the audio file again. They listened carefully, trying to pick up further clues but there just seemed to be vague chatter that kept cutting out. A man was asking about rope and a woman's voice was talking about guns but nothing that would help give any firm details away.

Florence rocked back in her seat and frowned. She looked up at her notes on the whiteboard to see if any of the information tied in with her earlier investigations, but there was no obvious link. They were all using codenames on the audio tape so it was impossible to identify who they'd be looking for anyway.

Sam slumped back in his seat too. He was getting a bit bored listening to the audio file; he was pretty sure he'd never seen *Starsky & Hutch* sit at a desk listening to a tape for two hours. It sounded like they were wrapping up their conversation anyway. One of the guys had checked out already and the old guy was saying goodbye and good luck to the others.

"...Show no fear, young prodigy. Your mission will soon be complete and you will be welcomed into the brethren of the Crimson Guardsmen. You'll return home as a hero of Crypteia."

Florence leant forward with interest. Crypteia? That was an organisation she hadn't heard of before. Perhaps they were dealing with someone new, but who was this *prodigy* he was talking to?

"I will not fail you, Your Exthellenthy," replied a different voice on the tape. *"And we have nothing to fear from their thpecial intellgenth thervices."*

Sam and Florence both sat bolt upright and stared at each other. They definitely recognised that voice.

* * *

Sam and Florence were stunned. Hearing Leo's distinctive mispronunciations on the audio file had sent a chill down both of their spines.

"What the actual fuck?" asked Florence. "That bad-speaking goofball *is* mixed up in this. Is he really their secret prodigy?"

"He seemed so nice," replied Sam. "He literally makes the world's tastiest baclava."

"Right, listen Sam. I'm going for a cigarette then I'll let Milquetoast know what we're doing. You scan these two hotels on the Black Knight satellite and figure out a backway in. Then we'll go and check out room 1012 in both of them." Florence picked up her cigarettes and lighter and threw her jacket on.

"And don't go anywhere without me, Sam. We ship out in ten minutes."

Florence left Sam in the office, jumped in the lift and waited for it to plod slowly up to ground level. She hurried through the video store and out onto the pavement where she paused to light up her cigarette.

She inhaled deeply and then started meandering slowly up the street so that she wasn't smoking directly by the Videodrome entrance. Sub-consciously Florence clocked a police van parked up across the street, but she gave it no further thought.

She wandered as far as the end of the block and then stopped at a street corner absent-mindedly exhaling smoke rings. A pair of killer heels in the window of a shoe-shop caught her eye, and Florence gazed at them through the glass pane as she finished her cigarette.

Although her eyes were drawn to the shoes, in her head all Florence was doing was replaying the words she had heard Leo say on the tape. '*...We have nothing to fear from their thpecial intellgenth thervices.*'

Leo had made no attempt to hide the fact he was Greek, but as far as she was aware there were no particular terrorist threats to the UK from that particular part of the Mediterranean. If anything the Greeks were considered strong allies. So who were these Crypteia clowns and what were they after?

As she continued to gaze through the shop window and ponder, she didn't notice the police van that had quietly relocated. It pulled up slowly behind her and swung open its rear doors. Florence gradually became recognisant of a vehicle engine purring somewhere in the background.

As she happened to glance back, a hood was pulled rapidly over her head. Before she could react, her arms were snapped behind her back and a set of cable ties jerked her wrists together, knocking the cigarette out of her hand. Florence banged her shin as she was bundled roughly into the rear of the van. She heard the doors slam shut behind her as the engine revved and the van sped away noisily.

* * *

Florence had left the computer on her desk unlocked to allow Sam to scope out the internal layout of London's

Mayfair Plaza Hotel using the Black Knight satellite. He did a quick scan and quickly figured out a rear door they used for unloading laundry would be the best route in without having to go through the hotel's main entrance foyer, and a service lift could get him up to the twenty-second floor relatively inconspicuously.

He was about to start planning a similar route for the Park Royal Hotel but then got distracted when he noticed an awful lot of other files on Florence's desktop which looked much more interesting. They all had rather intriguing filenames, but Sam knew he mustn't start nosing around - it would be terribly unprofessional if he snooped through her computer files. And it would surely breach some kind of security protocol. Surely?

He swivelled in Florence's chair, wondering when she'd be back. She'd already been gone ten minutes and would no doubt stroll back through the door any second. The thing is, it wasn't like these were encrypted files that were hidden away anywhere. They were right there, just sitting on her desktop.

Maybe he could just take a quick peek?

No thought Sam, he mustn't. He was better than that. Even if he was bored waiting for Florence, and feeling a little nosey, he really must show some restraint and resist the urge to snoop.

Well okay, let's have a look at just one, thought Sam. He chose a folder with a curious name; *Xenu*. He opened it up and then picked out a document to scan through.

Classified: Confidential..............
Casefile: Xenu

Xenu was a crazy intergalactic dictator who lived nearly seventy five million years ago. Xenu sent billions of aliens out into the galaxy because his planet was getting

overpopulated, and some ended up on planet Earth which was a prison planet he called Teegeeack. Once they were there, he activated countless volcanoes and other disasters, which just left behind the floating souls of the aliens. These souls, called the Thetans, were forced to watch a propaganda movie for thirty six days, implanting them with complex memories. These memories can be shed only through sacred knowledge which will enable individuals to acquire superhero powers such as mind-reading and psycho-kinesis.

What the hell was this, wondered Sam. Was Florence investigating some kind of sinister alien invasion? He read further down the document, where he found that Florence had added some comments of her own;

Level 4 Investigation - Xenu Executive Summary

Wow. This is some huge horseshit right here. Not so much as a conspiracy, but more of a scam. These scriptures from the cult of Scientology were the original work of science fiction writer L. Ron Hubbard and have since been used as the basis for this new age religion. Unlocking this sacred knowledge costs followers of this religion thousands and thousands of pounds. Funny that. I wonder if Xenu planned on it being so expensive 75 million years ago.

Filed under scams - No further action required.

Agent Lawrence

Dept. of Conspiracy

Sam closed the file down and figured he'd better not snoop any more right now in case Florence walked back in. He swivelled on her chair some more, wondering how much longer she would be. *Surely she should be back by now*. He decided to see how many times he could swivel in twenty seconds. After four attempts his average appeared to be seven times per twenty seconds.

He looked up at the clock. Florence had been gone for nearly thirty minutes. *Where the hell was she?* Perhaps he should go and look for her? Or maybe he should go and check out one of the hotels on his own? No, *stay here until she's back*, she had said to him. He decided to open up another file to help take his mind off waiting for her.

Classified: Restricted.............. Casefile: Stargate

Australian exo-political commentator Michael Salla claimed the United States and its allies invaded Iraq in order to take control of Saddam Hussein's access to alien weaponry through a Stargate. Salla claims that aliens from a secret tenth planet in the solar system have been interfering in human politics.

Sam knew he was no expert but predicted that this theory was also bollocks. He skimmed through Florence's executive summary which quickly drew the same conclusion.

Level 2 Investigation - Stargate Executive Summary

I'm not sure why these wingnut investigations keep getting sent down to my Conspiracy Department. This one looks like

nonsense written by a prepubescent teenager.

Filed under Timewasters - No further action required.

Agent Lawrence
Dept. of Conspiracy

Sam looked up at the clock. Maybe he should make himself a cup of coffee and just be patient. He went over to the machine in the corner, placed a cup under the spout and decided to rely on his proven lucky dip technique. The lights on the machine twinkled, the teeny tiny chimney went *pssshht* and the cup filled with an inoffensive light-brown liquid.

Sam sat back at his footstool where there was less temptation to snoop, and slowly sipped from the cup, correctly identifying the brown liquid as tea rather than coffee. He wasn't really a 'tea' kind of guy but decided to eek it out in order to try and pass some time. Sam found that apparently it was possible to make a cup of tea last twelve minutes if you limited it to a small sip every twenty seconds.

Jesus, where was she?

He decided to call her on her mobile phone — if she got cross with him for interrupting her smoke break, then so be it. He looked up her number on his call list and waited for it to ring. Seconds later it started ringing, from a phone inside her drawer.

It was at that moment that one of the TV screens on the office wall caught his eye. The channel was tuned into Sky News and the scrolling news banner read 'UK Prime Minister Gone Missing'. Sam immediately grabbed the remote control and turned up the volume.

A news correspondent standing outside Chequers was reporting that the PM Henry Morley had mysteriously disappeared from his country home that morning.

Apparently his shoes and socks were found in a wooded area within the grounds but, other than that, there were no clues and they believed he may have suffered some kind of mental breakdown. Sam realised this was more than likely linked to the audio file he and Florence had listened to. Milquetoast was right - they had been targeting the prime minister.

Sam couldn't wait any longer for Florence to return. He scribbled a message to her on a *post-it* note and stuck it to her desk: 'Didn't know where you were. Milquetoast was right! Check out Sky News!! Gone to investigate the Mayfair Plaza Hotel, See you there, ~~Love~~ ~~Luv~~ From Sam.'

He grabbed his bum bag, left the office and hurried up to the Betamax store. Once he got there, he tried to figure out how he would summon the correct underground lift to transport him to somewhere near the Mayfair Plaza Hotel.

Fortunately for Sam, he'd correctly ascertained that the Mayfair Plaza Hotel was located just around the corner from Paddington, London. He scanned carefully through the children's section until he stumbled across a box set of the 1975 stop motion BBC TV series *Paddington Bear*.

Sam took the cassette out if its cover and slotted it into the video player, hoping his hunch would work. At the very least he was hoping the lift wouldn't deposit him in deepest, darkest Peru. Luckily, after a brief but uncomfortably noisy underground lift journey, he found himself emerging through a door on to Platform 1 of Paddington Station.

* * *

Meanwhile, the white police van that had Florence bundled in the back was being driven erratically through the side streets of London. The driver was swerving in and out of traffic and narrowly avoiding pedestrians. As the tyres screeched around corners and bounced off kerbs, Florence found herself flung from one side of the van and then back again. She managed to regain her balance and wedged herself into a corner. After a five minute journey, the van finally pulled into an empty car park and the engine fell silent.

Florence, with the hood still firmly in place, composed herself and managed to sit herself upright on one of the bench seats. For somebody who had just been kidnapped, she was remarkably unflustered. It wasn't her first time. She listened carefully as the rear doors reopened, two people stepped into the back with her and then the doors slammed shut again.

One of her assailants spoke with an Italian-American accent. "We're gonna make you an offer you can't refuse," he started.

"Oh for fuck's sake," replied Florence. "Is that supposed to be a mafia accent?"

"Look, you're in a lot of trouble, lady!" said the assailant, angrily.

"Listen you pair of idiots. I know exactly who you are. Can you take this stupid hood off?"

Neither of the assailants said anything, wondering if this was some kind of bluff.

"Josie Griffiths, I saw you driving, you twat. And Red Kendall, that is the worst Italian-American accent I've ever heard from a Scottish person. Take the fucking hood off before I kick both of your arses."

Josie and Red looked at each other, a little disappointed that their plan had lasted as little time as it had. Josie pulled the hood off Florence's head.

"Well you're still our wee prisoner and we've got questions for you!" threatened Red, trying to retake the upper hand.

"Sure, sweet cheeks. What's on your mind?"

Red wasn't okay with being called sweet cheeks. This wasn't how he felt interrogations should normally go.

"Now you listen to me ya wee strumpet. You're about to get dragged behind this van if you're not careful lass."

Florence smiled, sweetly.

"Red, don't," whispered Josie.

"What? I thought we were gonna do that good cop/bad cop thing on her?"

"Yeah I know. But I don't think that's going to work now."

"Look morons," interrupted Florence. "I've been kidnapped three times before, I've been interrogated twice and there's really not much you can threaten me with that I haven't heard before. So ask me what you want to ask me so I can get out of this shit heap. I'm extremely busy today."

Josie took a deep breath and cut to the chase. "Fine. Why did you set us up?"

"We didn't set you up. Your friend set you up," replied Florence.

"Who? Agent bloody Juniper?"

"No, not bloody Sam. We think your friend Leo has something to do with all this. We're not sure yet, but we think he might be the insurgent we've been looking for."

"Leo? Why the hell would Leo set us up? We're on the same side!"

"As I said, we're not sure yet. But we think he left a trail of breadcrumbs that was designed to implicate all of you. Unfortunately he got away, and you guys ended up carrying the can for him. We think that's what he has been working on for months - to find some stooges to use as decoys. He's not as dumb as he seems."

Red and Josie studied her face carefully as she explained, trying to sense if she was telling the truth this time. After the bullshit they'd been told in the café, they weren't so sure.

"And did Sam know that you were sending your bloody stormtroopers in? Did he know they were going to shoot Elijah?"

Florence sighed. "Sam didn't know anything about it. He doesn't know his arse from his elbow most of the time. But no, the order was given from up high. You shouldn't be blaming him."

Florence paused and looked down at the floor of the van. Then she looked at Red, directly in his eyes.

"Look, I'm sorry about your friend Elijah. The situation escalated so quickly, and we managed it so badly. Sometimes we have to make decisions very quickly but, in this case, we made a lot of bad decisions in a short space of time. I was the one trying to supervise the mission in the control room, but it was a mess. Comms were shit. Sam shouldn't have been put there. And I handled it badly. I'm sorry."

Red eyed Florence carefully but said nothing.

Florence then looked at Josie. "Sam might be a lot of things; childish, irrational, clumsy, gullible, inappropriate, confusing, dozy and also a bit odd sometimes. But he isn't the one you should be blaming. It's me you should be blaming. I didn't want a partner, but I had one. And I should've done a better job looking out for him."

Josie was a little relieved to hear she hadn't entirely misjudged Sam's character but was still suspicious about him.

"But he lied about his name, didn't he? Where the hell did Jennifer come from?"

"That was me too." Florence sighed. "Look, I know what you think of us, and I understand what you think of our organisation. But you've got to understand, it's a dangerous world and we're fighting shadows every single day of our lives. Our enemies aren't obvious anymore and we never know who's telling the truth or who's lying to our faces. Unfortunately, you were caught up in a web of lies this time. Speaking of which, aren't you two supposed to be in jail?"

Josie and Red ignored her questions and sat in silence, pondering what they were going to do with their hostage now.

"While you two decide what you're going to do next, do you mind if I have a cigarette seeing as you interrupted my last one?"

"Umm. No, I guess not. Go ahead," said Josie.

Florence's arms were still bound behind her. In a single swift movement, she rotated her shoulders and swung both arms straight up and over her head, and then slipped her hands easily out of the cable ties. "I've always had surprisingly thick wrists and shockingly tiny hands," she winked.

Josie and Red froze, realising she was suddenly no longer incapacitated. Florence calmly took the inscribed zippo lighter and cigarettes out of her front pocket and lit one up. She took a puff of her cigarette, turned a dial on her lighter and then pointed it directly at the rear of the van.

"I've really got to go," Florence said. She flicked a trigger on her zippo lighter and a jet-powered blast of nitrogen instantly fired out of it blowing the doors clean off the back of the van. Florence stepped out through the gap where the rear doors once were and into the car park.

She took another puff on her cigarette and casually started walking back to the office.

Josie and Red watched her leave and said nothing.

Sixteen Candles

The drugs were wearing off and the Prime Minister of the United Kingdom was starting to become lucid. His memory was clouded and he had a throbbing headache, but he tried hard to keep his eyes open and to focus on his surroundings. As his senses realigned themselves he realised he was already standing naked on an antique coffee table and seemed to be in the somewhat regal setting of a mock Tudor hotel room.

"I trutht you are comfortable, Prime Minithter?"

"Who? Who's there?" Henry's vision was struggling to identify the blurry figure across the room who was speaking to him.

"I suggest you try not to move, Prime Minister. If you happen to topple off that table, the noothe around your neck is likely to make your stay here conthiderably shorter."

Henry realised a thick rope was forming a noose around his neck. He looked upwards and saw the rope was secured to a timber beam above with his wrists bound by a silk sash behind his back. Although he was mostly naked, he could feel something covering his modesty. He looked down trying to make out what it was he was wearing. Was it a pair of shorts? Was it a large pair of pants? He tried to crane his neck forward to see over his flabby belly. It was a nappy.

He pieced the fragmented information in his head together. The last thing he remembered was walking through the sunny glade at Chequers, and now he found himself standing on a vintage coffee table, with a noose around his neck, wearing a giant adult nappy.

"I hope you have a bloody good lawyer, whoever you are," growled Henry.

"Be assured Prime Minister, you really are not in any position to threaten me."

The nausea from the drugs was wearing off but Henry's legs were trembling, and beads of perspiration were starting to trickle from his brow. Each time he moved he could feel the noose tightening around his throat.

"You see Prime Minister, you will not be leaving this room alive. When I remove that table thupporting you, your neck will thnap like a twig, you will defecate profusely in your nappy and your body will be discovered sometime tomorrow by a shocked maid."

"This is nonsense. You can do what you like to me, but I am British, we are made of sterner stuff! You think you can destroy my legacy with your vile scheming?"

"Your only *legathy* will be to be remembered as the Prime Minister who killed himthelf partaking in an orgy of auto-erotic asphyxiation. Your reputation Prime Minister, will be dethtroyed along with you."

"You're mad," snorted Henry. "You've lost your bloody marbles!"

"Yes Prime Minister! You are abtholutely right! We have lost our marbles, haven't we? Or more correctly, they were taken from us weren't they!"

"What? What are you blathering on about?!"

"You have something that belongth to us don't you. The Parthenon Marbles, Prime Minister."

"You mean this is about the Elgin Marbles?! The bloody Elgin Marbles?!"

"Indeed. And after two hundred yearth, it is time for you to pay dearly for your theft."

"This is ridiculous. There are channels of negotiation for such things. Your petty terrorism will have no effect on this Government or our country. You are an insignificant fool!"

"Inthignificant am I, Prime Minister?" Leo sneered at Henry's outrage and started blowing into an inflatable doll. With each breath, the flesh-coloured balloon person started to take her shape.

"Say hello to your new girlfriend, Prime Minister. Your DNA will be liberally shared with her after your untimely death. And you can exthpect her to be wearing the clothes and wig of your mother when they find you. You dithguthting man, you!"

* * *

After watching Florence dramatically blow their back doors off in the car park, Red and Josie decided they would do their best to patch up the van. Red had found a leather tool bag stowed with the spare wheel. He used it to peel off the adhesive vinyl stickers identifying their van as a police vehicle, and then removed the blue lights and sirens from the roof. Meanwhile, Josie had done her best to re-attach the rear doors with a mixture of woodscrews, copper wiring and gaffer tape.

They were now sitting in Peckham High Street eating cheese and tomato sandwiches.

"So, you think anybody is actually looking for us, Red? We're sitting in a stripped out police van with the rear doors half-hanging off in the middle of Peckham eating a meal deal."

"Aye, I'm really not sure Josie. If we are on the run, I dinna think they're trying very hard to find us."

Red spotted a female police officer meandering along the pavement towards them. "Okay, there's only one of her. Watch to see if she calls for back up on her radio. If she tries to arrest us, I'll twat her and you get us out of here sharpish."

The WPC was chatting to an old man standing outside the fish shop. She then wandered a bit further and gave a cheery hello to the people inside the greengrocers, before looking across at Josie and Red in the van. She frowned briefly, walked up to the driver's side and tapped on the window.

Josie wound the window down two inches. "Yes?"

"Hello there!" beamed the WPC. "Just so's you know, you're parked in a loading bay, sweetheart. If you're not unloading, you're going to want to move on."

"Erm... okay."

"Hey, don't panic," she smiled. "It's not like I'm a *traffic warden* or anything, I won't tell on you! Just don't want you lovely people to get yourselves a ticket!"

"Sure. We'll move right now," replied Josie.

They watched in the side mirrors as the happiest police officer in Peckham carried on her philanthropic patrol down the pavement.

"She didn't bat an eyelid," said Red.

"So what now?" asked Josie. "Maybe we should drive to Mrs Bimble's house? I need to go and pick up Ralphy."

Red and Josie finished their sandwiches and headed off southward in the direction of Croydon. It took about half an hour to weave through the traffic and, by the time they got there, it was starting to rain.

They parked on the road just outside, walked up Mrs Bimble's path and rang the doorbell. There was no reply after a minute, so they rang the bell again. They heard some bumping around inside, and then Mrs Bimble's husband Norman opened the door. Josie had never been sure Mr Bimble actually existed as he was reportedly always in his loft playing with his model railway, yet here he was blinking like a confused mole seeing daylight for the first time.

"Hello, young lady. Can I help you?"

"Hi. Yes, we're friends of your wife Mr Bimble. Is she in?"

"I'm afraid you've missed her, she went off with another one of your little gang. A chap, the one with the funny voice."

"Leo? She went off with Leo?"

"That's the fellow. Would you like to come in and wait?"

Josie and Red exchanged worried glances. Florence had warned them that Leo might be dangerous. If Mrs Bimble was with him, she could be in trouble."

"Sure, we'll come in and wait," joined in Red, hoping they might get some idea of where they had headed off to.

Mr Bimble opened the door wider to allow them in. "I'll make us all a nice cup of tea."

Ten minutes later, Red and Josie were sat in Mr and Mrs Bimble's lounge drinking lukewarm milky tea.

"So do you know where they might have been going?" asked Red.

"I have no idea, young man," replied Mr Bimble. "I'm afraid Iris doesn't tell me all her comings and goings. She likes to go to her church near Hyde Park on Sunday mornings but other than that I'm usually the last to know what she gets up to."

"Iris, that's a pretty name," Josie had only ever been introduced to her as Mrs Bimble and she'd never volunteered her first name.

"Yes, I suppose it is a pretty name now I think of it. I remember years ago she told me that Iris was the Greek Goddess of the Rainbow. Rather sweet, really."

"Is she Greek then? I never knew that?"

"Well most people wouldn't, she left a long time ago. But yes, she was born in Mystras, a little village just outside Sparta. We met there back in the 60s when I worked for the Foreign Office."

"A real life Spartan, eh?" laughed Red. "I'll bet she was a fearless warrior in those days!"

Mr Bimble smiled. "Oh yes. Quite the gladiator she was!"

Josie sipped her disgusting tea. "So, she didn't mention when she would be back?"

"I'm afraid not. I just heard the door slam and off she went with that young chap and the dog."

"Ralphy, of course!" Josie's eyes lit up. "Red, Ralph is chipped! If I can log in we should be able to figure out where they are!"

Red handed Josie the phone from the van, and she signed onto her *Dog Finder* account. "Got him!"

Josie thanked Mr Bimble for the tea and Red left his untouched on the side. They hurried back out to the van and plotted a route to Ralph's location.

"Josie," said Red. "If Leo really is holding Mrs Bimble captive, we could probably do with some back up."

"Like who? I don't fancy calling the police in case they are actually on the lookout for us."

"I think you know who."

Josie was puzzled for a second. Then she reached into her pocket and took out the elegant looking business card with just a telephone number on it. She started dialling the number.

* * *

Sam ran through the concourse at Paddington Station and headed towards the Mayfair Plaza Hotel. As he got to the trade entrance around the back, he saw a trolley of laundry sitting by the rear door. He rifled through the pile of fabrics and pulled out a chef's jacket and matching hat. He put them both on and strutted confidently into the hotel.

"Who the fuck are you?" called a voice.

Sam looked round and saw a guy dressed as a bellboy looking at him. "I'm the back-up chef, you fucking benny," replied Sam, trying his best to sound like Gordon Ramsay.

"You're late, Fabricio is looking for you in the kitchen!"

What would Gordon say, wondered Sam.

"Fabricio can suck my balls," he shouted back, "I've been making prawn fucking vol-au-vents."

Sam carried on walking through the laundry room trying his best to look like he knew where he was going. He'd tried to memorise the layout of the building that he'd downloaded from the Black Knight satellite images but was stumped when he got to the two doors on the far side of the laundry room.

"You do know where the kitchen is don't you?!" shouted the bellboy across the room.

"Of course I bloody do, I'm a chef." Sam opened one of the doors, which turned out to be a cupboard full of brooms.

"Then what are you doing in the broom cupboard, you twat?!"

"Well I need a fucking broom don't I, you… shit… minge!" Sam was quite enjoying the impromptu foul-mouthed chef alias he'd spontaneously invented for himself. *This is what it must be like being Florence*, he thought.

Sam grabbed one of the brooms, closed the cupboard and then opened the adjacent door. He followed the corridor up and found the goods lift he was looking for. The lift doors opened, and Sam quickly stepped in. A woman in a tightly fitting maid's uniform was already in the lift, adjusting the hem on her skirt.

"Oh hey!" the woman said, standing upright.

"Hi," said Sam.

"What floor you headed to?"

"Uh, twenty-two please."

The woman in the tight maid's uniform leant across him and helpfully pressed the button for level twenty-two. Sam couldn't help but breathe in her perfume - he thought it smelt like pic'n'mix. They both stood and waited as the lift started to rise up the shaft.

"Why's a chef going up to twenty-two?" she asked.

Christ, more questions thought Sam. "Uh, I've got to… cut up some… sandwiches."

"Right. What's with the broom?"

"Huh? Oh, this? I need to sweep up… some… lettuce. From the sandwiches."

"Right."

They both stood in silence and waited some more as the lift slowly continued to rise. The silence was causing Sam some tension. Sexual tension. *Jesus, what was it about a maid's uniform that made him feel all unnecessary?* He pulled the strap on his bum bag around the side of his waist so that the pouch was sitting over the front part of his trousers.

The maid looked at his bum bag and stifled a giggle. "Nice little package you got there. What do you chef guys keep in there then?"

What the fuck does a chef keep in his bum bag? thought Sam. Steak knives? A cheese grater? A spatula?

"It's for… emergency… herbs."

"Emergency herbs?"

"Yeah, you know. Tarragon, oregano, thyme, frankincense. That sort of thing."

"You know frankincense isn't a herb, right?"

"It's not? I mean, sure it's not."

"Of course not. They put it in perfume, you loon."

"Yeah, I know that. We use it for the cutlery. We rub it… on the cutlery. To make it… you know… smell nice."

The maid screwed her face up as she tried to comprehend if this explanation made any sense whatsoever. The lift pinged as it reached level twenty-two. Sam stepped out through the doors, being careful that his bum bag stayed in position. As the doors closed, the maid continued up the building and Sam breathed a sigh of relief.

* * *

Florence got back to the Conspiracy Office and saw that Sam wasn't there. She looked at the missed calls on her mobile phone and the *post-it* note Sam had left for her on her desk.

'Didn't know where you were? Milquetoast was right! Check out Sky News!! Gone to investigate the Mayfair Plaza Hotel, See you there, ~~Love~~ ~~Luv~~ From Sam.'

Dammit she thought. She looked up at the TV screen and realised that Sam was referring to the breaking story about the mysterious disappearance of Henry Morley. She knew if Sam did catch up with Leo he could be well out of his depth.

"Right, let's find out exactly where you are, Sam."

Florence activated the London pigeon-cam fleet and tuned them in to pick out Sam's likeness.

Pigeons across London stopped their pecking at the pavement and immediately took to the skies, swooping between buildings and circling crowds of people. Where a pedestrian's likeness was not visible to an individual pigeon's camera, they were programmed to release a harmless liquid deposit on the person to encourage them to hold their position and look up towards the sky. There were an unusually high number of people tweeting complaints about pigeon-poop that morning.

"Gotcha!" said Florence as pigeon-cam No.402 picked him out going into the hotel near Paddington Basin.

Florence grabbed her Mk VII Surveillance kit, threw it in her purple rucksack and then scanned her desk, considering what else she might need for surveillance. She picked up the portable speaker that was still linked to the dog-mic, threw in a burner phone and then grabbed her Luger pistol out of her drawer, sliding it into her waistband.

Satisfied she was suitably kitted out, Florence headed straight up to the Betamax section where she noticed that the plastic cover for the 1975 boxset of Paddington Bear was still open on the desk. *Good lad* thought Florence. She had imagined that Sam might have got himself a taxi or something and was impressed to see he'd used the much swifter underground lift system.

"Hang in there, buddy," she said to herself. "I'm on my way."

* * *

"Felicitations of the day to you, this is Mr Milquetoast at your assistance. How may I be of service?" Milquetoast was a stickler for rigorous good manners, even more so when answering the phone.

"Huh? Is this Mr Milquetoast?" asked Red, rubbing his forehead.

"It most certainly is. And what is thy bidding, may I ask?"

Red looked at Josie who could see he was confused by the voice on speakerphone. She decided perhaps it would have been better if she had made the call after all. "Mr Milquetoast. This is Josie Griffiths. We met in the prison van when you… umm… helped us escape?"

"I most certainly did no such thing young lady! If I remember the incident correctly, I merely elected to take up the offer of a lift from a kindly security officer. If those fine men subsequently displayed esquivalience in their responsibilities to escort you to prison, then I'm afraid that really is no business of mine."

"Esqui-va-li…?"

"Esquivalience, dear girl. It's a word that means the wilful avoidance of one's official responsibilities. Or, more interestingly, it's actually not a word at all! It's actually an entirely fabricated word, invented by the authors of the New Oxford American Dictionary for the purpose of identifying plagiarism of their fine manuscript. Quite the ruse if you ask me."

"Mr Milquetoast, we really have no idea what you're talking about. But we think we need help. And we're not sure who else we can ask?"

"In a bit of a pickle are you? Well perhaps I may be able to assist in unpickling you."

"We think an old lady called Mrs Bimble might be in danger. You see, she was looking after my dog Ralphy when we got kidnapped by those psychos in the helicopters."

"I'm quite sure you weren't kidnapped Ms Griffiths. Arrested, maybe. Detained, certainly! But kidnapped - goodness me, no."

"Whatever. Listen, my dog is chipped, and we've been tracking him. He's somewhere driving around London at the moment, near Paddington I think. But Mrs Bimble doesn't drive.

"And I assume neither does Ralphy?"

"What? No! Of course not. But her husband said Leo was at their house. If he's as ruthless as your *Agent Florence* says he is, then both Mrs Bimble and Ralphy could be in danger."

"I see."

Red backed Josie up. "We're not scared of dealing with that barmcake Leo on his own, Milquetoast. But if he's part of some sort of splinter cell, then we'd need some back up. And it's not like we can just call up the police is it?"

"Given you are currently *on the run* as it were, I would suggest not Reginald."

"So can you help us, Mr Milquetoast?" asked Josie.

"Well, let's see now. Near Paddington, you say. Where exactly do you think this rascal Leo could be headed? Does he have an abode in that area that you know of?"

"No, his house was the one that burnt down in Croydon. I know Mrs Bimble goes to church near Hyde Park on Sundays, but Leo's never mentioned going to it."

"Hmm." Mr Milquetoast went quiet for a few moments, considering his options. Red and Josie looked at each other, wondering if he might have fallen asleep.

"Ok," said Milquetoast. "Here's what I think…"

* * *

Sam tried to look as innocent as possible as he searched around the twenty-second floor checking the room numbers. He didn't want to attract any more attention from nosey staff members. 1004, 1006, 1008. Sam followed the sequence till he got to room number 1012. Once outside he put his ear to the door to see if he could hear anything to indicate if Leo was inside, but he could hear nothing. He glanced up and down the corridor to see if anyone was around - the coast was clear.

Sam reached into his Mk IV Surveillance kit and pulled out the torch. He pressed the red button and pointed it through the hotel room door. The torch instantly provided visibility through to the other side of the door. Sam could see it was a particularly grand suite — not your standard hotel room.

The invisibility torch wasn't powerful enough to see through more than a single wall, so he couldn't make out if there was anything occurring on the far side of the suite, behind the central partition. But from what he could see there didn't seem to be anything too suspicious going on in the sleeping area. He could see a couple of Winchester armchairs, a Corby trouser-press, some neatly folded clothes on hangers and a blonde woman lying fully clothed on a four poster bed.

Darn, thought Sam. He should've gone to the Park Royal Hotel first. Maybe he should try and call Florence again and get her to head straight there. He walked back towards the lift and got his phone out, when he suddenly heard an angry shout.

"God damn it, you're not having the bloody maaarbles!!"

Sam spun around on the spot and ran back to the door. The voices inside were raised now and he could hear a vicious argument breaking out inside.

An old man in a dressing gown opened the door to neighbouring room 1014 and stuck his head into the corridor. "What the bugger is going on out here?" he shouted.

Sam didn't have time to explain. He darted towards the man's suite. "Room service, sir?" he asked, barging past him. Sam raced through to the old man's bedroom area and turned the torch on again, this time pointing it through the wall adjoined to room 1012.

Sam and the old man in the dressing gown both stared in disbelief as they looked straight through the wall into the next room. Inside 1012, they could both clearly see the Prime Minister Henry Morley standing semi-naked on a small table with a noose around his neck. Next to him was an angry looking Leo, with his foot up on the table ready to kick it away.

"Well, I say!" exclaimed the old man, scratching his head.

Sam didn't have time to explain and couldn't wait for help. He hoped the stud walls dividing the rooms would be thin enough to let him burst through with his raw brute strength. He took a few steps back and psyched himself up. He had space for about eight full paces in order to get up to full sprinting speed and shoulder barge his way through the wall.

"C'mon, c'mon, beast-mode here we go…" he said, psyching himself up, and then proceeded to launch himself at full pelt towards the wall, dropping his shoulder just before he made contact.

Sam hit the wall hard, rebounded straight back off and landed flat on his arse. "Motherfu—" he stopped himself, as the old man in the dressing gown already looked a little shocked. Sam quickly reached into his bum bag and pulled out the lip balm. Eugene's instruction echoed in Sam's head; 'twist clockwise for balm!"

Sam pointed the lip balm directly at the wall and twisted it *anti*-clockwise. A blazing red flare fired out of the tube and shot straight into the wall, crashing through the plasterboard and spiralling out of control as it rocketed through into room 1012.

Leo's shocked face stared back at him through the newly-made hole. Sam launched himself towards the cavity attempting to perform a breathtaking swan dive, but his torso got jammed in the hole, ruining his dramatic rescue.

Leo was dancing around trying to avoid being struck by the flare as it fizzed and screeched in circles around the hotel room. The prime minister was trembling as he turned his head just enough to see Sam dangling helplessly, halfway through the wall.

"Push me!" shouted Sam, hoping the old man in the dressing gown would give him a shove the rest of the way. Sam felt the old man's bony hands on his backside, followed by a lacklustre push.

After ten seconds of whizzing around the room, the flare shot out through the window, raining debris on the cars down below. Leo stopped cowering and walked menacingly towards the coffee table.

"Leo don't do this!" pleaded Sam, still wedged as the old man thrusted at his buttocks.

Leo looked at Sam, and then back at Henry. "Tho long, Prime Minister!" He kicked the table from under him, dropping all of Henry's weight onto his neck.

The old man in the dressing gown gave one last, mighty push on Sam's buttocks sending him tumbling through into Leo's room. Leo grabbed the inflatable woman off the bed and threw it towards Sam in an effort to distract him, and then turned and scrambled out of the room, colliding into the Corby trouser-press on his way out the door.

Sam rolled himself back onto his feet and ran towards Henry as his body jerked and convulsed on the rope. Sam threw his arms around him at nappy height and lifted as hard as he could, trying to take the weight off his neck.

"Are you sure you're room service?" asked the old man in the dressing gown, poking his head through the hole.

"Get help," gasped Sam. "I'm not sure how long I can hold him."

The old man did as he was told and picked up the phone on the bedside table. Sam kept his arms clamped around Henry, trying desperately to lift him up towards the ceiling.

Henry's face was turning beetroot red, and he was gurgling and spluttering.

"Hang in there, sir," encouraged Sam, "I won't let you go."

Two hotel staff ran out of the lift and arrived at the door of the room together. Quickly recognising the desperate situation, one of them immediately helped Sam support Henry while the other stood on a chair to untie the knot attaching him to the rafter above.

As the rope came loose, Sam's strength gave way and Henry collapsed onto the floor, gasping for air. One of the hotel guys was already calling to reception for back up and an ambulance while the other stared at the hole in the wall, confused.

"Sir," said Sam, "Speak to me, are you okay?"

"Don't worry about me," croaked Henry. "Don't let that bastard get away!"

* * *

The underground lift system should only take a minute or so to get to Paddington and from there Florence knew she would quickly be able to catch up with Sam before he got out of his depth.

Florence pulled the iron shutter closed and waited as the gears engaged and the lift-car started to vibrate along the shaft. As the gears rattled and pulleys heaved, she checked the time on her watch. *Great, he couldn't have got far.*

The lift car suddenly clunked, the lights flickered and then the whole contraption fell eerily silent. Florence froze and listened for signs of movement.

"Shitting hell."

She banged the lift-car wall, expecting her magic fist would inspire the lift back to life again. The lift stayed dormant. She pressed some of the lift buttons randomly, then pressed all of the lift buttons, and then finally resorted to punching the collective lift buttons with her fist. Irritatingly, it still wasn't fixed.

Much to Florence's annoyance, she decided she would need to press the 'Call for Help' button. She held her finger on the amber button and spoke into the small microphone adjacent to it.

The voice of Agent Krueger, the security teenager based in the video store, responded quickly and efficiently, "Yello?"

"Krueger, this is Florence. The fucking lift has stopped. What's going on?"

"Mmm," came the reply. "Hang on, let me take a look."

Florence rolled her eyes at nobody in particular and waited while she could hear Krueger tapping into the keyboard of his computer.

"Mmm, yeah. Lift is stuck."

"I know it's stuck Stephen Hawking. Could I trouble you to unstick the fucking thing?"

"Mmm. No-can-do at the moment. Looks like the tertiary generator has gone down. All lifts are stuck."

"Don't you dare *no-can-do* me, Krueger. Get this sack of dogshit moving or so help me, I'll climb out this shaft, come up to the video store and shove your testicles in the tertiary generator."

No reply came from the microphone.

"Krueger, are you still there?"

"I think I'm finding your tone a little inappropriate for the workplace."

"Krueger, this is urgent, stop pissing around."

"I refer you to Section 42 of the human resources Handbook."

"Listen to me Krueger, I've got a junior agent out on a solo reconnaissance mission at this precise moment. If something happens to him then I swear to God I will batter you to death with your human resources Handbook."

No reply came from the microphone.

"Krueger?! Don't you go silent on me!"

"I could put a ticket in to the IT Helpdesk for you?"

Florence took a deep, deep breath. "We are going to have serious words later, Krueger." She let go of the amber button and suppressed a scream.

* * *

Sam was bounding down the fire escape stairs of the hotel in a bid to catch up with Leo, who was several flights of stairs in front of him. Sam's rhythm of three steps at a time was effective and he was hanging onto the balustrade at the bottom of each run in order to swing his body round the corner on each landing like a Waltzer at the fairground. He heard Leo burst through the fire exit doors at the bottom of the stairwell and out onto the street. Twenty seconds later Sam came clattering through the same doors into the fresh air after him.

The hotel stairwell had led out onto the Edgware Road and Sam could see Leo sprinting southwards away from him. Sam made off after him, dodging between confused looking pedestrians and swerving around inconveniently placed lamp posts. At each junction he danced between taxis and even jumped over a slow moving basset hound. Leo was fast but Sam was closing the gap. An old man sitting outside a shisha café shouted at Sam angrily as he clattered into a pavement table, toppling the man's coffee and smashing his glass shisha pipe.

"Sorry!" shouted Sam, stumbling away. "Gotta get my steps in!"

Leo stopped up ahead and turned to face Sam. *I've got you now* thought Sam, continuing to hurtle down the pavement like a man possessed.

Leo took a pistol out of his waistband and fired two shots in Sam's direction. Sam dived for cover behind a recycling bin as people on the pavement around him scattered into doorways at the sound of gunshots. Sam peered around the bin only to see Leo turn away and dart off into a side passage. He leapt out from his hiding place and ran to the corner of the alleyway. He cautiously leant his head around the edge and instinctively pulled back as another bullet ricocheted off the brickwork. Sam waited until he could hear Leo's footsteps sprinting away. He peeked around the corner again, and then chased after him down the alley.

As he broke back into a sprint, Sam thought he felt his lucky three-leaf clover slip out of his pocket. He glanced back to see it fluttering to the ground and considered whether to stop and grab it - he needed all the luck he could get at the moment. *No,* he thought. *No lucky charms. I'm a grown up and I don't need lucky charms.* Florence had said it needed four leaves to be lucky anyway.

Sam ran out of the alleyway which led out at the other end onto a road with lock-up garages flanking either side. He sprinted past the garage block and towards the leafy Sussex Gardens estate. He caught sight of Leo up ahead dive bombing over a stony wall into the grounds of St. John's Church. Sam ran up to the same wall and attempted to execute a similar slick manoeuvre, only with significantly less skill, ultimately landing with an undignified thump into a plume of stinging nettles. He touched his cheeks and could feel his face swelling up and tingling uncomfortably. He peered up through the nettles to see a glimpse of Leo disappearing into the old timber doors at the front of the church.

He approached the arched entrance carefully, readying himself in case Leo ambushed him. He wasn't sure if Leo was still just inside the door ready to pounce. He picked up an empty flowerpot from one of the gravesides and rolled it across the front of the entrance. Two further shots immediately fired out from the doorway, shattering the flowerpot.

"Leo!" he shouted. "It's me, Sam." Leo knew full well it was Sam. "You've got to give it up. I've got reinforcements coming!" Sam didn't have any reinforcements coming. "Why don't you come out so we can talk about this. We could… have a coffee?" Leo wasn't coming out, Leo didn't want to talk, and Leo didn't like coffee. Sam wasn't great at negotiations.

"You shouldn't be here Tham, you don't know who you're dealing with!" shouted Leo from inside the church. Sam was regretting his decision to use his lip balm emergency flare to blast through the wall at the hotel. He could have really done with some back up right now.

He didn't want to risk charging through the front door whilst Leo had his gun at the ready inside. He looked around for another way into the church, hoping he might be able to sneak up on Leo from behind and perhaps catch him off guard. He spied a drainpipe leading up the side of the church wall towards the top of the bell tower. He figured if he could manage to shimmy up it and reach the open window halfway up, maybe he would be able to slide down one of the bell ropes inside and take Leo by surprise.

Sam reached as high up the drainpipe as he could, grasped it, and then pulled his body up before clamping his knees tightly around the pipe. He reached up again, one hand at a time, and shifted his knees up once more. He held his body close into the pipe and pulled himself higher and higher up the exterior of the church.

As he got closer to the window, he couldn't resist tentatively looking down at the eery gravestones below that looked so much smaller from twenty feet in the air. His arms trembled as the steel pipework started to creak. This might not have been Sam's greatest idea after all. Leo heard Sam clunking up the pipe and stepped out from the doorway to see what he was up to.

"Where on earth do you think you're going now, Tham?" he laughed, pointing his revolver up towards Sam.

Sam clung tightly to the drainpipe, bracing himself waiting for Leo to shoot. Chunks of the old masonry suddenly crumbled as the drainpipe buckled and came loose from its wall brackets. The top half of the pipe started to fold downwards with Sam still clinging onto it like a petrified limpet. Seeing Sam and the collapsing pipework tumbling down towards him, Leo instinctively ducked, firing wildly into the air.

Leo proved to be an excellent cushion, breaking Sam's fall and preventing him hitting the unforgiving concrete. Leo tried to scramble to his knees as Sam did his best to put him in a headlock. Leo punched him in the balls, causing Sam to lose his grasp as he winced in pain. Leo staggered back into the church trying desperately to get some distance between himself and Sam.

Sam meanwhile tried to clamber to his feet, while nursing his throbbing testicles. *You never, ever punch a man in the balls*, he thought. *Who does that in a fight? That was a line crossed. And now, Sam meant business.*

He reached into his bum bag and took out his pen.

* * *

Sam stepped warily into the church, holding his pen out in front of him for protection. He peered cautiously into the main nave which consisted of a traditional central aisle with neat rows of timber pews on either side leading all the way up towards an imposing altar.

Magnificent stained glass windows loomed up within the grey stone walls on either side, framed by full-height, purple, velvet drapes. Hefty timber rafters spanned across the lofty roof and a dramatic, double-height stone statue of Jesus being crucified was affixed behind the altar. Other walls were adorned with similar evocative religious carvings, and the blue and red bell ropes were neatly stowed at the foot of the tower.

Sam noted an ornate font over towards the far end of the aisle, presumably containing holy water. He made a mental note to remember that, in case Leo turned out to be a vampire. *Was holy water for vampires? Or was that for werewolves? No, it was sunlight for werewolves, and a stake in the heart for vampires. So who does the holy water kill? Was it zombies? Or maybe vicars. No, that didn't sound right either.*

"Thurprise!" Leo jumped up from behind the font, pointing his revolver directly between Sam's eyes. Sam pointed his pen back at Leo in retaliation.

"Never bring a pen to a gunfight, Tham!" Then he looked momentarily confused. "What the fuck is wrong with your face?"

"Stinging nettles!" replied Sam grimly, refusing to be distracted.

"Ouch! That lookth like it really hurt?"

"I know, right? It's *really* sore." Sam prodded his face with his finger. "I think I need some calamine lotion or something?"

"Yeah, you should get that looked at."

That was nice, thought Sam. *It never hurts to be civil, even during a gunfight*. But Sam knew he had to stay focused on Leo's gun.

In the movies they would always count the number of bullets that had already been fired by the baddie, anticipating that their magazine might be empty. Sam tried to remember how many shots Leo had fired already. *Was it five? Or was it six? And how many bullets does a revolver hold? Sam was sure it was six. Or maybe it was eight? No, hang on, sausages come in packets of eight. And hot dog rolls come in packs of ten. Why was that?* he wondered. *It would be easier if they sold sausages in packs of ten, or alternatively sold hot dog rolls in packs of eight so they matched.*

Leo gritted his teeth and then pulled the trigger. Sam flinched, but there was no bang, just a hollow click.

"You should *always* keep count of your sausages, Leo!"

"Huh?"

"Bullets! *Dammit*, I meant keep count of your *bullets*." Sam kept his pen pointed directly at Leo, watching him carefully as he steadily walked towards him.

Leo lowered his empty gun and looked at the pen with confusion. "What are you going to do now, Tham? Draw on me?"

"This isn't just a pen, Leo. This is a licensed MI-51 Mark IV flamethrower pen. And you my friend are under arrest."

Oddly, Leo seemed distracted. In fact, it didn't seem like Leo was actually looking at Sam at all. He seemed to be looking at something over Sam's shoulder - something behind him.

"Aah, I'm not falling for that," smiled Sam. "The ol' *what's-that-behind-you* gag. Honestly Leo, I thought you were better than that."

Leo was still looking past him towards the door that Sam had just arrived through, as a creepy smile started to spread across his face. Sam tried to keep his eyes on Leo, as he slowly turned his head to check behind, just in case there was something sneaking up on him. As he did so, a thundering hail of machine gun bullets rattled out around him striking the pews and the walls and the floor. And the font. And the lectern. And also the Jesus. Sparks flew off the floor and pieces of wood splintered into the air as the torrent of bullets continued to pepper every available surface around him.

Leo was cowering back behind the stone font and after what seemed like enough time for Sam's life to flash before his eyes several times, the gunfire finally subsided. Sam looked down at his own body and was mildly shocked to note that he had not been peppered with bullet holes. He slowly turned around as the wispy smoke behind him cleared.

"Welcome to Sunday school, Samuel. Here endeth your first lesson!" Mrs Bimble was standing at the entrance behind Sam, holding two smoking Kalashnikov semi-automatic sub-machine guns. Behind her there were twelve armoured soldiers clad in striking red uniforms and one small dog clad in scruffy brown fur.

As the twelve soldiers spread out and surrounded him, Sam dropped his flamethrower pen and signified his surrender by placing his hands behind his head.

Mrs Bimble was being escorted by her personal Praetorian Guardsmen. They consisted of a squad of armed guards sporting distinctive crimson uniforms and cradling automatic rifles menacingly. Their identical blood red jumpsuits and matching balaclavas were punctuated by ammo belts slung around their torsos, grenades hanging off their waistbelts and daggers strapped to their thighs. Other than appearing to represent a rather ruthless paramilitary branch of the Manchester United Supporters Club, Sam duly noted that this small band of muscle was ruthlessly efficient at housekeeping.

Specifically, upon Mrs Bimble's instructions they immediately deployed throughout the church with the co-ordination of a motorcycle display team. One was guarding the front door, one was by the rear door, and another three were busying themselves strapping Sam's feet together with a thick rope. Another one had disappeared towards the church office and subsequently returned wheeling in an old television set on a trolley, and was busy tuning it in.

* * *

Whilst all this activity was going on around him, Ralphy the dog was sniffing under a row of pews and had found himself a biscuit worth further investigation. Usually he would wolf such treasures down with enthusiasm, but right now he wasn't really feeling himself.

Although Ralphy missed Josie since she unexpectedly disappeared a few days ago, that wasn't what was bothering him. Mrs Bimble had been looking after him and she had been feeding him lots of nice things. But Ralphy had been enduring a bit of a tummy ache for several days now, and it was nothing to do with the food. He'd felt like this before, usually when he'd swallowed a bone that he couldn't digest properly, but on this occasion he hadn't had any bones for ages.

* * *

Once the guards had finished tying Sam's feet together, they threw the loose end of the rope up over one of the ceiling rafters and hoisted him up feet first. In moments, Sam found himself dangling in front of the stone statue of Jesus, viewing the entire church upside down with blood rapidly rushing to his head. With Sam safely trussed up like the last turkey at Christmas, Leo had conveniently emerged from his hiding place behind the font and felt comfortable enough to start gloating again.

"How's the view up there, Tham?" he mocked.

"Oh do be quiet, Leonidas," scolded Mrs Bimble. "If you had done your job properly, I wouldn't be here clearing up your mess."

"Got to say, Mrs Bimble," said Sam, his swollen face rapidly turning pink, "Really impressed with your one-handed Kalashnikov technique. Very *Tony Montana.*"

"Thank you, young man. I haven't always been a little old lady you know. Where I come from, women are revered for their strength, not relegated to being regarded as the fairer sex."

"Sure." Sam's face was getting really itchy from the nettles. "And where would that be? Themyscira? The Amazon Islands? Newcastle?"

"Thilence!" yelled Leo. "How dare you mock our *queen*."

"Oh, she's your queen! My apologies, Leo. What exactly is she the queen of? Queen of the Red Oompa-Loompas presumably? Queen of the People Who Can't Pronounce Their S's?"

"These men are not oompa-loompas! These are the legendary Crimson Guards of Thparta! And I will soon be one of their number."

"That's nice Leo. Really, I'm happy for you. It's just my nose is starting to get blocked."

"I warned you that you didn't know who you were dealing with, you intholent fool," sneered Leo. "We are here to return the Elgin Marbles to Thparta."

"Marbles? You're doing all this just to get the Elgin Marbles back? That's what this has all been about?!"

"Oh do be quiet," butted in Mrs Bimble. "It's nothing to do with the bloody marbles Leonidas, stop being such a drama queen."

"Yeah shut up Leo. You're such a drama queen!" echoed Sam.

* * *

Ralphy the dog was still industriously sniffing around under the pews but had decided against the mouldy biscuit. Something definitely wasn't right with his tummy, perhaps a little poop would help? He decided to disappear to the back row of seats for a little privacy, squatted his back end down and started to strain. He had long felt rather indignant about the uncomfortably awkward pose that dogs had to maintain in order to avoid getting poop on their fur, so he was pleased nobody was paying much attention to him. He strained as hard as he could and as if by magic, a little poop dropped out.

Only, it wasn't a poop. Ralph looked at the curious metal device that had just dropped out of his bottom and recognised it immediately. That was the thing that the crazy lady and had shoved up his backside when he was tied up outside that café.

Ralph noticed his tummy suddenly felt a lot better now. Great, whatever it was that just popped out, he was very happy it wasn't inside him anymore.

As Ralph wandered off feeling satisfied, the little metal device started transmitting again.

* * *

On the other side of the church, the guard tuning in the old TV set finished what he was doing and handed the remote control to the old lady. Mrs Bimble turned the volume up so the man on the screen could be heard.

"My beloved, Iris," said the elderly man on the screen with the creased Mediterranean complexion. "How pleasant to see you again, my dear wife."

"And you, my cherished Agis. The tyrant prime minister has escaped our clutches, but we have captured another little fly in our web." Mrs Bimble stepped back so that the old man could see the ensnared Sam.

"So I see. And where is Agent Leonidas?"

Leo leaped across the aisle and presented himself in front of the screen to the king. "I am here, Your Excellenthy!"

"Hmm. Leonidas. I am extremely disappointed in you. You have allowed the prime minister to escape, and have therefore categorically failed in your mission. Your ineptitude is not worthy of a true Spartan Hoplite," he said slowly.

"Your Excellenthy, forgive me. I have served you loyally. Give me one more chance, I beg you."

"Spartans do not get *one more chance* to prove themselves worthy of joining the Crimson Guards, Leonidas. You have failed."

Leo dropped to his knees and clasped his hands together "I'm... I'm so thorry! Give me another mission Lord, anything. Let me prove mythelf!"

"Iris, kindly resolve this matter. We have no need of this fool any longer."

Leo's eyes widened and started to flood. His body shivered as panic set in. "My queen, I beg of you! Forgive me, I'll do anything!"

Mrs Bimble walked across to the guard standing nearest to her. She reached into the guard's scabbard and pulled out his dagger. "You have been a great disappointment to us, Leonidas."

Agis continued to watch from the screen and said nothing.

"No! My queen, please! You don't have to do thith!"

Mrs Bimble calmly walked towards Leo, holding the steel blade. "For Sparta," she said quietly.

She placed one hand on Leo's cheek and swiftly drew the blade across the front of his throat with the other.

Leo's eyes rolled into his head and the colour quickly drained out of his face, as his body collapsed to the floor into a pool of his own blood.

"Good," said Agis.

The remaining Praetorian Guards looked on with sterile ambivalence as Mrs Bimble wiped the blood from the dagger's blade on the fabric of Leo's shirt.

Sam stopped joking. If he hadn't been hanging upside down, his jaw would have dropped open. "Who *are* you people?"

"Who are we?" replied Agis, staring out of the TV screen. "Who *are* we, boy? The people you see before you are the men and women of the *legendary Crypteia.* We are the ancestors of the great Lycurgus, we are the hunters of the Helots, we are the special operations unit of the mighty Spartan Army. We are the ones who live in the shadows, and we have done so for over two thousand years."

"You're... the Spartan Army?"

"We are the Crypteia," clarified Mrs Bimble. "And it is time for the Spartan Empire to rise once again."

"What are you talking about? Rise up against who? No one even knows you exist!" Sam was starting to feel delirious as his head rushed with blood.

"Empires across the globe have celebrated our fall since 400 BC," replied Mrs Bimble. "You watched as our people were eradicated, and you mocked our decline while your new empires took our place. The Romans, the

Turks, the Spanish, the Dutch, and most of all, you pompous British. You all grew in strength over the centuries as our culture slowly died."

"You're crazy." Sam couldn't take his eyes off Leo's gruesome, lifeless body on the church floor. "You think killing people like Leo is going to make a difference? You think that destroying politicians is going to make people take you seriously?"

Agis snarled back at Sam through the camera. "You people plundered our riches over a millennia and you think to lecture us? We have blood debts that are owed to us from empires across the globe. We are only just beginning by destroying your corrupt British Government. Others will follow your downfall soon." His gaze flicked across the screen towards Mrs Bimble. "Iris, we have no need of this cretinous child any longer. Kindly dispense with him also."

"But my cherished one, he is part of British Intelligence," she replied. "I thought he may be a useful bargaining chip as a hostage, no?"

Agis paused as he gave her new strategy brief consideration.

"No I don't think so, Iris. Slit his throat."

Stalag *17*

Florence was becoming increasingly agitated as she waited for the underground lift system to kick back to life again. The eery silence from within the tunnel stretched on and the lights remained stubbornly off.

Florence started to become aware of distant voices, muffled and indistinct. She placed her ear next to the bulkhead, trying to identify if there were people outside in the tunnel. Then she realised the voices were coming from behind her, from within her purple rucksack. She pulled it off her shoulder and zipped open the rear compartment. The voices were coming from the portable speaker that was still tuned into the microphone she had shoved up that dog's butt. Somehow it seemed to have come to life again and was now clear as day. Florence put the speaker to her ear.

"Who are we, young man? The people you see before you are the men and women of The Crypteia. We are the ancestors of the great Lycurgus..." Florence listened intently as the gravelly voice ranted on threateningly. Then she heard Sam's voice! Wherever he was, he was in serious trouble and needed help. Florence looked around at the lift car that entrapped her causing a familiar feeling of regret to wash over her. She became uncomfortably aware of the zippo lighter in her pocket, the one gifted to her from Ben Cornelius, all those years ago.

Florence grasped hold of the cast iron concertina grill of the lift-car, hauled it open and stepped out into the blackness of the tunnel. She flicked on her torch revealing the overhead chains draped along the roof of the tunnel, and rails fixed to the floor providing a track to guide the route of the passenger cars. She looked ahead of her into the shadowy gloom. She had no idea how far along the track she'd gone before the lift system had malfunctioned. She felt sure it had been clanking along for at least a minute or two, so in theory she could nearly be at her destination in Paddington Station by now.

She hurried off down the tunnel, trying not to slip in the oily puddles or step on the scurrying rats. After a minute or two she started to become anxious as there seemed to be no sign of an obvious exit point. There was one last roll of the dice. Florence pulled her mobile phone out of her backpack and called the one person she hated asking for help from.

Milquetoast answered instantly with his customary greeting and ostentatious waffle. Florence quickly briefed him of the re-emergence of the microphone, the voices she was hearing from it and how she thought Sam could be in danger. Annoyingly, Milquetoast sounded remarkably unperturbed.

"Worry not, young Florence. I not only comprehend your predicament, but I am currently gallivanting forth like the proverbial White Knight to aid our erstwhile companion."

"Milquetoast. I don't think you understand, you're going to need serious back up. This is much bigger than we thought."

"Verily, my dear girl. Leave it to Milquetoast."

The line went silent. *Ugh* she thought, who on earth still says '*verily*'?

* * *

"Wait! Wait!" yelped Sam.

Mrs Bimble was holding the blade to his upside down throat. "What?"

"I've got a question."

Mrs Bimble paused, momentarily retracting her blade and raising her eyebrows.

"Why the church?" he blurted out. "Of all the places you could use as a hideout, why a church?"

Mrs Bimble looked up at the masonry carvings and stonework of the ancient building. "This is no random church, child. This monument has belonged to the Crypteia for generations. Your clueless British security services are rarely suspicious of wrongdoings on such sacred ground which has just served to help us conceal our identities for so many years."

"Ah, see now that's clever," nodded Sam. "That's good thinking right there. You see that's why the Spartans were good. Good logistics, good planning, sneaky—"

"We're most flattered." Mrs Bimble held her knife back to Sam's throat.

He tensed as he felt the cold steel against his skin. He tried to stare into the distance so he wouldn't cry. It was one thing having your throat cut when you're hanging upside down in front of Jesus, but he really didn't want to be remembered as the guy who was crying whilst it happened.

As he stared, Sam caught sight of a pigeon quietly glide through the open doors of the church, and gently perch on the back of a pew. The silent pigeon stared at Sam, without expressing any emotion. Just silently watching.

"WAIT! WAIT! That wasn't my question!"

Mrs Bimble's lip curled up as she pulled her blade back just a fraction. "What?"

"So, your guys. Those ones all dressed up like psycho jelly babies. How come they're all wearing red jumpsuits and balaclavas?"

"What do you mean?"

"Well, I mean the Spartans — the real Spartans — they were naked, weren't they? I always thought that was where the whole *spartan* word came from? Nothing much there?"

"You have been watching far too much Hollywood, young man. I can assure you our ancestors fought wearing as much armour as they could carry including a helmet, cuirass, codpiece and thigh armour. Their crimson capes were a flourish designed to conceal any wounds to the evil immortal hordes."

"Is that so?" enthused Sam. "Well, I didn't know that. So your bouncers over there are wearing red as a kind of traditional thing, right?"

"My Praetorian Guard wear crimson as a homage to their kin. And you, little government weasel, need to stop trying to distract me."

"WAAAIITT!"

"No more waiting."

"No really, what's happened to Ralphy? Ralphy's gone!"

Mrs Bimble kept the blade steady next to Sam's throat and turned to look if she could see Ralph. "Ralphy! Ralphy darling, come to mommy!"

Ralph, free of any fangled internal microphones, came happily bounding from under the pews, although he came to a stunned halt as he saw Leo's corpse lying in a grisly pile of blood. *Marvellous*, thought Sam. *Why couldn't Ralph have stayed hidden for just a tiny bit longer?!*

"Enough of this!" yelled the old man on the TV screen. "Iris, kill this irksome simpleton now."

* * *

Florence finally found a steel ladder fixed to the wall inside the lift tunnel and was clambering up it as quick as she could. She wasn't sure precisely where it would bring her out but being above ground would definitely be better than running blindly through the pitch darkness with the rats.

As she got to the top of the ladder, she reached a heavy manhole cover which she shunted out the way and then pulled herself up into a tiny dark cupboard. She dragged the manhole cover back into place and tried to feel around for a light switch. She flicked it on to find herself surrounded by mops, brooms and a variety of cleaning liquids stacked neatly on shelves. She put her ear to the door to figure out where she had emerged.

"Two filets, one nuggets, one chips and a milkshake please."

"What flavour milkshake?"

"Vanilla. No, chocolate. No, vanilla! Definitely vanilla!"

Florence opened the door and strode confidently out of the fast food joint's broom cupboard into the restaurant area. A few people in the queue briefly looked at the random woman walking out of a cupboard, but nobody really seemed to register it as particularly unusual behaviour.

As she walked out the front of the bustling fast food restaurant, she saw the sign for Edgware Road tube station and quickly got her bearings. In the distance she heard a series of cracks which she recognised as gunfire. She sprinted down the pavement in the direction of the noise, as confused-looking shoppers meandered in her way.

* * *

"Wait, what's that noise?" asked Sam.

"There is no noise. Hush now, stop making this difficult." Mrs Bimble pushed the blade against Sam's neck.

"There is, there is! Listen!"

Mrs Bimble frowned and tilted her head slightly, realising that actually she could hear a faint, grumbly noise that wasn't there before. The distant droning sound rapidly escalated in pitch before exploding into a thundering engine roar as a white van battered through the old oak doors at the front of the church. The backfiring engine echoed through the church as the van careered up the aisle before coming to a skidding halt at the altar. Mrs Bimble staggered backwards, dropping her blade as one of the purple drapes flailed down onto her.

The van's rear doors burst open, and Red sprayed bullets out of an automatic machine gun sitting on a tripod. "Eat lead, ya knuckleheads!"

The scattered Crimson Guards reasserted themselves and immediately returned fire at the van. Josie avoided their gunfire by laying her body flat inside the cab, and then momentarily popping up to fire back with her own rifle, whenever she sensed they were pausing to reload.

The Crimson Guards panned out across the church, finding pockets of cover to fire from, as Mrs Bimble angrily berated them and demanded they immediately kill the two attackers in the van.

Josie clambered low across the passenger seat, opened the van door and slid down behind the vehicle so she could use it as a barricade from their return fire. Red's machine gun in the back ran out of ammunition so he also retreated back through the inside of the van, grabbed a satchel on the way and huddled down next to Josie using the van for cover. Together they reached into the satchel, and each pulled out a grenade. They looked at each other, Red nodded, and they simultaneously pulled the pins before lobbing them over the top of the van into the middle of the church.

Sam was still busy dangling from his ankles. He tried to wriggle himself free, but the momentum just resulted in him spinning around in circles rather uncontrollably. This gave Sam the unfortunate disadvantage of only facing the developing pandemonium momentarily before he revolved back around each time to find himself facing the statue of a disapproving Jesus.

Sam tried to make sense of the escalating chaos as he spun around; *Van smashed through doors — Jesus — Van doors burst open — Jesus — Hey, there's Red! — Jesus — And Josie too! — Jesus — Shitload of gunfire everywhere — Jesus — two grenades drop on the floor and roll towards him — Oh shit!*

As he rotated back around, he wriggled furiously before the two grenades could explode in his face. His ankles weren't budging, and he just couldn't stop himself from spinning. He clenched his teeth and braced himself, waiting for the impact of the grenades as they exploded.

After a few seconds, he realised the grenades hadn't exploded, they just kind of fizzed and fizzled until thick grey smoke plumed out of them and spread across the church, forming a cloudy barrier obscuring the van Josie and Red were hiding behind. The crimson guards quickly dropped back out of the smoke but continued to fire randomly into the cloud.

Mrs Bimble crouched by the TV set. "Iris, let the guards deal with this. Get yourself out of there!" commanded the old man on the screen. Mrs Bimble beckoned one of her guards to come over to her and ordered him to cut Sam down from the rafter so he could be used as a human shield as she made her escape from the building. As the guard's machete sliced through the rope suspending him, Sam slumped to the floor headfirst, concussing himself.

The guard grabbed Sam by the collar and hauled him unceremoniously up onto his feet. Mrs Bimble picked up Ralphy and signalled for the guard to follow her with Sam as she sneaked off into the vestry. Once inside, she unlatched a small door in the far corner and carried Ralphy outside to the graveyard. The guard followed on behind, with one hand on Sam's collar, and the other holding a gun next to Sam's head.

"Follow me to the garages," demanded Mrs Bimble. "Time for me to depart."

* * *

Meanwhile still inside the church, Red and Josie were busy repositioning a row of pews to form an added barrier from any stray bullets.

The Crimson Squad Leader shouted at his team to form a phalanx and maintain suppressive fire while two of the guards loaded up a rocket-propelled grenade launcher. As one of the guards mounted the bulky tube onto his shoulder, his counterpart slotted a projectile into the muzzle.

"Fire in the hole!" he shouted, pulling the trigger. The missile propelled itself deep into the smoke, spiralling in Red and Josie's direction. Before they could react, the rocket struck the grey statue above their heads, exploding the Virgin Mary into a shower of concrete shrapnel. The explosion sent Josie and Red tumbling through the air towards the pulpit.

Josie hit a concrete pillar and then crumpled to the floor, dazed and struggling to focus. Her ears were ringing, and her face was covered in chalky dust. She looked across at Red who was lying motionless on his back. Both of his legs had been grotesquely blown apart from the knees and an arm was missing.

"Red!" She crawled across to him and grabbed his shoulders. "Red, wake up!" She put her face to his, willing him back to consciousness with tears in her eyes. "Come on you ginger, Braveheart twat, don't you fucking die on me."

Red's eyes slowly opened. "Well ye can stop bloody dripping snot on me for a start." Josie held on to him tightly and put her head close to his.

"Josie, I can't feel my legs."

"Your legs are fine Red," she lied.

"I feel tired…"

"I know you do, Red, I know you do. Hang in there."

Josie heard the click-clack of two rifles being cocked close behind her and turned to see two Crimson Guardsmen with their gun barrels pointed towards her and Red.

* * *

One of the Crimson Guardsmen tilted his head towards a walkie-talkie on his shoulder, ensuring his rifle held steady on Josie.

"We've got them both disarmed, request instructions?"

The Squad Leader's voice came back over the radio loud and clear. "Standby. Red Four is wheeling the TV across."

One of the other Crimson Guards promptly arrived having manoeuvred the television on the trolley across the rubble strewn church floor, trying hard not to trip over the cable. The old man on the screen looked particularly grumpy now. "Meddlesome fools. Kill them both immediately."

The two crimson guards gave an affirmatory glance at one another then zeroed their sights at Red and Josie. Red closed his eyes. Josie still had tears in hers.

Behind the two guards, Josie could see the sun's rays streaming in through the huge stained-glass windows, creating beautiful, vivid, multi-coloured rainbows across the void of the church. She didn't have the strength to roll away or fight or scream. She laid herself across Red's chest, surrendering to their tragic fate.

As she gazed past the guards, the rainbows faded as the multi-coloured beams were suddenly replaced by stark, white rays of sunlight. A silhouetted figure came crashing through one of the stained glass windows, fracturing the coloured mosaic into a thousand tiny glass fragments and flooding the church with bright daylight. Simultaneously, another figure flew through an adjacent window, sending more shards of coloured glass splintering across the interior of the church. Then another, and another.

The two Crimson Guards hesitated and turned their heads in response to the shattering glass and were each swiftly met with a bullet to the chest, knocking them off their feet.

Josie sat up to see the church filling with more and more silhouetted figures in black, storming through every door and window and rappelling down from the rafters. Their bullets quickly picked off another four Crimson Guards in positions at the back of the church, with effortless pinpoint efficiency. There must have been at least a dozen E-Squadron soldiers streaming into the church. No, two dozen or maybe three dozen. Josie couldn't count, there seemed to be so many of them. She patted Red on the chest. "Red, look!"

Red managed to squint his eyes open and craned his head forward. Captain Flex shouted orders at his team, coordinating his ruthless orchestra. "Fan out left! Suppressive fire! You two, cover me!" His men responded unflinchingly, darting around and picking off all of their targets in red.

The last few cowering Crimson Guards tried to fight back by firing their guns in panic at the marauding black clad soldiers, but they were quickly overrun by the ruthless precision of Captain Flex's onslaught.

Moments later, the bodies of soldiers in red balaclavas and red jumpsuits lay strewn across the church, draped on rubble and propped lifelessly against the stone walls.

Captain Flex quickly scanned the area to ensure there were no more pockets of resistance, and when he was satisfied, he ordered his men to stay vigilant but lower their weapons.

The church fell momentarily silent, then another man tentatively stepped through the rubble at the front doors of the church. The familiar figure in a hat and spectacles strode past Captain Flex towards Josie and Red, jubilantly swinging his walking cane.

"Well you took your fucking time," said Josie, still clutching Red in her arms. "I thought you were supposed to be backing us up?"

"Some would say it was perfect timing, young lady."

"Perfect timing?! Look at the state of Red!"

"Such tosh!" replied Milquetoast grinning. "There's barely a scratch on him. Flex! Get the Bionics Engineer over here, this man needs medical assistance."

Captain Flex signalled to his medic, who came sprinting over with an emergency pack and immediately got to work stemming the blood from Red's limbs. Josie stood up and stepped back to give him room to work whilst Milquetoast turned his attention towards the man on the crackling TV set.

"Well now, *Crypteia* eh? We haven't had you chaps on our radar before. It appears you've been leading us quite the merry little dance for the last few weeks, have you not?"

The old man in the TV set leant into the camera, his wrinkled Mediterranean features creasing as he shook his fist angrily. "You may think you have defeated us, Englishman, but the Crypteia are legion. You *will* return our Elgin Marbles, we *will* have our vengeance on your pitiful government, and the Spartan Empire *will* rise again!"

"Oh tish and pish. You are nothing more than a rag tag bunch of armed miscreants. And as for your bloody marbles, you'll get them back when *we're* good and ready. We're still looking at them, old boy!" Milquetoast flicked off the TV set with satisfaction and walked over to Josie. "A most heroic effort from you, my dear. My organisation is very impressed, and we are most indebted to you. Both of you."

Josie was anxiously looking over the medic's shoulder, trying to see if Red was still conscious.

"Don't worry about young Reginald," continued Milquetoast. "E-Squadron specialise in battlefield injuries, you may have noticed most of them are a mish-mash of bionic parts. So where is our other erstwhile hero, Samuel?"

"You didn't find him?" asked Josie, "My god, we lost sight of him during the battle. So, where the hell is he?"

* * *

Florence sprinted down the Edgware Road in the direction of the gunfire. The sound of E-Squadron's gargantuan black helicopters hovering a few blocks away were a welcome relief as she realised that Milquetoast had successfully arrived on scene with the cavalry.

She charged past a shisha café but then hesitated at the next junction, trying to figure out which way to head. She glanced down and noticed a small laminated three-leaf clover laying on the concrete pathway. She picked it up from the floor and stared at it.

"Genius!" she said to herself. That was smart thinking from Sam to leave a trail of breadcrumbs for her like that.

Florence sprinted off down the alleyway and came out across the front of a block of garages. As she did so, a large black 4 x 4 pulled out of an open garage, slamming into her thigh and rolling her onto the bonnet.

Florence was momentarily stunned. She'd been so wrapped up with catching up to Sam, she hadn't been paying attention to where she was going. She gasped and held her hand up apologetically to the driver, accepting responsibility for her own lack of attention.

The driver was emotionless in response. Florence lowered herself off the bonnet and took a second look at the driver. As she stared harder through the tinted windscreen, she realised the driver was only expressionless because he was wearing a red balaclava over his face. She could make out his eyes, *but what the fuck was he wearing? Was that an ammo belt slung around his chest?*

This was too much of a coincidence so close to where Sam was in trouble — she instinctively pulled out her Luger and pointed it at the driver. "Out! Turn the engine off and get *out* of the car!"

The driver turned his head to say something to the person in the back seat. It looked like an old woman sitting back there. Then the driver turned back towards Florence, and from below the dashboard swiftly pulled up a Kalashnikov, pointing it through the windscreen towards her.

Florence instinctively ducked just as the driver pulled his trigger and fired a stream of bullets, which shattered the windscreen and rained glass out across the bonnet as bullets flew over her head. The engine revved loudly, spurring Florence to roll her body to the side of the vehicle before the wheels could accelerate over her. The tyres screeched as they tried to grip the tarmac causing smoke to emanate from the rear wheels. The vehicle suddenly lurched forward, then swerved onto the road.

Florence saw Sam's face in the back seat through the side window, sitting next to the old woman. He held up his handcuffed wrists so Florence could see them and squished his face up to the window as he mouthed the word 'help'. Unable to grasp how he had ended up in there, Florence resorted to intuition and pointed her pistol directly at the driver. She knew she had one chance to make a clean shot before the 4 x 4 sped away into the distance.

She braced her firing arm with her other hand and closed her left eye. Target practice from the prone position was standard, but lying on her side on concrete was always trickier. She held her breath as she squeezed the trigger and a single shot echoed out between the garages. The driver's side window cracked, and a splash of blood belched out from the driver's head before he slumped forward onto the steering wheel. The car jerked and swerved wildly before careening into a lamppost and coming to a rest burrowed into some large, industrial, refuse bins.

Florence breathed out, relieved her marksmanship skills were still on point when it mattered. She rolled back onto her feet as one of the car's rear doors swung open. The old lady stepped out of the back, pointing an Uzi semi-automatic towards Florence. Florence had her Luger pistol trained on the old woman, now certain that this pensioner was some sort of kidnapper rather than a hostage. She kept one eye on the old woman as she tried to look past her into the back seat of the car.

"Sam? Are you okay in there?"

"Hi Florence! I've had better days." He held up his wrists again, assuming that would be a suitable explanation.

"Ok Sam. You hang in there, buddy. Got a bit of a Mexican stand-off going on out here," she turned her gaze back at the old woman, watching her carefully across the top of her pistol. "And who the fuck might you be?"

Sam decided to interject. "Oh Florence, you two haven't met have you? Mrs Bimble, this is my partner, Agent Florence. We're work partners only, not like partner-partners."

Mrs Bimble didn't answer. Her focus was also on Florence, and she wasn't going to allow herself to be distracted like before.

"And Florence, this is Mrs Bimble. Also known as Iris. Also known as the Queen of the Crypteia. Who themselves are known as the ancestors of the Spartan Army. Yes, *those* Spartans. The ones from Sparta. Honestly, I've learnt so much today."

"Have you now," replied Florence, quietly. "And what is the Queen of Sparta doing pointing a gun at me off the Edgware Road?"

"Getting ready to blow your pretty helot head off," replied Mrs Bimble, equally quietly.

"She says she's getting ready to blow your pretty helmet head off!" clarified Sam, loudly.

"My pretty *what* head?" shouted Florence back.

"Your pretty *helmet* head!" confirmed Sam.

"I said *helot*," scolded Mrs Bimble. "Her pretty *helot* head."

"Oh. She says you've got a pretty *helot* head Florence. Not a *helmet* head!"

"What the fuck does that mean? What's a *helot head*?" Florence kept her steely gaze on Mrs Bimble, ready to shoot if she saw a flicker of movement.

"Mrs Bimble," whispered Sam. "What's a *helot head?"*

"It means *slave,* you imbecile. The helots are the Spartan's slaves and that's what you and your countrymen are going to be when the Spartan Empire rises once again."

"Oh I see. Thanks," replied Sam. "Florence! She says it means *slave*! We're all going to be slaves for the Spartans!"

"Oh, are we now? Well not on my watch, Mrs Bimble." Florence gritted her teeth. She'd spotted Mrs Bimble's forefinger tensing onto the trigger of the Uzi. Florence dived to her left, breaking into a commando roll as the machine gun muzzle flashed and chattered to life. Bullets flew through the air and sparked off the concrete, tracking towards Florence as she continued rolling across the tarmac to stay ahead of them.

As she rolled, Florence managed to fire off a single shot in retaliation, which deflected off the car door and went skywards. Bullets continued to rattle back at Florence who had no time to reload her pistol. Instead she reached over her own shoulder into her rucksack to pull out her lipstick.

With both his wrists and ankles bound, Sam wasn't able to help Florence much but managed to swing both legs up onto the back seat and wriggle his way closer to the open door. He curled his knees up to his chin and then thrusted both feet to full stretch into Mrs Bimble's back as hard as he could. Mrs Bimble staggered forward, firing the Uzi into the ground as she did so. Florence saw her chance and in one swift movement pointed her lipstick and twisted the cap anti-clockwise. A bright red flare fired out of the lipstick, streaming a tail of red flame. As the flare struck Mrs Bimble in the chest, the old lady burst into flames and then exploded into a stunning vermillion starburst.

Florence ducked as bits of Mrs Bimble flew into the sky and started to drop a few seconds later, showering the 4 x 4 and the surrounding garages with flaming pieces of old lady.

Sam leaned forward out of the car as Florence stood up. "Are you okay, partner?"

Florence smiled. "I am now. Partner."

As charred fragments of pensioner smoked on the road, three helicopters emerged and hovered overhead, having spied the release of Florence's flare from the sky. Seconds later, the rapid footsteps of the E-Squadron troopers could be heard as they sprinted around the corner from the churchyard.

"Ma'am, we didn't realise you were here!" said Captain Flex.

"It's okay now, Captain. All under control. Although could you get someone to untie him." Florence gestured towards Sam who was busily trying to bite himself free of the handcuffs.

"I'm on it." Flex shouted at a few of his guys to attend to Sam before he gnawed his own arms off. Other members of the E-Squadron team fanned out round the block in order to cordon the area off from civilians.

"Well Ms Florence, it would appear you've been rather busy today after all!" Milquetoast appeared to be twirling his cane with particular enthusiasm as he strolled around the corner, flanked by Josie.

"Apparently so, you waffly old badger." Florence smiled and held her hand out towards him. "Thanks for your help Milquetoast. We really needed you there today."

Milquetoast removed his hat, gently took hold of her palm and bowed his head low. "At your service, madam."

Josie ran up to Sam as he was finally untethered and briefly flung her arms around his shoulders. "I'm glad you're okay Sam. I'm sorry I called you a two-faced piece of shit last time I saw you."

"That's alright," said Sam. "Maybe we can start again. We could catch a movie sometime?"

Josie smiled but was simultaneously slightly repelled. "What the fuck is wrong with your face?"

"Oh, it's the stinging nettles I think. Also I've been hanging upside down for a while. And had a knife stuck to my throat. And been shot at. And fell off a drainpipe. And got stuck in a wall. And got punched in the balls."

Josie looked mildly impressed. But only mildly. "What happened to Ralphy, Sam? I can't find him anywhere."

Sam tapped on the boot of the black car. "He was very brave. He'll make a great police dog one day, you know. Needs to choose his friends better though."

Josie lifted up the boot hatch. Ralphy was curled up in the back, snoring his furry head off. He'd had quite a day.

Epilogue

Florence was sitting at one of her two desks drinking an unfeasibly strong black coffee. Sam was perched on his footstool workstation by the door, putting the finishing touches to his report on what was now being referred to as the 'Spartan Investigation'.

"So what happened to Mrs Bimble's husband? Did he know she was a psychopathic Spartan bigamist all along?" asked Florence.

"God, no. He didn't really believe it at first but after a while he was quite pleased actually. He's spent the last twenty years happily building that model railway in his loft. Now she's gone, he says he's going to extend his track downstairs."

Sam's knee was cramping up. He stretched his leg out and wiggled his foot around. "Is there anything else I should include about the mysterious Crypteia? That creepy old dude is still out there somewhere plotting his revenge. Are we going to go out there and set up a stakeout on him or something?"

"No need." Florence rocked back in her chair and rested both her feet up on her desk, looking uncharacteristically relaxed. "The White Rabbit has decided to take himself on a little *holiday* out to Greece. I've no doubt he'll be paying the resort of Sparta a visit while he's there."

Sam stopped writing and thought for a moment.

"I never did say thank you, Florence. For rescuing me."

"I'll try not to leave it so late next time Sam. Besides, you're the one that busted them. I should really be thanking you."

"Interesting you should say that!" Sam adjusted his buttocks on his stool. "So I was thinking, given that we're kind of even now, and given that I'll probably get another medal from the White Rabbit for this, and given that you have *two* desks, and given that I have *no* desks…"

"Say no more, Sam. You're going to ask me if you can sit at this desk now, aren't you?" Florence waved her coffee cup towards her spare desk.

"Well, yeah. I kind of was?"

"Ok then. Ask me."

Sam sighed. "Florence, can I please have the other desk, so I don't have to sit on this stupid stool?"

"Unfortunately not Sam. I might need it."

"What the fuck do you need another desk for?" A wad of papers fell out of Sam's report file and scattered across the floor.

"In case we have any new starters. They wouldn't have anywhere to sit, would they?"

"*I don't have anywhere to sit!*" Sam tried to reach down to some of the scattered papers without getting off his stool. "And as if we're *ever* going to get any new joiners! You didn't even want *me* in your team."

The door to the office swung open and smacked Sam in the head.

"Oh, I do apologise old bean. I didn't expect you to be sitting behind that door… " Milquetoast said.

Sam rubbed the corner of his head. "Neither did I," he replied grumpily.

"… but I thought I'd escort your new trainee down here personally!" Milquetoast took a step to his left and swirled his hand theatrically.

Josie walked through the door, high fived Milquetoast and flopped down triumphantly at the spare desk. "Thanks for saving my seat, partner."

"No problem, you earned it," replied Florence. "Glad to have you onboard, *Agent Griffiths*."

Sam looked at Josie and couldn't stop a smile creeping across his lips. Then he scowled at Florence. "Are you kidding me? You're giving *Josie* the desk and I have to sit *here*?!"

Milquetoast tried his best not to look mildly amused. "Well my work here appears to be done. If you'd all excuse me, I have other trainees starting today who are due to attend their inductions…"

Milquetoast referred down to his clipboard, checking his next appointment. "… Ah yes, here we are. Reginald Kendall has been patched up nicely by the bio-engineers and has agreed to be assigned to E-Squadron."

As Milquetoast closed the door behind himself, Sam glanced back at Josie and smiled excitedly.

Florence caught the look. "We're not going to be having any of *that* between you two, just so you know. There's not going to be *any* fraternising in my team."

"Of course not," agreed Sam earnestly.

"Certainly not," confirmed Josie.

Florence eyed them both suspiciously. "I mean it. *No fraternising.*"

"Absolutely not," agreed Sam.

"Definitely not," confirmed Josie, who then winked at Sam.

The red phone rang and Sam, Florence and Josie all stared at it, unsure whose job it was to answer phones. Whoever did pick up the receiver would probably become the permanent phone-answerer. And that would probably be the same person who became the permanent coffee-maker. And then that person would probably also become the permanent go-to-the-deli-to-get-bagels person. It would probably never end.

Sam looked at Florence wearily. Then he looked at Josie and sighed, accepting his fate. He stepped up, cleared his throat and lifted the receiver.

"*Department of Conspiracy. How can we help you?*"

The End

Printed in Dunstable, United Kingdom

67207068R00180